Tara Moss is a bestselling author, human rights activist, documentary host, and model. Her novels have been published in nineteen countries and thirteen languages, and her memoir *The Fictional Woman* was a #1 national bestseller. She is a UNICEF Goodwill Ambassador and has received the Edna Ryan Award for her significant contributions to feminist debate and for speaking out for women and children, and in 2017 she was recognised as one of the Global Top 50 Diversity Figures in Public Life. She is a PhD Candidate at the University of Sydney, and has earned her private investigator credentials (Cert III) from the Australian Security Academy. *The Cobra Queen* is her thirteenth book and fourth Pandora English novel.

TARA MOSS

THE
BLOOD
COUNTESS

echo

echo

Echo Publishing
An imprint of Bonnier Books UK
80-81 Wimpole Street
London W1G 9RE
www.echopublishing.com.au
www.bonnierbooks.co.uk

First published by Pan Macmillan Australia in 2010.
This edition first published by Echo Publishing in 2020.

Cover design by Lisa Brewster
Typesetting and reformatting by Shaun Jury

Typeset in Baskerville
Printed in Australia at Griffin Press.
Only wood grown from sustainable regrowth forests is used in the
manufacture of paper found in this book.

A catalogue record for this book is available from the
National Library of Australia
ISBN: 9781760685874 (paperback)
ISBN: 9781760686536 (ebook)

echopublishingau

echo_publishing

echo_publishing

For my husband Berndt

CHAPTER
ONE

*M*y mysterious host did not greet me. Instead, I found a tall, expressionless chauffeur.

I arrived at the sprawling airport with my maps and directions and dreams, animated with an uneasy cocktail of excitement, relief and...terror. I had finally escaped my small hometown of Gretchenville for one of the biggest and most famous cities in the world. This oft-imagined fantasy of mine was now reality; a reality of unknown circumstances and vast possibilities. Everything was new and unfamiliar. Everything was changed. And it was all thanks to the offer of a lifetime.

New York.

My plane was late, delaying this triumphant life change by half an hour. When I finally disembarked at JFK I found myself faced with an aggressive throng of strangers. They were talking on cell phones or shouting at airline staff, striding this way and that, swinging briefcases and bags. Amid this clamorous human maelstrom stood a tall figure dressed in an impeccable black suit and dark sunglasses. This man had a deathly pallor, I thought, and he seemed eerily still and silent despite the chaos around him. He held a white sign marked with my name.

P. ENGLISH

When you see *P. English* you immediately assume P is for Patricia, right? Or Penny? Well, you'd be wrong. My mother was an archaeologist, my father was an academic and these two otherwise intelligent people had the combined wisdom to name their only child *Pandora*. That's right, I share my name with the lady in Greek mythology who opened a box and let all the evil into the world. And if you picked up the past tense when I was telling you about my parents, you would have guessed that they are either retired, or I am an orphan.

It's the latter.

My parents died in an accident in Egypt when I was eleven. I'd had a bad feeling about the trip beforehand, but of course I was only eleven, so I could hardly stop them going. I wasn't with them when it happened. I was with my Aunt Georgia, and there I stayed. I was already considered weird (for a number of reasons), and growing up as the ward of my father's older sister did nothing to increase my popularity with other kids my age. Aunt Georgia is a good, decent woman, but she is the math teacher at the only school in Gretchenville, and known for being strict. The older townsfolk call her a 'spinster', and the kids call her something less kind. Aunt Georgia thought it best not to remind me about my parents or the accident, so as not to upset me, thus there are no photos of them around her house. And to 'avoid embarrassment' (hers, not mine) caused by the negative associations with my name she insists on calling me 'Dora'.

(Please don't call me Dora. I really hate it.)

'That's me. Pandora English.' I smiled cheerfully at the stranger to disguise my excited panic. Though of average height, I barely came up to the man's chest. Maybe it was just my nerves, but I thought, *He is so still. If he's breathing, I can't tell.*

Without a word of acknowledgment the towering chauffeur took my briefcase and walked off. I followed the man through the part he formed in the horde of airport patrons. He led me to the baggage carousel, and grabbed the suitcase I indicated – still without a single utterance. This lack of conversation was, I figured, either due to my being too important to converse with, or too unimportant. I would like to think it was the former, but that would be unlikely. I'm a nineteen-year-old who went to a small town high school. I'm not rich, not famous and not influential. I don't currently have a cell phone or a blog or a BBF (Best Best Friend or is it BFF? Anyway, I don't really have one). My suitcase is not Louis Vuitton, or whatever the cool big city people use to transport their things these days. No, mine is a battered suitcase of faded and scratched leather, marked with some of those stamps and stickers you used to find on old steam trunks. It's not battered from my own adventures. I haven't had my own adventures yet. (Though just between you and me, that is about to change.) The suitcase belonged to my mother, the archaeologist, and I treasured it and the idea of all the adventures it had seen with her.

6 · TARA MOSS

I followed in the wake of this silent chauffeur and arrived at a long black car parked at the kerb outside. A bit like the sunglasses the man didn't take off, the car gleamed with a sleek foreign quality, tinted and impenetrable-looking. Everything here gleamed, I thought, compared with home. He opened the right rear door for me and passed me my briefcase. I took his meaning and got in, and sat with my briefcase in my lap, while he placed my mother's tattered suitcase in the back and closed the trunk with a neat click. I was surprised and frankly flattered that anyone would deem me worthy of a chauffeur. I'd never so much as seen a chauffeur before, except in the movies, and here I was being driven by one in this city, of all places – the city of my dreams.

I sat in the back of this clean, impressive car in my good jeans and my new grey suit jacket (a little wrinkled from the flight), and clutched my freshly purchased briefcase in a way I hoped made me look like a New Yorker. I didn't have anything in my briefcase yet, except my wallet and my one-way ticket and a dog-eared paperback novel I'd been reading, but I soon hoped to have it filled with writing assignments. This was the town where I would have my career as a journalist. I would write for the big magazines. I would investigate interesting stories and interview celebrities.

I would be a famous writer.

I hoped.

We battled through a swarm of traffic that honked and stopped and started in ways I had never seen back home. Eventually our sleek black car escaped the airport and flew down wide, fast-moving roads on a maze of freeways. As we crossed the 59th Street Bridge into Manhattan I gasped in awe at my first glimpse of New York, a sight I had been waiting so long to see. Before me was the postcard image of 'The Big Apple', an island of giant monoliths built of concrete and glass. This was the concrete jungle where King Kong had swatted planes from the pinnacle of the Empire State Building. This was where countless Woody Allen protagonists lived out their socially awkward lives. This was the romance of an *Affair to Remember* and the terror of *Cloverfield* all on one island. I could make out the Chrysler Building and the Empire State. It was nearing sunset, and my fabled Manhattan throbbed with an electric buzz, the skyline glowing with thousands (millions?) of cubes of lit windows, a red sky looming above.

Over the bridge and into the maze of its skyscrapers we went.

I stared wide-eyed out the car window as tight grids of traffic swallowed us. Street after street, buildings sat shoulder to shoulder. Strangers were shoulder to shoulder, too, moving in erratic patterns across the winter sidewalks, in a scene every bit as chaotic as that I'd witnessed at the airport. There were neon signs, advertising posters and billboards. Cars honked. People shouted and walked and stood, wielding umbrellas and shopping bags, talking on cell phones or to themselves. I spotted the kind of subway grilles Marilyn Monroe once posed over. (They weren't so glamorous without her.) We headed uptown along Madison Avenue and into what I knew from my maps to be the Upper East Side, where skyscrapers gave way to five- and six-storey walk-up apartment blocks with fire escapes trailing down the outsides. We turned left and crossed the unexpected green oasis of Central Park along a single-lane road that weaved through the trees and benches, and eventually we entered a small tunnel, dark and filled with a curious fog. When the strange fog lifted perhaps a minute later we were on a dark residential street. The homes seemed older here, and quiet. The driver slowed and pulled up to the kerb of a gothic-looking corner building.

Number one, Addams Avenue.

The engine stopped.

This was the tiny Manhattan suburb of Spektor, the one I hadn't been able to locate on my maps. This was the home of my Great-Aunt Celia, my mother's mother's sister, my only living relative apart from Aunt Georgia. I had not met Celia and I'm pretty sure my Aunt Georgia hadn't met her either. From what little I did know of her, I expected a very old and quite possibly eccentric woman who had long ago lived the high life as a fashion designer for Hollywood movie stars and now lived a quiet life holed up in her New York penthouse. She'd be in her nineties by my calculation.

'It's generous of her to take you,' Aunt Georgia had explained. 'But you'll have to earn your keep. Help her across the street, get her medications and bring home the groceries. She'll be very old and frail...'

These warnings had sounded depressing, sure, but the excitement of starting my career in New York and the chance to strike out on my own seemed more than a fair trade for any geriatric unpleasantries. It wasn't every day that a letter arrived in the mail offering an orphan a new life in Manhattan. Aunt Georgia had taken some convincing, but she knew I wanted desperately to live in New York, and this was the only way I could do it. This was my ticket out of Gretchenville. It was also my chance to break free of Aunt Georgia's incessant algebra and the oppressive weight of my little family tragedy. From age eleven I pretty much had 'Poor Little Orphan' tattooed on my forehead, along with the aforementioned 'weird kid' tag, so if this generous relative I hadn't met happened to be a geriatric stranger in her eighties living in a pocket of Manhattan that didn't exist on the maps I looked at (and was about as lively as a ghost town by all appearances) I didn't care. The main thing was, I had escaped Gretchenville (population now 3999, with my unprecedented departure).

I got out of the big black car and fumbled for some money to tip the driver, who silently refused with a shake of his pale, expressionless head. He effortlessly deposited my suitcase at the jaws of the strange old building where I would live for the foreseeable future. And then he strode back to his car, got in and drove off.

I peered upwards.

The building appeared narrow and stretched to the dark sky, pointing up in a series of stone arches, turrets and spikes. It stood five storeys in total, with ancient-looking heavily embellished window arches placed in twos and threes across the front. The details of the intricate stonework had faded to stained variations of grey, and the overall effect was a little eerie to behold, especially as – unless it was a trick of the light – it appeared that the windows on the middle floors were boarded up.

Right...

I found the bell panel next to the arched, iron-gated entrance, and rang the top floor. In mere seconds there was a cheery but indecipherable reply and the gates unlocked with a buzz. I tried to haul open the wooden door inside the archway but it was heavier than the entry of a tomb, and seemingly as often used. *Could that be?* My mysterious driver had already vanished, so I put down my briefcase and gave the door a yank with both hands and all of my questionable muscle. How could an old lady live beyond such a door? How could she leave the house? Or perhaps she didn't leave the house. Perhaps she *couldn't.* Maybe that's where I came in.

Dear me. What am I getting myself into?

I pulled again. 'Oh, please open...' I murmured in frustration, and managed to crack open the door. Inch by inch I pushed inside; one foot, then an ankle, a leg, and my slim torso, until my suitcase, my briefcase and I had gained entry. The thick door creaked shut as soon as I let go, and sealed me in with a dull thud and a puff of dust. The temperature inside was several degrees cooler than on the street, which was hardly balmy. I found myself standing in an oval entranceway with a high ceiling, decorated with once-majestic tilework and gilded wall sconces, now in a state of dusty disrepair. A circular staircase snaked up towards the sealed wooden door of a mezzanine floor, and the presence of an old lift was announced by a call bell and an elaborate cage of ironwork, including spiked fleurs-de-lis, one of which was broken and balanced on an angle. Above me, a cobweb had formed across an impressive crystal chandelier, which hung slightly askew. It was the only source of light.

It seemed my Great-Aunt Celia's building was as creepy inside as it was out, not that I have anything against creepy, particularly. After all, I'd been obsessed with old cemeteries for a while. I'd photographed the one in Gretchenville perhaps a hundred times. One grave in particular.

In the tomb-like silence there was the clink and grind of old machinery, and in minutes the iron lacework of the lift doors slid back to reveal a slim woman. She stepped into the dim circle of light thrown by the dusty chandelier; a sophisticated figure dressed in a black and blood red silk dress cinched at the waist by a thin, glossy belt. For a surreal moment it seemed as if a *Vogue* fashion image from the 1940s or 50s had come to life. She wore Mary Jane heels, not flats. Not compression stockings – *silk* stockings. Her long fingers were cased in dark suede gloves, fashioned with a little cut-out at the wrist and fastened with a red leather button.

Wow!

'Darling Pandora! Is that you?' the woman sang with more vitality than I had anticipated of anyone's great-aunt. Her lips were varnished in a dark, glistening red lipstick, held wide in a smile. 'Pandora!' she said again, swaying as she stepped forward. She wore a small black hat with a thin mesh veil that obscured her face from the chin up. Yes, my Great-Aunt Celia was a widow, I now recalled, but I had not seen anyone wear one of those hats except in black and white photographs. She had left Gretchenville in the early forties to travel the world designing for top fashion houses and Hollywood movie stars, and been married briefly to a New York photographer who died of a heart condition or something. Unsurprisingly, she had never moved back to Gretchenville. (And why would she? I wouldn't.) That was what little I knew of the woman I had come to live with. Or that was what I *thought* I'd been told about her. But wouldn't that make this woman far too young to be Celia?

'I'm Celia,' she confirmed just when I was sure it had to be someone else sent to greet me. She extended her gloved hand and I blinked.

'Um, I'm Pandora. Thank you so much for having me,' I replied awkwardly and shook her hand. The suede felt velvety under my fingertips.

Doubtless I'd mixed up my histories. Was she my Aunt Celia, perhaps? My mom's sister? She didn't have a walker or anything, though now that I was looking, I noticed there was a cane in her left hand. It was made of carved mahogany and polished silver, and it shone. Somehow, though, it had the air of a prop, rather than an aid.

'Welcome. Please come,' Celia said, and beckoned me to the elevator. 'I trust my driver found you without difficulty. I hope you weren't waiting here for long?'

'Not at all. You were so quick.' She had been somewhat

quicker than I'd expected. 'Thanks so much for sending the driver. That was very generous of you.' He'd seemed so strange and silent. Perhaps that was normal. I wasn't used to New Yorkers, after all, and I'd heard they could be a bit impersonal.

'Generous?' Celia replied. 'Nonsense. That's what he is for. I can't very well leave my driver idle, can I?'

I lacked a suitable response for such a statement.

Smiling nervously, I hauled my mother's case into the small lift. Celia pressed a button, and the gothic machinery around us rattled closed. Slowly we ascended, passing the first floor, which was visible through the lace ironwork of the lift. Things were dusty and quiet on the landing as we passed. The next floor was much the same, only with an impressive cobweb dangling like white lace across a doorway. I had the distinct impression that some of the flats in this building were uninhabited.

And then, in a flash, I had one of my peculiar feelings. It started as a cold, hard thing in my stomach.

Someone died here. Someone died here, the wrong way.

The thing is, either I have an active imagination, or I see things others cannot. It's been this way since I can remember. My 'active imagination', as my dad used to call it, involves active dreams, prophetic visions, odd feelings, and it used to involve a great deal of frustration for my parents, not to mention a few child psychology bills. After I apparently foretold the death of the local butcher at age eight – and claimed to hear from him afterwards – people stopped coming to our house. It didn't matter that I was kinda smart and kinda pretty; I was the local weird kid.

These feelings of mine – or whatever you choose to call them – have always been strong when they come, but after the episode with the butcher, I learned to suppress them – with limited success.

Most importantly, I learned to keep my mouth shut.

'It's Victorian,' Celia said of the building, noticing I'd grown silent.

My great-aunt waited patiently for me to respond. I managed to nod and say, 'Mmm,' while I worked at suppressing the dread in my gut. *Death.* The feeling was strong and unmistakable.

I wondered if my Aunt Georgia had warned her about my peculiarity.

'It was built in 1888 by Edmund Barrett, the architect and scientist,' Celia went on, and gave me a meaningful look as if I ought to know something about him.

'How interesting,' I replied, recovering myself. Barrett didn't ring a bell. 'It's lovely.'

'I'm afraid it's fallen into some disrepair since my tenants passed on,' Celia told me. 'I don't recommend you explore the other floors.'

There was that cold feeling again.

'The building is structurally sound, I trust?' I smiled when I said it, as if I might be joking. I wasn't.

'Oh, darling, quite. You needn't worry about anything like *that*,' Celia said with a wave of her gloved hand.

'It's ... beautiful,' I blurted as a way of covering my little ripple of unease. 'In a gothic sort of way,' I added, and watched the deserted-looking third floor pass beneath us.

'Yes. Gothic Revival,' Celia informed me, unfazed. 'The style was popular around that time, though you aren't likely to come across many buildings quite like this one. It is unique.'

I could see that.

'I hope you didn't have too much trouble with the door?' my host ventured. 'It doesn't like visitors.'

I frowned at the choice of words. 'Yes, it is quite heavy,' I agreed. 'How do you manage it?'

'There's a trick.'

The little elevator stopped at the top floor. We had arrived. The doors slid open, and we found ourselves faced with a set of double doors like those I'd seen on each of the other landings, only in this case the doors were painted a deep, glossy midnight blue. No dust. A carved table with a silver tray stood to one side. We stepped out of the lift and the door rattled closed behind us. Aunt Celia stepped up to the doors and paused. 'Would you like to come in and see your new home?' she asked me.

'Thank you,' I said, and she smiled pleasantly through her veil.

Celia opened one of the doors with her key and I followed her inside.

I gaped.

My Great-Aunt Celia's spacious penthouse apartment was stunningly beautiful, and quite unlike anything I'd ever seen. The ceilings were high and domed in the centre and the floors were polished wood. The large main lounge room was filled with row upon row of tall bookcases bursting with beautifully bound books. I saw glass-fronted sideboards filled with curious artefacts, objets d'art and exotic plants I had not seen before. I thought I recognised a Venus flytrap, something I'd only seen in books. The furniture was antique. In fact, everything appeared old, but wonderfully appealing to the eye – a bevelled Edwardian mirror, curved lamps of stained glass, dark portraits of unsmiling nobility, exquisite tables and chairs with creatures carved into their wood. Every bit of the decor, every object, every piece of furniture seemed as if it had been crafted with the utmost care. Victorian. Edwardian. An Art Deco touch here and there. Details within details. Carvings within carvings. Celia had wonderful taste, and the different period styles blended seamlessly, though the result reminded me a bit of a beautiful library, or even museum. What Celia's penthouse lacked in 'lived in' warmth and hominess, however, it certainly made up for with elegance and curiosity. My Aunt Georgia's humble home with its modern, utilitarian furniture seemed strikingly dull by contrast. (Well, it had seemed rather dull before, I'll grant.) No cobwebs here. No sense of disrepair. The chandeliers gleamed and twinkled.

'This is my private area,' Celia told me as we reached a locked doorway at the end of a long hallway. 'I would prefer you not use this area.'

I nodded. 'Of course.'

We walked back down the hallway towards the other end of the penthouse, past the kitchen, the dining room and the vast, open sitting room/lounge room. At the far end we reached an open doorway, the end of our little walking tour. The lights were switched on inside the room, and it smelled invitingly of freshly cut flowers.

'This will be your room, Pandora,' Celia said. 'If you don't object?'

Object? Celia's guestroom was palatial in a way you rarely saw in modern bedrooms. The ample high-ceilinged space contained a grand, four-poster bed made up with lace-edged pillows. There was a tall antique wardrobe in one corner and a beautiful oak dresser on which a vanity mirror and a crystal vase of deep red roses were placed. Next to it was the open door of an ensuite bathroom with a black and white tiled floor. Two narrow, arched windows opened on to the residential street at the front of the building. A small Victorian writing table with a hinged, sloping desktop sat under one window, and an old gramophone was on the floor next to it. I wondered fleetingly if it would play. On one of the flat surfaces of the writing desk was a platter of fruit and a sandwich.

'I thought you might like a snack before you go to bed,' she explained.

'Thank you so much.' I was ravenous.

Next to the platter was a small photograph in an antique silver frame. Even from across the room I recognised it instantly, thought I had not seen it since I was very, very young. This was a portrait of my parents on their wedding day. They were gripping each other and grinning. My father wore a white shirt and tie, and my mother's veil was pulled back, circling her head in a snowy halo. They looked so young, so happy. I felt a tug at my heart.

'Welcome, Pandora.'

Once again, I gathered myself. 'Thank you so much. This is wonderful,' I told my great-aunt, and meant it wholeheartedly. I placed my briefcase and my mother's suitcase inside the door. If this was to be my new room, it was better than I could have asked for and far more than I'd expected. It was easily three times the size of the spartan room I had been living in at Georgia's for the past eight years.

'Help yourself to anything you like in the kitchen, and in the apartment. I want you to feel at home here,' Celia told me. 'However, there are some rules.' Beneath the veil, her face became serious, and I stood at attention, as if to let her know I would take her rules on board like a good cadet. 'Knock before you enter, please. And don't venture into my side of the flat, as I said. I don't like to be disturbed.' She watched to see that I was taking note, and I certainly was. 'And I *don't* recommend you explore the other floors of the building,' she concluded.

There was something ominous about that third rule, something ominous and important. I'm a pretty good girl, and I've never thought of myself as a rebel of any sort, but this was the second time Celia had mentioned that I shouldn't snoop around the other levels of the old building, and I admit it gave me a naughty urge to do exactly that. I put that urge firmly away. It was a simple request, and one I knew I should honour.

I nodded earnestly. 'Yes, Great-Aunt Celia.'

Celia lifted her delicate chin and gave me a reassuring smile. 'Now, darling, you may have heard that New York is dangerous. Nonsense. There are some fine folks here in Manhattan. But don't wander the streets alone at night unless you want trouble. Things change around here when the sun sets.' She patted me gently on the arm and I thought she actually winked. 'But of course you are a big girl, and you can look after yourself.'

She searched my face as if for some sign or recognition of something, though I couldn't imagine what she thought she might see.

'If you need anything you can't find here at home, there's a corner store just down the street.' Celia pointed to the left of the two tall arched windows to indicate direction. 'It's open all hours. Harold runs it. He'll get you any supplies you may need. Put them on my tab.'

'Oh, I hope to find a job very soon, and then I'll pay my own way,' I promised. I didn't want anyone's charity. 'And I'll pay you back for the car and any groceries and things.'

My great-aunt smiled through her veil. 'Of course you'll have a job soon, dear, but payment won't be necessary. You are family. Use the tab. Make yourself at home, Pandora. I think you'll like it here in New York.'

'Thank you so much. May I use your phone so I can let Aunt Georgia know I arrived safely?'

Celia leaned glamorously in the doorway and cocked her head. 'Oh, darling, did Georgia not tell you? There is no phone here. I abhor the things, and they never seem to work in this old building, anyway.'

'Oh,' I replied, floored. I knew she preferred letters, but no phone at all? I guessed that meant she didn't have Internet either...

'And no Internet,' Celia confirmed, and I flinched. 'Darling, I am sure your aunt would love to receive a letter from you in your beautiful handwriting,' she suggested. 'Why don't you write one tonight? Or in the morning?'

I nodded. 'I'll do that,' I said, thinking how very eccentric she was to live without such common modern conveniences. I guess older people didn't always email. Never mind. Getting a cell phone would certainly be a priority as soon as I got a job.

'Oh!' I exclaimed suddenly, as something moved unexpectedly against my ankle. I took a little hop back and then looked down. 'Oh, you have a cat,' I said, relieved. I kneeled down, grinning. I love cats. And dogs. And pretty much all pets. Aunt Georgia never allowed me one. I offered a hand, and the feline sniffed my fingers delicately. She was a beautiful and unusual-looking creature – snow white and short-haired, with not even a single dash of colour on her soft coat. She looked up and I saw her eyes were like pink opals. Even her eyelashes were ivory.

'Yes,' Celia replied. 'She is Freyja.'

'Freyja' was a name I recognised from my mother's books. Growing up, I'd read every book in the house several times, and though I preferred my paranormal romance novels the best, my mother's books on ancient cultures, mythology and folklore were a close second. Freyja was the name of a Norse goddess, if I remembered correctly. She was often depicted wearing a flowing

feather cloak of some kind, driving a chariot pulled
by cats.

'I think it's a great name,' I said, and Freyja purred
and circled my ankles before strutting over to her mistress.

'I think she was investigating your room. It's been a
very long time since we've had anyone stay. We hope
you'll like it here, Pandora.'

With another gentle pat of my arm, my great-aunt
left me for the evening. Freyja walked after her with her
tail up. I smiled to myself at the sight of them. I was
desperate to sink into that four-poster bed, but not before
I wolfed down the sandwich she'd prepared and enjoyed
a long soak in the exquisite claw-foot bath of the ensuite.

I found some bubble bath and got the tub steaming
hot. Georgia's house in Gretchenville had one shower and
no bath, and I soon realised how much I'd missed bathing.
I luxuriated, shaved my legs, washed my long, naturally
light-brown hair with some lovely rose-scented shampoo,
and ate the most delicious strawberries I'd ever tasted. I
stared at the bathroom ceiling, wet and smiling. Once
soaked and sated to the point of bliss, my hands wrinkled
like prunes, I towelled off and dried my hair. By the time
I flopped onto my new bed I was already in a deep lull. I
reached over to switch off the bedside lamp, and through
heavy eyes noticed a stack of fashion magazines on the
bedside table. How thoughtful of Celia to put them out
for me. There were top fashion magazines that never
even came to Gretchenville. I noticed some older ones,
too, issues of *Vogue* from the 1950s. I couldn't wait to read
them. But not yet. A hazy view of the elaborate ceiling

cornices was fading in and out of my consciousness. My white linen nightie felt cosy and warm against my clean, scented skin. My new bedroom was beautiful and not at all cobwebby or musty. I was relieved that Celia didn't seem like the invalid Aunt Georgia had described. Things were so much better than I'd feared when I'd first seen the building.

New York. I am finally here.

In the morning I would go to *Mia* magazine for my first job interview. *I will wow them*, I thought optimistically as I drifted off. *I'll have a job here in no time.*

I flicked the bedside light off, and closed my eyes. I figured I was settling in pretty well for someone who had never travelled to a big city on her own.

And I was.

Until I woke to find a man in my room.

CHAPTER
TWO

*S*omewhere in my dream I became aware of a presence.

I was in the grip of a deep sleep, and it was a struggle to lift my heavy eyelids. Through snatches of vision, I thought I made out a pale silhouette against one wall, illuminated by the low light coming in under the curtains. *Odd.* I wondered if I was dreaming, or if some item of furniture in Celia's guestroom formed the vague outline of a man, and I hadn't noticed it before I went to bed. A coat rack? One of her gothic paintings, perhaps?

Then the silhouette moved its head.

'Hey!' I shouted, and leapt out of the four-poster bed, putting it between the intruder and myself.

I remembered with sudden embarrassment that I was dressed in my nightie, and I covered my breasts with my arms as a reflex before deciding to sacrifice modesty in favour of a ninja-style pose. I held my fists up, body rigid, ready to fight. I turned my head away from the stranger for just a moment to yell, 'Celia!' through the closed door.

The man placed his hand over my mouth.

Strangely, it felt like being touched by a cloud. My resultant scream became muffled. Somehow he had traversed the bed in a flash.

'Shhh,' came a low, reassuring voice. 'I'm really sorry to have startled you.' He smiled in the half-light, and even laughed lightly, seemingly delighted about something. He had a slight accent, though I couldn't pick what it was.

I frowned, confused.

'Sorry,' he repeated, dropping his hand from my mouth. 'It's just that...I'm so glad that you can see me.'

'I'm not blind. Of course I can see you. You're in my room!' I declared, baffled. 'Celia!' I yelled again.

'She's not home yet,' the man told me.

Well, *that* was not reassuring.

'You shouldn't wake up the whole building,' he advised.

'Shouldn't I?' I challenged.

He shook his head. 'No. Though there aren't a lot of people here these days, are there?'

Great, he knew the other flats were unoccupied. That was not reassuring either.

'Are you trying to scare me or something?' I challenged boldly. 'Because I'm not scared of you.' I thought this was a bluff, but immediately upon saying it, I realised it was true. I was not particularly frightened. The man standing before me seemed kind of *calm*, and the look in his eye was not lusty or crazed or any of the things I had been led to expect of a man who would break into a woman's bedroom in New York in the middle of the night. I used to sneak into a lot of horror movies in the Gretchenville

Village Cinema when I was younger, and this person did not fit the stereotype of horror movie villain. And now that my eyes had adjusted and I was really looking at him, I noticed the other obvious thing; how he was dressed. No balaclava. No scary hockey mask. He was actually wearing a full uniform, like a military man of one of the great wars of years gone by. And he was *handsome*. (Yes, I am perfectly aware that good-looking people can be serial killers, and it is weird and unhealthy for a girl to notice the physical attractiveness of a guy who has apparently broken into her room, but there it is.) This guy looked to be in his twenties, perhaps his late twenties, and his jaw was so strong it brought to mind an anvil. He was lean and tanned, and his eyes were the brightest blue I had ever seen. They almost seemed to glow. Though clean-shaven, he had sideburns, which seemed a little retro to me. Beneath his cap, his hair was sandy and worn a bit long over the collar.

'How did you get in here?' I asked, my faux-ninja stance softening a touch. Neither of the two windows appeared open or broken. My door was closed.

'I've, um, been here for a while,' the young man replied vaguely, clenching that magnificent jaw and casting his eyes about. *He's been in this room for a while...?* 'No. Wait. That came out wrong,' he apologised. 'It's a long story.'

'You know my great-aunt?' I ventured.

He nodded. 'Celia? Sure.'

So he knew her name at least. Though given I'd called it out, it wasn't exactly hard to guess.

'Prove it,' I dared. 'Prove that you know her.' I crossed

my arms over my chest and set my face sternly to let him
know I was no pushover. A few seconds followed while
he appeared to be thinking about how best to respond.
'And why are you wearing a uniform?' I added. I guess
I was a little nervous with the strained silence. I wasn't
someone who'd had a lot of men in my room before, and
certainly never after dark, and with myself dressed only
in a flimsy nightie.

(I told you I had to get out of Gretchenville.)

'You can see my uniform?' the handsome visitor
asked, again seeming surprised. 'How clearly, exactly?'
He looked down at himself.

'Well, it's right in front of my face.' *Obviously*. This
guy might be good-looking but he was none too sharp,
was he? 'You are in the military,' I observed. 'Or is that
a costume?' He wore a dark cap of some kind, and his
dark blue uniform was impeccably tailored, and tapered
at the waist, with shiny buttons up the front. It brought
to mind the dress uniform of a marine, but that wasn't
it. His uniform seemed distantly familiar, and it set off a
thought in me that wouldn't quite form. I knew it would
come to me later. His cap was worn on a slight angle,
and I thought it gave him a bit of a movie star look, like
he was from an old war film and Humphrey Bogart was
about to waltz in.

The man smiled at me, seeming amused about
something. 'Well, yes I am...well, *was*.' Then he looked
around the room, deciding...deciding what, I couldn't
tell. His expression changed. He came over earnest-
looking, those luminous blue eyes large.

'Um...look, I am sorry to have startled you, Miss. You should forget you saw me. I will, um, make myself disappear,' he said awkwardly.

And he did just that.

My eyes must have fooled me. I could have sworn the stranger actually disappeared.

'But...' I began, and then stopped.

I glanced at the round bedside clock. It wasn't digital, but it was one of the few modern items in the room. The hour hand glowed at the two position. *Great.* It was just past two in the morning the day of my first job interview in New York City and I was standing in my host's guestroom in my nightie like an idiot, talking to the air. I half expected Celia to come in and see what the trouble was. In fact, I had half expected my mum to come in and hug me and soothe me and put me to bed again like she had when I was younger. I had always had vivid dreams – nightmares, sleep walking, sleep talking – since I was old enough to speak. But now I was far from that childhood home, my mother was long since gone, and if I had strange dreams about hunky military guys showing up next to my bed, well I would just have to deal with it on my own.

I crawled back into the big bed and stared at the ceiling for what seemed like forever before dreams finally took me.

CHAPTER
THREE

I woke from my slumber sometime before my seven o'clock alarm, disoriented. I had, for some reason, been dreaming of beautiful soldiers.

My eyes moved sleepily over the old-fashioned ceiling and light fixtures above me. This was the first foreign room I'd slept in for eight years, and as my eyes lit upon each new detail I thought I might still be in a dream. The wardrobe. The gramophone. The narrow, gothic windows.

New York!

It came to me in a flash, and I bolted out of the huge bed, practically tripping over one of the lace pillows.

My first morning in New York!

I parted the curtains, threw open one of the windows and the sounds of the city poured in on me with an exhilarating rush. Well, maybe not *quite* the exhilarating rush I'd expected. Addams Avenue was actually motionless outside, the residents evidently still asleep, but in the distance, through a light fog, I could see the towering Manhattan metropolis I had been driven through the night before. That was where I was headed. That was where I would find my career.

I was anxious to make the right first impression at my interview. So anxious, in fact, that the simple task of getting dressed became a disconcerting exercise in indecision, even though I only owned one measly suitcase of clothes. My Gretchenville clothing felt too casual for big New York and my only 'businesslike' option seemed sort of boring. In anticipation of this new life I'd bought my first ever suit in the only decent boutique in Gretchenville not one month earlier, but the mirror here in Manhattan told me it wouldn't do. I had never taken more than thirty minutes to shower, change and make myself up before, but this morning I tried each outfit on, discarded it and then tried it on again after exhausting all other options and combinations. It was humiliating. At seven forty-five I was finally ready, if a little ashamed at the time it had taken. I stood before the full-length mirror of the old wardrobe in my room for one last appraisal and sighed at what I saw. Grey suit pants. Matching grey jacket (yes, the same one I'd worn on the plane). Black square-neck knit top. Flat, ballet-style shoes. I had made some effort to tame my tresses, which now fell down my back with a slight bend, and I had put on light makeup and lip gloss.

Boring. You look boring.

I didn't exactly look like I worked for a glossy magazine like *Mia*, but at least I didn't look like a Gretchenville high school student. Luckily, I am blessed with my mother's figure (slim legs, tapering waist and a 'very nice' bust, or so my only ever boyfriend assured me). The grey suit, if not exactly stylish, at least hung on me well. It would have to do.

Enough already.

I was famished by the time I entered the kitchen. Waiting on the counter was a note from my great-aunt, left under a key:

Dearest Pandora,
Please help yourself to anything you like. I look forward to seeing
you tonight.
Best regards,
Great-Aunt Celia

The note's formality brought a smile to my lips.

Despite my hunger I decided that I was too excited to eat. I took the key, packed my map in my briefcase along with my résumés and some unpublished articles I'd written, rechecked and pocketed the address for *Mia*, and set off with an umbrella.

I was determined to walk.

Surprisingly – considering my Manhattan map didn't cover the Spektor area – I had no trouble finding my way into nearby Central Park and then across to Third Avenue. It was as if my feet already knew the way. I took my time, kept to myself and walked the many blocks to the midtown address I'd been given. It took me over an hour, and would probably have taken me less time if I hadn't been gazing up at the buildings and loud advertising around me. Before ten I was standing outside the address I had been given, warming myself up with a takeaway coffee. The address for *Mia* magazine was in Times Square, in an area of huge glass and concrete skyscrapers, and for every way that Spektor seemed old, gothic and mysterious, the towers that surrounded me were modern, over-lit and formidably sleek. I dumped my empty styrofoam cup in a garbage bin and ran a hand over my hair. It felt like it had tangled on the walk, so I pulled my brush out of my briefcase and smoothed my hair out quickly, attracting a few strange looks.

I paused.

Two women stepped through the glass doors wearing security tags around their necks with the word VOGUE written at the bottom. They seemed to shimmer in the cool winter daylight, all glossy hair, toned long legs and designer clothes. Every inch of them was manicured, groomed and expensive. I looked down at myself, with my second-rate briefcase and umbrella, and the plain grey suit I'd bought in Gretchenville. I didn't like what I saw.

Suck it up, Pandora.

This was my only scheduled job interview in all of New York. I had to be positive about it. I had never really fit in anywhere, and I hoped, no *prayed*, that this would be somewhere I could finally belong – here in this building with these people. I tried to imagine myself coming here to work, walking through those spotless glass doors and into that large reception area, around which several large light boxes illuminated the latest magazine covers of the various publications with offices inside. Each seemed more glamorous than the next – *Style*, *W*, *Allure*, *Glamour*, *Vanity Fair*, *Vogue*.

And then there was *Mia*, with a display in a less prominent position next to some teen titles and a men's magazine. It was only in its fourth issue, and I liked the new cover. It featured a young woman in a striped shirt and blue jeans. Her pixie haircut was spiked up in all the right places. She wore a leather satchel effortlessly, her stance confident and a little androgynous, thumbs hooked in the waistband of her jeans. Her eyes were outlined like a cat's, her face beautifully unconventional. Like each of the other cover girls I'd seen *Mia* use (I'd special ordered every issue and pored over each page back home), this cover model had a certain *je ne sais quoi* that appealed to me. More than the celebrities and supermodels on the bigger magazine covers, I wanted to be *this* girl. I imagined her satchel to be filled with interesting notes, journals, books, perhaps even a camera she used to document her fascinating life. She was anonymous, smart-looking, and yes, *cool*.

Mia had a mission statement that included 'real' interviews with celebrities (never the made-up stories that filled so many other publications), and rejected overly airbrushed images and pointless articles about how to 'get a man'. These were just some of the reasons why I wanted to start my writing career with them.

Ever since I first started going with my mother on her trips to the supermarket as a kid, I'd been fascinated by the glossy magazines in the checkout line. We didn't have expensive magazines in our town, like *Vogue* (there was no one there to buy it), but all the pages of cheap glamour thrilled me nonetheless. My father disapproved, of course, but my mother sometimes let me sneak one into the cart. During high school I took a part time job at Bettina and Ben's Book Barn – a new and used bookstore. It was a great resource for my voracious book reading habit, but they also had stacks of used fashion magazines at the back – fancy ones, if out of date. What I found there was inspirational, but translating couture looks to real life was not realistic. Those kinds of clothes just weren't available in Gretchenville. And then, sadly, despite being the only bookstore in town, Bettina and Ben's Book Barn closed. I guess they'd never turned a big profit, and when the online stores took off locally it put them out of business. By then I'd graduated and I wasn't keen to wait tables or flip burgers, so I gave away my cell phone and became extra careful with my spending while I held out for a writing job at the local paper. (I'd always had to be careful with money. My parents had been thrifty, and Aunt Georgia took frugality to new levels, so I didn't find it too hard.)

Amazingly, Celia's letter came soon after my unemployment, and now here I was about to walk into *Mia* magazine. It was surprising how things could come together.

I entered through the sliding doors feeling somehow smaller than I ought. My flat shoes were nearly silent as I traversed the marble floors. The man at the long marble reception neither noticed me, nor responded as I approached.

'Um, hello. My name's Pandora English, I'm here for *Mia* magazine,' I said.

The man swivelled towards me, and his eyes flickered over my torso. 'Law offices are on the second floor,' he muttered. 'First set of elevators.' He reached for a visitors tag. He hadn't met my eyes.

I shrank into my grey collar. *It's the suit. I should never have bought this stupid suit.*

'Excuse me, I am here for *Mia* magazine, please,' I said, more firmly.

He looked at me and, seeing my face, brightened slightly. With a muttered apology he handed me a security swing tag with the word VISITOR emblazoned across it.

'Eighteenth floor. First set of elevators. Return the tag when you're done,' he instructed.

'Thank you,' I replied.

I found the appropriate bank of elevators and got in the first lift that opened. It wasn't empty. At the back, a hulking young man was trying to talk on his cell phone, but was evidently thwarted by a lack of reception. He said a couple of words, frowned at his phone, seeming all frustrated, and then held the device in his hand helplessly. When he looked up and caught me gazing at him, he smirked.

My heart sped up. This New Yorker's face was charming, as was...well, the rest of him from what I could see. He seemed impossibly tall; perhaps six foot six, with the build of an athlete. He had dark brown, close-cropped hair. He was rather easy on the eyes, and mine kept drifting back to him. Before the doors closed, a petite, svelte woman of about thirty got in, dressed head to toe in black and cream, and scented with Chanel No. 5. She looked and smelled expensive. *Mr Easy on the Eyes* looked her over approvingly, and disheartened at this, I decided to stare at my flat shoes.

The elevator stopped at the second floor. No one got in. 'This is you,' came a cool male voice, just as the doors were about to close.

I turned. 'Excuse me?'

Mr Easy on the Eyes had spoken. At my response, his smile dropped a fraction.

'The law offices?' he said, seeming a little bored.

'*Mia* magazine,' I corrected him. I could have sworn the Chanel lady chuckled.

Stupid, stupid suit. I look like a law clerk? I resolved to spend my first pay cheque shopping for something more appropriate for my new career.

The elevator continued to ascend. The Chanel woman got out at *Vogue*, and as soon as she was gone I removed my grey suit jacket like it was covered in freshly spilled manure. I tried to sling it casually over one arm, and managed to flick the man in the face. A noise escaped his throat and he rubbed his eye.

'Oh, I'm so sorry! Are you okay?'

'I'm fine,' he said unconvincingly, and looked away. He was indeed tall (were all the men in New York tall I wondered) and he had hazel eyes. One eye was a little red, I noticed. (Oops.) He had the appearance of a jock, all fit and outdoorsy. His jacket smelled pleasantly of new leather and fine cologne, and when his scent hit me I was inside another of my peculiar feelings, seeing with vivid clarity this man's muscled torso and a hand sliding up his chest – my hand. I sensed as if it were real his warm mouth, his kiss, his hard body under mine...

Oh good grief.

I gasped.

'Are you okay?' he asked, and frowned at me. Now he was looking very unimpressed. He must have thought I was crazy. I could only nod. Heat crept into my cheeks. I didn't even know the man. What was I to make of all *that*?

'This is my floor,' he said, and stepped out, seeming eager to escape. 'I hope you get the job,' I heard him mutter as an afterthought.

I winced again, this time at the inference that I looked like a job applicant. I tried to tell myself it was just the visitor's tag, but I knew I looked like a fish out of water in this building of glamorous media types. Unable to look away, I watched the handsome man walk into the reception area of a magazine office. He was soon silhouetted by twin moons of tanned cleavage featured on the cover of the subtly named *Men Only* magazine, and that was my last glimpse of him before the elevator doors slid shut.

I decided that any man who worked for such a publication wouldn't know anything about women anyway. I didn't care if I had embarrassed myself, and he thought I looked like a law clerk. And I was sure the strange feeling I'd had didn't mean anything. It didn't mean anything at all.

They aren't always premonitions, I reminded myself. Just mostly.

On the eighteenth floor, my introduction at *Mia* magazine did not exactly go as planned.

The receptionist informed me that I was not expected, she didn't know who I was, she didn't care who I was, and no, I most certainly could not leave a résumé or meet with the editor and show her my work. Helen Markson, my contact, no longer worked there, it seemed. No one had bothered to inform me. I was baffled and deeply embarrassed. This mortifying conversation took place below an oversized version of my pixie-haired cover girl heroine, as if to add further insult to injury. No matter how I tried, the receptionist wouldn't let me past that cover girl to enter the office. She had no use for me at all. Eventually, I had to leave.

After composing myself in the ladies down the hall, I recovered the boldness to brave *Glamour* magazine. I'd come all this way – I had to try, right? The receptionist there took one look at me and said they weren't hiring. She was, at least, more polite about it. The Chanel woman manned *Vogue* magazine, as luck would have it, and she wouldn't let me in the door. She even seemed to enjoy ignoring me through the glass panel, the entry buzzer at her manicured fingertip. I had no interest in trying *Men Only* magazine, of course, despite feeling like I'd practically lost my virginity to one of their staff in the elevator. (I hoped his eye would recover.)

And that was it. Rejected outright, I returned the security tag without a word.

Have you ever felt so low you didn't know what to do with yourself?

I had nowhere to go, and I took my time getting there. There wasn't anything to do at Celia's penthouse except recount my failure, and I didn't have money to spend on shopping, so I walked around Times Square and gawked until I couldn't stand all the noise one moment longer. And then I walked some more.

Walking was cheap, and I discovered I had pretty good instincts for finding my way around this big city, despite my lack of experience. I walked into the Art Deco foyer of the Empire State Building, amazed to see that this famous structure was, after all, also an office building. Offices were listed on the wall. Imagine working in the Empire State Building? The idea was beyond me. I got into one of the elevators behind a small group of chatting tourists and found I was able to smile again after my miserable experience at *Mia*. As the elevator ascended and my ears popped from the altitude, I recalled black and white footage of Robert Wadlow, nearly nine feet tall, the world's tallest man, standing atop the world's tallest building with the then governor of New York. It had left such an impression on me when I was a kid. What would it have been like to be so tall? Of course, Wadlow had passed away at only twenty-two, and this was no longer the world's tallest building. It wasn't even the tallest in America, but it was still a wonder of the modern world, and I was here, *within it*, travelling to the top. I rubbed my hands together.

Good thing I don't suffer vertigo, I thought when I stepped out onto the windy observation platform.

I'd never in my life been so high off the ground, except for the aeroplane trip that had brought me to New York. This amazing tower pierced the sky one quarter of a mile over Manhattan and the view was even better than I had imagined. The enormous buildings below seemed less formidable from this angle, like dense clusters of man-made stalagmites. The geometry of the island finally made sense from the sky. From this angle the grid of streets appeared strikingly ordered. Fifth Avenue was wide and straight as an arrow. I gazed at the Chrysler Building, and the Statue of Liberty in the distance. I began to feel that I was really in New York, after dreaming about it for so many years.

I leaned forward and gripped the mesh surrounding the platform. At some point in the years since Robert Wadlow had towered over the governor here at the top of New York, they'd had to erect this mesh and a large guardrail to stop jumpers. I stepped back from it. Despite all the people, and the spectacular view, something about the moment ignited a deep, pressing loneliness.

It was then I noticed the familiar coldness in my belly, and I frowned. Something was happening. I should have felt elated, exhilarated to finally stand on this platform and take in the sights of the town that would make me all

I could be. All around me were tourists, happy, smiling, and taking pictures. And yet something was wrong.

He is much better off without me, came a voice.

I stood at attention, spooked, and darted my eyes from side to side. Who'd said that? A blur of ivory and apricot caught my eye. There was movement at the edge of the platform to my right. A woman. I saw that she was climbing up to stand on the thick concrete railing next to one of the round, coin-operated sets of binoculars. I realised I'd sensed her grief, not mine. It wasn't my own loneliness I'd felt, but hers. She intended to jump.

I rushed towards her, and a child and her mother stepped back to let me pass.

'Rude,' I heard the mother say under her breath, but I was too panicked to care. Couldn't anyone else see what was happening? I looked for help, but no one else had noticed her. If I hesitated, it could be too late.

I stopped only two feet from the woman. Her purse was on the ground at my feet. She'd left it on the platform.

This young woman was only a few years older than me, and was dressed in a forties-style matching apricot jacket and skirt, with a pair of ivory gloves and a scarf, looking every bit as elegant as Grace Kelly. The wind pushed at the waves of her hair. Aware of my presence, she turned, still balanced on the rail. She regarded me with a sad, haunting smile.

'Please come down,' I told her gently, my arms extended and palms open.

I wouldn't make a good wife for anybody, she told me, though I could see that her lips hadn't moved. It was then I realised I could see through her to the buildings below. The edges of her form were indistinct somehow.

'I'm sure that's not true,' I said in a low voice, confused by what I was seeing. 'You would make a great wife.'

The wind caught her ivory scarf, and it lifted away. We watched it drift and fall towards the street below, eighty-six deadly floors beneath us.

When she turned to face me again, I thought I saw a flash of recognition. *How sweet you came*, she told me.

'What's your name?' I asked, wishing like hell that someone would help me talk her down. I could grab her arm but she might still jump and try to take me with her if she was desperate enough.

I'm Evelyn, she explained to me. *Evelyn McHale. You are the chosen one, Pandora*. She seemed fascinated by that. Her heartbroken expression lightened just a little.

'How do you know my name? What do you mean by "chosen"?' I asked, and then I decided I didn't care about any of that just yet. I wanted her to step down off the rail, away from the edge. 'Please come down,' I pleaded. 'Take my hand,' I said, and reached out slowly.

Evelyn looked to my outstretched hand but didn't accept it. *Don't worry, Pandora*, she assured me. *I've been doing this every day for years.*

And before I could stop her, she turned and leapt *through* the mesh.

In a blink she was out of view. My heart stopped and all the breath ran out of me. I didn't dare lean to the edge to watch her fall. I closed my eyes.

When I opened my eyes I was still alone. Inexplicably, Evelyn's purse was no longer at my feet. There were only milling tourists, and me. I'd cleared a small section of the platform. The other tourists were giving me space because they thought I was crazy, I realised. I'd been talking to myself.

I pressed my cold fingertips to my temples.

Evelyn McHale. She jumped in 1947. A famous photo had been taken of her body in the crumpled wreckage of a car. I had seen it in *LIFE* magazine. I was sure of it.

Active imagination. It's your active imagination, Pandora.

I walked back to the elevator with my stomach in knots. I tried not to think of what my father would say.

I sent my Aunt Georgia a postcard informing her that I had arrived safely, and that my new home was lovely. I also mentioned that I would call her when I had my own phone. (When I could afford it... once I got a job...)

I chose a black and white postcard image of the Empire State Building, with the words 'Empire State 1947' written in one corner. I hoped Evelyn would have liked it.

❧

Central Park was where I spent most of my day. It was beautiful, and free. I loitered there for hours, and fancied that any lone figures I spotted were also rejects from small towns, wandering through New York in search of a place to belong. I ate a simple hot dog and sat on a bench near a deserted carousel, resting my feet while I finished reading my novel. I watched dog walkers, joggers and strolling couples pass me as though I were invisible. It wasn't cold enough for the celebrated Central Park ice rink, but the joggers made clouds with their breath as they ran. I froze slowly, degree by degree as the hours passed, until I felt like a stone statue. Upon the end of my novel (which featured a Viking vampire and a hot werewolf, with a romantic ending quite unlike any I'd personally experienced) I got up and walked off the chill in my bones.

At one point in my wanderings I crossed a single-lane road with light traffic, and thought I saw a car very like the one Celia's silent chauffeur had driven. I almost waved, but of course that would have been silly. I didn't know anyone in this place.

In the late afternoon the weather grew a bit strange. I was at the northern end of the park, walking a path through the trees and thinking of how much my feet were beginning to hurt, when I found myself enveloped in a surreal wall of fog. The fog was thick and odd-smelling – like the scent of old books and mothballs – and I was unable to see more than six feet ahead of me. Then, as quickly as the fog had appeared, it lifted and I found myself on the quiet streets of Spektor, standing in front of the corner store Great-Aunt Celia had mentioned.

HAROLD'S GROCER the sign in front of me said.

It was one of those old-fashioned shopfronts with a hand-painted sign, and there was something familiar and pleasant about the sight of it. I looked down the street and saw Celia's large, Gothic Revival building on the corner. My sense of direction could not have been better. I took a breath. My briefcase felt like a dead weight after all my meandering. If I was going to do that much walking, I'd need a satchel, I decided. (*Like the one on the cover of the magazine that didn't hire me.* But I wasn't going to think about that anymore.)

I stepped inside the musty store, and a bell tinkled to announce my arrival.

I looked around. The shelves were lined with basic grocery goods, though I didn't recognise the brands. There were a lot of old tins and things in boxes. The shop had a really cool cash register, though, I noticed; one of those big old metal ones with typewriter-like keys and white number tabs that pop up to show the total. A real antique. Behind it, a man was bent over some shelves, searching for something.

'Hi there, you must be Harold,' I said.

At the sound of my voice the man turned.

Oh good lord.

Harold the grocer was round and short, and he wore a plaid shirt tucked into work pants. His leather belt was straining under the bulge of his stomach. Most of all, I was struck by his virescent complexion. The apples of his cheeks were green instead of red, and the whites of his eyes were yellow. I stepped back.

'And you must be Pandora English, Ms Celia's friend.' The man smiled with Granny Apple cheeks and I nodded uncertainly.

'Uh, yes.'

'Ms Celia has really been looking forward to your arrival. She is one great lady.' He was lost in his thoughts for a moment. 'Now, what can I get you, young lady? I can get you anything you want.'

That seemed unlikely.

I swallowed. 'Um, I don't really need anything.' I wanted to leave. I'd just head home and make myself something in the kitchen. 'I was just—'

'Oh, Pandora, don't be afraid. You've got no reason to be afraid of me.'

I shook my head, mortified at the astuteness of his observation. I suppose I looked as terrified as I felt. 'Oh, no, I'm not afraid. I'm fine. Just a bit out of sorts with all the travel,' I told him, not wanting to admit that in my current fragile state his complexion was peculiar enough to send me running.

'Yeah, that's some little town, Gretchenville.'

'You've heard of it?'

'Oh yes. Celia talked about it. Population of three thousand nine hundred and ninety-nine, with your departure, huh?'

'That's right.' Exactly right. Creepy.

'Now what can I get you, young lady?' he pressed.

I looked around the store. 'Well...I'll need some fresh milk, I guess. And do you have any cheese?'

'Milk is in the fridge over there. Just tell me which

cheese you want and I'll make sure I have it for you next time you're in.' He moved forward a step and leaned on the counter with one elbow. He didn't have a lot of hair, and the faintly green wisps atop his head moved a little as he spoke, like seaweed in a soft current.

'Oh, I don't want to put you to any trouble,' I said.

'You, trouble me? No! This is just what I'm here for, Pandora. Just tell me what type of cheese you like.'

I had half a mind to ask for something unusual, like Stilton or something, but I'd never tried anything like that and I just wanted plain old cheddar. I told him so.

'Come in any time and I'll have it ready for you,' he assured me, and smiled at me with such genuine kindness that I found I could overlook his unusual appearance. 'Anything else you can think of? Anything at all?'

I bought some soft drink, some milk and a small box of cereal and Harold put it on Celia's tab without even giving me an option to pay. I felt funny about using my great-aunt's tab, despite her insistence, but I was determined to pay her back as soon as I had a job. (Whenever that might be.)

'Now you come back tomorrow, okay, Pandora? Any time. I'm open all hours.'

I nodded. 'Thanks, Harold.'

'And remember not to go wandering after dark unless you are looking for trouble, okay?' he said.

I nodded at his warning, grabbed my shopping and briefcase and made my way out of the store.

'But of course, you can look after yourself,' I heard him say as the door shut behind me.

I waved at him through the glass pane in the door and thought it odd that Celia had said almost exactly the same thing.

CHAPTER
FOUR

The winter sun was beginning to set by the time I heaved on the bafflingly heavy door of Celia's building, my arms filled with groceries and my heart battling with the day's disappointments. After all that rejection, I was in no mood for further resistance.

'Oh, come on door, open,' I muttered at it, and it gave slightly.

I struggled inside, cursing under my breath, and dragged my groceries and myself into the lift along with my *I-thought-it-was-fancy-when-I-bought-it* suit and briefcase, which was decidedly bereft of assignments and full of as many résumés as it had contained when I'd left that morning. To add to my melancholy, I was sure my flat shoes were half an inch flatter than when I'd left in the morning. And I'd given myself blisters. A fit of sadness hit me as the elevator ascended, and I did my best to brush it aside. It wouldn't do to feel sorry for myself. I had a lovely and generous host. My first day in New York had not gone how I'd hoped, but that was probably to be expected. I'd been naive, that's all. I would get there.

But with no Helen Markson, who will I see about a job?

I arrived at Celia's penthouse, used the key I'd been given, and stepped inside. Such was the day I'd had, it felt like it had been weeks since I'd left the place bursting with optimism and too excited to eat. The apartment was dark and I guessed my host was out, or perhaps having a nap. I flicked on a light in the open lounge room, and put down my bags.

'Oh!' came a cry. It was my Great-Aunt Celia, who was reading an enormous novel in the small halo of light of her reading lamp, half hidden in a book-lined alcove in the lounge room. Freyja the white cat was curled up on the hassock next to her resting feet, and in a flash she leapt up and hid behind the chair. Celia, too, sprang quite suddenly from her upholstered chair, and her book fell to the floor with a dull thud as she literally leapt away from her reading lamp and slipped into the shadows beyond it with a deceptively youthful agility.

'Great-Aunt Celia?' I asked. 'Are you okay?'

'Oh, darling Pandora, you startled me,' she said from the shadows. 'I hoped you would knock.'

I'd forgotten. 'I'm so sorry,' I apologised, and then stopped short.

My eyes were adjusting to the darkness, and what I saw amazed me. Celia wasn't wearing her hat and veil, and I could see that her face was *beautiful*. Her skin was white and luminescent, her eyes wide and dark, and though I would have deemed it impossible, she seemed barely to possess a crease or a wrinkle. Celia's eyebrows were high and sharp, as were her cheekbones. With her crimson lips and her glossy dark hair set in perfect waves she looked like a 1940s movie star. It was impossible to guess her age, but even in the low light I was utterly shocked by her appearance. This was *Great*-Aunt Celia, who would have to be around ninety years old by my calculation? *No way.* She looked younger than my own mother would be, were she alive.

'You startled me, my dear,' Celia repeated, reaching blindly behind her. The fingertips of one elegant hand found her black hat, and in seconds she had fixed it expertly to her head with a bobby pin. Once again, the thin mesh veil fell over her face, obscuring her luminous skin and oddly youthful features. She took her cane in one hand.

'I forgot you asked me to knock,' I said, quite stunned. 'I'll remember in future.'

'Thank you,' Celia said, arranging herself to lean casually on the head of the cane she didn't really seem to need. 'How did you go today?' she asked, expertly changing the subject.

'Good,' I said automatically. But that wasn't true. 'Actually, not so good,' I corrected myself. 'I don't think there was any interest at the magazines I went to, and my contact at *Mia* no longer works there and no one had bothered to inform me.'

My miserable first day of job hunting was upsetting, as was the embarrassment of bursting in on my generous host and startling her, but most of all, I was distracted by the vision of Celia *sans* veil. I thought about the face I had just seen. I thought about reasons why a woman would wear a veil all the time, even indoors, and reasons why a woman would jump up and act all odd when she was seen without it. Perhaps this wasn't my Great-Aunt Celia at all? Perhaps this woman had done something to Celia and was living here under false pretences? *Is this woman an impostor?* But, if so, what possible reason could she have for allowing me to stay?

'Celia, I have to say, you look beautiful without your veil,' I told her, and watched her face. 'You *are* my Great-Aunt Celia, right?'

She smiled through the little squares of fine netting. 'Well, yes. Thank you, darling Pandora, but I think you are the one who needs complimenting. You have lovely features. Great bone structure, just like your mother.' She moved forward into the light and touched the edge of my hairline, sweeping the hair back behind my ear.

I did look very much like my late mother when she was my age. That was true.

'Yes. Now, let's see what you are wearing. This is a new suit?' Celia tilted her head, examining me. 'Hmm. Polyester. The fabric is inexpensive, but the colour suits your complexion.'

From a former fashion designer, I didn't really mind the comment about the material. It was made in China, I knew. But still.

'You didn't make the impression you wanted to today, did you, Pandora?'

I pursed my lips. 'No,' I replied tightly.

'These magazines interviewing you, they are fashion magazines, yes?' she asked.

I nodded, a touch guilty. Even when I was ten, my parents had disapproved of their sole offspring's preference for glamorous magazines rather than the *Journal of Archaeological Science* or the *Annual Review of Applied Linguistics*. Mostly, this was a disappointment to my father, from what I can tell. (One of a few disappointments, actually, my 'active imagination' being the primary one.)

Celia nodded thoughtfully. 'I see.' She placed her hands ever so lightly on my shoulders, then my waist and my hips. Her touch was quick and efficient. 'I have a couple of things I'd like you to try on,' she told me.

'You do?'

Celia disappeared and returned a few minutes later with some garments folded neatly over her arm. In one hand she held a pair of Mary Janes, a bit like the ones she wore herself. This pair, however, were ruby red.

Oh...

My eyes widened at the sight of them. 'Those are really back in fashion,' I said, recalling that I'd seen something like them on the cover of *Vogue* (I remembered how the Chanel woman had so rudely kept me out of the office, then hastily banished the thought...)

Celia placed the clothes over the arm of her chair. She shook her head gently. 'Fashionable? Oh, darling, *fashion* is merely an exercise in spin,' Celia told me. 'True style is not about fashion. Style is individual. Style is part of the great theatre of life.' As she spoke, she gesticulated in the air with one hand. It was a theatrical movement, and she performed it with elegance.

I didn't understand this distinction. Weren't fashion and style the same thing?

'You'll see what I mean,' my great-aunt assured me. 'You like these shoes, I see. What is your shoe size?'

'Um, an eight.'

'Ah, you are a true Lucasta. The Lucasta women, we've always been the same size. You can have these shoes. My gift to you.' She handed them to me and I must have lit up like a kid at Christmas, because she smiled broadly through her veil. I held the shoes by the lip of the heel, and studied them as I would a sculpture. They were in excellent condition, but aged slightly in ways that seemed to give them more character. The leather was softly worn inside. I wondered what they'd seen. I wondered where they'd walked. They seemed to have a magical quality about them.

But this wasn't all my great-aunt had for me. She held up a knee-length silk dress, cut on the bias. 'And this would suit you, also,' Celia suggested. The amber fabric shimmered in the light of the reading lamp. 'It will bring out your beautiful, cognac eyes.' No one had described my eyes that way before. 'And this jacket.' She said, and passed me a lightweight bouclé wool woven jacket. I recognised the iconic style immediately, confirmed when I saw a flash of the worn label: CHANEL. 'You could wear this with your jeans to your next interview.'

My eyes widened once more. Chanel was perhaps the most imitated and ripped-off label in the world but this jacket was the real deal, and it had life in it. It looked like it had seen things, experienced things. I thought it was much cooler than anything the Chanel lady from *Vogue* had been wearing. This jacket had history. I had half a mind to go back to *Vogue* wearing it, just to make her jealous.

'I'd love to wear it. Thank you,' I said, not bothering to hide my excitement and gratitude. Maybe these outward signs of belonging would help to get me through the door of one of the magazines I so desperately wanted to work for.

'Designed by Coco Chanel herself, not that Karl Lagerfeld fellow,' Celia explained. 'Coco was chief designer until 1971, and she invented the multi-layered pearls and smart jackets look that is still popular today. There is a matching skirt but I'd recommend you wear it with jeans, for a more casual look. You are only nineteen, after all. You don't want to look like you're wearing your great-aunt's clothes.'

I laughed, and she flashed a wicked smile.

'"Vintage" they call these now,' Celia mused. 'But the word *vintage* normally refers to the time that something of quality was made, like a wine, not the thing itself. Interesting, don't you think? We didn't call these clothes 'vintage' back when they were made, but this was when clothes were made with quality, to last. Good clothes never go out of style. You just have to change the way you wear them, that's all.'

'So fashion is just a trend, and style is something else?' I asked.

Celia nodded. 'Now you are beginning to understand.'

She'd given me an idea. 'I could write a piece on that.'

'Why don't you?'

I'd read an article in *Mia* (not that I was going to think about them anymore...) about how tons of unwanted newly produced clothing were unceremoniously dumped and destroyed rather than given away or marked down because a lot of designers wanted to keep their high-end brand-associated prices. Perhaps I could write a piece on vintage clothes? On the advice of a former fashion designer? On quality rather than newness?

I was so focused on the thought of what I would write that I almost forgot my questions about Celia and her identity.

Almost.

'So, how long ago did you last see my mother?' I asked casually, fingering the wool of the jacket she'd offered to lend me, and looking over my shoulder to watch her expression. An answer like 'last year' would alert me that something was amiss. I couldn't truly believe this woman was an impostor, but what other explanation could there be for her youthful appearance?

Celia sighed and laid one hand on my shoulder. 'Oh, darling, it is terrible what happened to them. It really is. When they died, I hadn't seen either of them for a few years. Travel was not what it is now. I wish we'd spent more time together.'

Well, that was pretty convincing, I had to admit.

'It must have been hard for you, foreseeing that,' she added.

I froze. What did she mean?

Celia gave my shoulder a little squeeze. 'You were only

a little girl when I last saw you, no older than three or four, but I could tell even then that you had the gift.'

I didn't remember the meeting. I was too young. 'What do you mean, "the gift"?' I asked.

'Your name, Pandora. Your name means *gifted*.'

I blinked. 'It does?' I knew all about the mythical Pandora, but I'd never had it put that way before. 'Gifted?'

'Yes. You are gifted,' she told me, and cocked her head. 'Your mother did not discuss this with you?'

I shook my head.

Celia seemed thoughtful. 'We have much to discuss then,' she said finally. 'But first, you are new to New York, so perhaps you are not familiar with the wide range of publications in the city. Did you know that there is a magazine here that shares your name?'

'It's called *Pandora*?' *Really?*

'Yes. Perhaps tomorrow you could present yourself and see if the editor will take you on.'

I laughed. She couldn't be serious. 'You make it sound so easy.'

'It is, darling.'

'You think I can just show up?' That certainly hadn't been my experience so far.

'I think that's precisely what you should do,' Celia said firmly, and gave me a knowing look I didn't quite understand. 'Tomorrow. Go to *Pandora* magazine.'

'A special jacket can only take you so far, you know,' I protested. But my great-aunt was a stubborn woman, I could see. There was no point debating it.

CHAPTER
FIVE

*M*y brain simply would not rest.

On my second night in New York I lay in bed in my white nightie and stared at the ceiling, thinking, thinking, thinking...

How can Celia be my great-aunt and look so young?

Celia sure seemed like the glamorous 1940s designer she was supposed to be, but it seemed impossible to me that she could be over eighty, or even fifty years old. I didn't know much about big cities, of course, but I didn't think there was anything in the water in Manhattan that could have that kind of effect. I couldn't ask my mother, and I sure didn't want to share my questions with Aunt Georgia, who had been reluctant to let me go. She had only agreed because Great-Aunt Celia was my only other living blood relative, and would probably benefit from having someone to help her around the house. There was no way I could risk being summoned back to Gretchenville, even if my initial impressions of New York were a little less than fairytale. As I drifted off my increasingly tired mind wrestled with the conundrums of

Celia's appearance, my strange and exciting surrounds, and my first terrible day of rejection.

It was sometime later that I realised I had not come to bed at all.

I was still sitting up with my Great-Aunt Celia in the lounge room, bravely asking her outright if she was an impostor. *'Are you the real Celia? Why are you so much younger than you are supposed to be?'* I probed.

Celia had her veil off again, and her exposed skin was luminous and beautiful. She was alluring in a way I had never been witness to before. I actually wanted to reach out and *feel* her cheekbones. The urge to touch her was almost irresistible. I couldn't take my eyes off her face. And despite our conversation, despite my questions and this bizarre trance I was in, Celia seemed forgiving and kind and gentle. She was unruffled by my interrogation.

'Darling...' she began. Celia held my hand as we conversed, her gloves off and her hands icy cold and soft as silk. She gave my hand a little squeeze. *'Darling, everyone's doing it. It's no big deal,'* she explained patiently, and when she smiled I saw she had enormous ivory fangs. As she continued to smile, her eyes began to glow red and she transformed before me – her forehead became monstrously bat-like, her hands turned to claws. *'Come on, Pandora, give it a try,'* she growled, turning more beast-like by the minute. She snatched me by the throat with her clawed hands, and held me still. *'Join me!'* she cackled triumphantly.

'Nooooo!' I screamed and struggled to break free from

her grasp. 'No, Celia! Don't!' I fought her off desperately, barely able to breathe.

My cries were muffled and when I opened my eyes again, predictably, I was in bed. One of my hands was clutching my own throat – both protecting it from my nightmarish vision of Celia and making it rather hard for me to breathe. My other hand was clawing my pillow quite uselessly. (I told you I have active dreams.)

'Psssst... Is everything okay?'

What?

'Do you need assistance?' came the voice again.

I sat up and looked around.

Am I awake this time?

My heart was pounding pretty fast, so yes, I decided, I was very much awake if not exactly fully lucid. It was night. I was in my room in Celia's penthouse, and the lights were out. The shades over the tall, narrow windows were not quite closed, and small shafts of streetlight illuminated the darkness. I could see Celia's clothes hanging from the wardrobe, the fancy Chanel jacket ready for me to wear. Where had the voice come from? My eyes lit upon a white shape near the door. It resembled a man, just as I had seen the night before, and again, as my eyes adjusted his features became clear; the tailored uniform and cap, the masculine jaw and bright blue eyes. This time the man held his cap in his hands, head bowed slightly as if he were addressing someone respectfully. He was tanned and clean-shaven, and his sandy blond hair sat in glossy waves, worn a little long over the ears.

This time I didn't bother calling for Celia.

'Miss Pandora?' the figure asked. He knew my name now.

'Yes,' I answered, more or less convinced that I was dreaming again. Still, dreaming the *handsome soldier* dream was an improvement on being sucked dry by *Countess Celia, vampire-at-large.* 'What's *your* name?' I asked in a whisper.

'Second Lieutenant Luke Thomas, ma'am.'

'Second Lieutenant Luke Thomas. Of course,' I grumbled and leaned back on my elbows. He looked young for such a rank. 'Well, Lieutenant Luke, I've just been having a ridiculous nightmare, and I'm not talking to you because you don't exist. Good night.'

I slipped back under the covers and closed my eyes. After a few beats I opened them again. He was still there.

'Do you wish for me to take my leave?' the young man asked, sounding a little uncertain. He still held his cap in his hands. The sight of it was sort of heartbreaking for some reason. 'You sounded like you needed assistance. You screamed,' he informed me.

I sat up on one elbow and frowned. 'Am I dreaming?' I asked the room.

'No, I don't think so,' Luke replied. 'You can see me?' This seemed to be a particular point of interest, if our last 'conversation' was anything to go by.

'Yes,' I replied. And I could. Luke was in the same uniform, the dark blue single-breasted coat – an old-style frock coat – worn almost to the knee and decorated with nine polished buttons from the high collar at the neck to the narrow, nipped waist. The uniform was neatly

tailored across his broad shoulders and trim physique.
His dark blue felt cap had crossed sabres embroidered on
it, and was decorated with two feathers. His pants were
sky blue, with a stripe up the side, and he wore handsome
leather riding boots, I now noticed. The overall effect was
somehow romantic. 'I really am seeing you, aren't I?'

'Yes, I believe so,' he replied, his head still bowed a
little.

'And you are a ghost?' I ventured.

'I am deceased.'

Goodness. I sat up fully, and rubbed my eyes. This
wasn't a dream/nightmare that was going to go away
any time soon, it seemed. 'I guess I'd better put something
on,' I decided. 'Would you look the other way please,
Lieutenant?'

'Yes, ma'am.'

I giggled a little at his formal reply – considering the
circumstance of the bedroom and all – and grabbed my
grey suit jacket from next to the bed. It didn't exactly
look right over my nightie – well – it didn't look right
anywhere it seemed – but I felt less exposed. 'It's okay.
You can turn around now,' I said.

My uniformed visitor turned back around to see that I
was sitting on the end of my bed, arms crossed, wearing
my polyester suit jacket over the white linen nightie. I
tried to think of something intelligent to say to him, while
still accepting that I was probably dreaming and would
be sure in the morning that I'd been talking in my sleep.

Talking to a dead military guy in my sleep. Such a typical
'me' way to spend a night, really.

'You said last night that you've been here for a while,' I recalled. This felt like a variation of *So, do you come here often?*

'I live here, yes. Well, I exist in the building.'

'Do you usually "visit" the visitors, then?'

'There aren't many here. There haven't been for a while,' he told me. 'Not, um...' he hesitated. 'Like you. Living.'

Creepy. Boy, I know how to give myself creepy dreams.

'And my Great-Aunt Celia?'

He must have seen the question on my face. 'Oh, no. No, not that I have any problem with Ms Celia, it's just that we don't... Um, she doesn't see me, I don't think. We've never spoken.'

This is a weird conversation. Very, very weird.

To the best of my memory and to the best of my knowledge I hadn't spoken to any ghosts since I was little, and those 'imagined friends' had got me in a lot of trouble. My mother, who was quite big on total honesty in parenting, had calmly explained to me that the 'Butcher Incident' nearly ended up with her and my dad getting divorced. My father was apparently stuck on the idea of having a normal child, and of course science and reason were all he had room for. My mother was more accepting, I think, and she had subtle ways of letting me know that it was okay if I was different. Over the years she decorated my room with ancient masks from all the countries she travelled to, and she explained that we could be anything we desired, depending on our will. Many nights I drifted off to sleep under the hollow eyes of the noble Sumatran chieftain mask, the Kwakiutl wild woman, and the African Pende mask for communicating with spirits, wondering who I would be.

Now, at age nineteen, I was a woman, not a child, and this conversation I was having with a dead man named 'Lieutenant Luke' might not be happening, but at least it was harmless. My father couldn't be offended. It wasn't going to break anyone up. And at least I'd dreamed up a handsome ghost, even if he appeared to have died some decades before I was born and probably wouldn't be a wealth of knowledge on pop culture or the things I needed to learn about fashion. (Fortunately I had a freakishly young great-aunt for that.)

'So, just to clarify, my great-aunt can't see you, but I can. And you are deceased,' I said.

Luke nodded. 'Yes. Since the Civil War,' he confirmed, quite deadpan, so to speak.

The Civil War. Of course.

I was no expert on the Civil War, but I knew that it had to do with the North and the South fighting, and it had to do largely with a dispute over slavery. It lasted for a few bloody years in the 1860s and the Confederate Southern states were eventually overcome, and slavery was abolished. I'd seen lousy re-enactments in video presentations at school when I was very young. But the subject was not exactly at the forefront of my mind, so I couldn't imagine why I would conjure a soldier from the war here, now, in New York. Why couldn't I imagine Alexander McQueen, or Gianni Versace, or someone else more helpful to my current predicament?

'And what have you been up to since the Civil War?' I asked casually.

He clutched his felt cap, his tone turning serious. 'I was a second lieutenant in the Lincoln Cavalry,' he said. Well, that explained the riding boots, and the frock coat. Abraham Lincoln was the President at the time, so I guessed that the Lincoln Calvary would have consisted of soldiers on horseback fighting for the Union army, against the Southern Confederate slave states. The Union colours were blue. 'I was in the Army of the Potomac in the Eastern Theatre,' Lieutenant Luke went on, but when he saw my blank expression he paused. 'I forget that was a long time ago. I am sorry. There have been other wars since. There are other wars now. These things would not interest you.'

'Please go on,' I encouraged him. 'Don't *you* be sorry. I'm sorry for my ignorance.' I should have paid more attention in history class. But then how could I have known I'd have a conversation like this in a dream so many years later?

'The Civil War broke out shortly after my wedding, and I was called to battle. My wife Edna was with child,' he said. 'A daughter, she believed.'

At that I got a little shiver. The smile was wiped from my face.

'It was bloody. Much bloodier than we had anticipated, and we were ill prepared.' The regret in his voice was palpable. I saw the pain flicker behind his eyes and wondered what horrors he was recalling. The men who volunteered would have been especially young and inexperienced. I recalled stories of unprepared troops. Starvation. Lack of organisation. 'I've always thought that was the reason I did not pass over – because I did not get to meet our daughter while I was alive. Somehow, after the pain of dying, I just ended up here wearing my dress uniform. I don't know what happened to the other men, or where my body was taken. I don't know what this building is. I don't know what happened to my family . . . my child.'

Gulp.

I realised my eyes had welled up. I kept them open so tears wouldn't cascade down my cheeks. I believed this could possibly be the saddest story I had ever heard. This was not what I wanted of hunky soldier dreams. Hunky soldier dreams were not supposed to involve sad stories. Hunky soldier dreams were supposed to involve the kind of lovemaking I read about in my novels – the kind of lovemaking I hoped to one day experience.

'My wife was around your age when we married,' he observed, smiling gently. 'She was very lovely, like you.'

I bit my lip. 'How old are you?'

'I am twenty-five years of age. That is, I was twenty-five in 1861.'

1861. I tried to take that in.

'Are you unwed?' he asked.

I blushed. 'Um, yes.' I looked at my hands.

'Oh, I am sorry. I have embarrassed you.'

'Oh no, it's fine. Yes, I am unwed.'

'I am sorry for my question. I sometimes only think

in the old ways. I don't have much experience in the new world. In fact, I can't pass outside the walls of this building.'

I tried to imagine what that must be like.

'That was all a long time ago and I have been here, just...waiting. For what, I don't know. For many years I expected to find my wife and daughter here, but they never arrived. I am alone.'

Wow. This illusion of mine was beginning to sound quite convincing. I pondered that. And I pondered why a ghost like Luke – if that's what he was, a ghost – couldn't escape these walls, couldn't get *free* even after all of his family must have passed over. What was it that held him here?

'It must get very lonely for you,' I said.

'Yes. In one sense. But there are sometimes others to talk to.'

I felt another shiver. 'There are?'

'Oh, I don't mean to alarm you, but yes, from time to time there are others. And I do see some of what goes on outside these walls, even though I can't be part of it. I can 'see' things, as it were. I can see the world changing around me. I experience things much differently to how I did before *this.*'

Before you were dead.

Interesting. This, at least, was something we had in common. I sometimes knew about things I couldn't rightly know about, and because I had no good reason to know these things, and no rational or scientific explanation for why I knew them, I was as good as a ghost. No one would believe me. My father had taught me to distrust my gift, and my mother, whether she intended to or not, had taught me the trouble it could cause. Those were the lessons of my strange youth.

'Can I ask you something?' Lieutenant Luke said, and paused.

I nodded, and watched him through eyes that were a touch blurry from fighting back tears.

'It is true, isn't it? *That we won?*' he asked, and seemed to hold his breath in anticipation of my answer.

I found I had been doing the same, and when I realised what he was asking, I exhaled. 'Yes. Your side won,' I told him.

Lieutenant Luke closed his eyes and nodded. After perhaps a minute he opened his eyes and smiled gently at me. 'I had heard, but...I wasn't sure.'

'The war lasted a few years, but yes, the Union side won,' I said. 'Of course, that was one hundred and fifty years ago now.'

Lieutenant Luke stiffened. 'Did you say that was one hundred and fifty years ago?'

I hoped I hadn't said anything wrong. Had he not known? Was this bad news for him? Had he believed it still possible that he would find his living daughter or wife?

'Yes. The Civil War ended about one hundred and fifty years ago,' I explained more cautiously.

At this apparently new piece of information, the young man appeared lost in thought. 'These are interesting times, then,' he said at last. 'Very interesting times.'

When he looked up his bright eyes searched my face with new curiosity. Had I said something significant?

'Thank you, Miss Pandora,' Lieutenant Luke said. 'Thank you for listening to me. I'm sorry if I saddened you. It was not my intention.'

I shook my head and a tear fell down my cheek. My guest ghost gently wiped it away with a hand that looked as real and human as any I'd seen, but felt like a cool, soft cloud.

'May I visit you again?' the handsome visitor asked.

I nodded, and at that he kissed my hand. His lips felt like a cool tingle against my skin and my body responded with a flush of warmth.

Oh boy.

'If you ever need me, just call for me. Good night, Miss Pandora.'

And he vanished.

CHAPTER
SIX

On my second morning in New York I woke with painful pins and needles in one arm, and an odd 'pulled' feeling in both armpits. I noticed that I had somehow worn my suit jacket to bed, over my white nightie. This was not the most comfortable or logical of sleepwear choices.

Then I remembered how it got there.

Luke. Lieutenant Luke.

'Pandora, honestly,' I berated myself aloud, and this time the 'room' did not respond. Was I so desperate for a man that I had to dream one up? I hadn't thought so. But then dreams could be revealing. On the surface, at least, I didn't like what the dream of Lieutenant Luke might say about me. And I certainly didn't like the dream about Great-Aunt Celia the vampire.

Why couldn't I dream of puppy dogs and kittens like most girls?

My eyes lit upon the Chanel jacket that hung from the wardrobe in my room. I recalled my conversation with the beautiful and wise former designer Celia.

Should I really present myself at *Pandora* magazine, as she suggested? Could I risk the second day in a row of heart-wrenching rejection?

I was still undecided when I shuffled into the kitchen, my hair askew. What I found there surprised me. There was a note waiting for me on the counter, beneath a string of costume pearls:

Dearest Pandora,
The offices of Pandora magazine can be found at the following address. See Skye between nine thirty and ten.
Good luck. See you tonight.
Best regards,
CELIA
PS Chanel Inspiration.

Hmmm—.

This note was accompanied by a piece of paper listing the SoHo address and details of *Pandora* magazine. Skye DeVille was the editor. The demographic for the magazine was said to be females aged seventeen to twenty-five, which I fitted well. Beneath this note and the address was a carefully torn page from a magazine. It was a picture of a young woman in a Chanel jacket worn with a white T-shirt, strings of costume pearls and faded blue jeans. She wore her hair a bit like I did, loose and natural.

I smiled. Inspiration indeed.

Just before ten I found myself eye to eye with the hollow twin orbital sockets of a full-sized skeleton in a shop window on Spring Street.

I'd followed the directions on my map to the SoHo address for *Pandora* magazine and found this strange display. I pressed my hands up to the glass to shield the glare and saw that beyond this skeleton were more skulls and medical models, taxidermied birds, bats, even an alligator's head. Venus flytrap plants lined the window with green mouth-like leaves open with what seemed like bared teeth. Was this unusual shop where Celia had purchased hers? What was this place? I took a step back from the glass. It was called EVOLUTION, according to the sign. Sadly it wasn't open yet. I'd check it out after my (quite possibly humiliating) trip to *Pandora* magazine.

South of Houston Street sure was interesting, and had a different flavour to what I'd seen on 5th Avenue and around Central Park. SoHo was once known as Hell's Hundred Acres, and had been filled with brothels, bars, factories and sweatshops. Former industrial warehouses were now artist residences and high-end fashion boutiques. On the way to *Pandora* I'd wandered past Bloomingdales, Dolce & Gabbana and Chanel; I walked with my head high, knowing I was wearing Celia's jacket designed by Coco Chanel herself. The fashion boutique that left the biggest impression was a store for Prada. It had a huge sloping window display as deep as a Gretchenville front porch, and decorated with gravity-defying couture-clothed mannequins.

I looked at Celia's note again and realised that I had not quite arrived at the right address. I was standing in front of number 120, instead of 120b, which showed as a narrow doorway next to the shop. I smoothed my hair down in the reflection of the shop window, approached the doorway and nervously pushed the buzzer for *Pandora*. Still warm from walking (which people seemed to do a lot of in New York), I waited on the wintry street in my T-shirt, jeans and worn ballet flats, wearing Celia's exquisite vintage Chanel jacket and pearls, all covered by a heavy winter shawl I would take off before presenting myself. My briefcase was armed with my résumé and I was armed with a glimmer of hope. I waited, a little warily, for a reply.

Buzzzt.

There came a brief babble of loud static and voices, and the door buzzed. I pushed on the unlocked door and gratefully stepped inside.

Pandora magazine was on the fourth floor of a six-storey walk-up, according to Celia's note, and the rubber soles of my ever-flatter shoes made dull little noises on my ascent through the cold and graffitied stairwell. There were signs over the doorway for each floor, indicating photographers and design studios, and I was panting lightly by the time I reached the doorway bearing the sign PANDORA MAGAZINE.

If nothing else, this city would keep me fit.

I pushed my way through the door and a soft chime

sounded. I found myself in a classic converted New York warehouse space with painted concrete floors, exposed metal beams and brick walls. The office was sparsely furnished but quite chic, with several large cubicles spaced out around the floor, and one walled office built into the corner, presumably for the magazine's editor. A broad, white reception desk was immediately in front of me as I walked in. Behind it sat a faux red-haired receptionist. She offered a distracted 'Hello,' seeming a little preoccupied with flipping through her Rolodex. She seemed a little panicked, actually.

'Hi there. Excuse me,' I started, staring at the dark part in the receptionist's dyed hair. After yesterday's record, I felt I had experienced rather enough rejection for a while and I wasn't keen to get started on the next phase of disappointment, but there was nothing for it but to get on with things, however they were destined to turn out.

'Oh dear, what a day!' the redhead exclaimed quite suddenly, and looked up at me with a dazzling, crooked smile. 'Hi. Ohhh, cool jacket. Is that vintage?'

I nodded.

'How may I help you?'

I recalled my rude reception at *Mia* and *Vogue*. This was a different experience already. 'I'm here for, um, a job...' I began, a little too uncertain for my own good.

'Oh! Oh, thank god you're here,' the young woman said, cutting me off. 'I'm Morticia. It's so nice to meet you! You were so quick!' She leapt to her feet and shook my hand.

This Morticia had a body that was tall and bent like Popeye's lady friend, Olive Oyl. She looked about my age, and despite her handle she didn't seem to be much like the Addams Family's matriarch, apart from her skin, which was as pale as parchment. She sported red, shaggy hair instead of straight black locks. No shuffle. No Gomez. This Morticia came around the reception desk, smiling. I took in the mini-dress and striped, opaque stockings she wore with Doc Martens, and some part of me immediately liked her.

'It's been absolute chaos this morning, as you can imagine!' I was told. 'I just couldn't believe it when I got the message. I think Skye will want to see you first, then we can get you settled in.'

Holy cow. I had to stop her there. 'I'm not sure if there is some mistake,' I explained. 'I would love to meet the editor but I'm just here looking for a position. My name is Pandora English. I don't actually have an appointment…'

I trailed off. Morticia was paying no attention whatsoever, and was instead ushering me past the sleek reception area to where the 'real' work of the magazine happened. The writing. The editing. The design. I counted five stylish young women and one man hunched over laptops. Half of them looked up when we walked in, and then quickly got back to whatever tasks they were absorbed in.

'My name's Morticia, by the way. Did I mention that?'

'Yes. It's a great name,' I told her.

'You can begin today?' she asked eagerly.

I nodded vigorously, and then stopped myself. This was simply too good to be true. 'I'd love to, but—'

'You speak English? No visa problems?'

I shrugged.

'Good. Now I think you'll find Skye a bit—' she began, but stopped when a petite, formidably groomed woman about ten years our senior stepped into our path and narrowed her mascaraed eyes at me. She had the air of a coiled snake, and although she was arguably much more stylish and sophisticated than either Morticia or myself, she wore her expensive clothes like a suit of armour. There was nothing fun about it, or about her demeanour. I wondered fleetingly if Celia would call it 'fashion' or 'style', or neither. Her hair was worn short, black and slick, and her lips were a thin line of pastel. I noticed angry lines around her mouth.

'Skye, this is Pandora,' Morticia began, her head bowed towards the fearsome woman's designer shoes. 'She's replacing Samantha. Isn't it great that her name is actually Pandora? Pandora *is* your real name, right?'

I nodded in reply, reduced to mute head motions by this surprising turn of events.

'*Samantha,*' Skye DeVille hissed. From the tone of her voice I gathered that the woman of that name had fallen out of favour before her sudden departure, or perhaps it was the suddenness of the departure that had caused her to fall out of favour? The editor's dark eyes moved to me and I was looked up and down with an X-ray-like scan. She seemed to sneer at my hair and unmanicured nails, but thankfully, incredibly, I seemed to pass muster. (Thank you, Celia.) 'So, you are the new girl,' she observed. 'Well, we have five days until deadline. Be on time and get the damn coffee orders right. Samantha didn't know her chai lattes from her double espressos.'

I wanted to laugh, but Morticia's expression warned me off the idea.

Skye's lecture seemed to be at an end, so it was my time to impress. 'It is such a pleasure to meet you,' I said, mustering my courage. 'I assure you that I am the right woman for the job. I am always punctual, and I am ready for any assignments you might have for me.' I fumbled in my briefcase then extended my hand. 'Here is my résumé.'

Skye raised an eyebrow. She did not accept my résumé. The air in the office seemed to have actually cooled. I looked to my shoes, all my bravery extinguished. This woman was Medusa, and could turn me to stone if I met her eyes.

'File those,' the editor demanded, and pointed at a pile of files sitting on a desk. I lifted my eyes just enough to see where she pointed. 'Morticia, sort out the paperwork for this girl.' With that she turned on her Prada heel and disappeared into her office. The door slammed and rattled. I noticed that the other staff had been watching from a (safe) distance. The office had fallen into a dead quiet, and now the buzz of work resumed.

My mouth felt dry.

'Your desk is here,' Morticia said gently, in almost a whisper. I was shown to my humble cubicle. Actually, it was a half-sized cubicle outside Skye's office door.

'Do you know how to make coffee?' she asked me.

Just great. 'Yup,' I replied. 'I know about coffee.'

If I was a more independent person, more proud, and with more options in this new city, I might have stormed out of there and told Skye to get an enema with her blasted chai lattes. But I didn't. 'You want me to start right away?' I asked instead, not quite believing my luck. I would rather risk facing Medusa every day than go back to Gretchenville.

'We need you to start right away,' Morticia replied, as if it were the most natural thing in the world. 'I'm glad the ad for an assistant was answered so quickly. You're perfect. You don't have a criminal record or anything, do you? You're not an illegal alien?'

'No. Nothing like that.'

'Perfect. Oh, you'll probably want to clean out Samantha's desk,' Morticia said apologetically.

I nodded and opened the first drawer. I found candy wrappers, dried gum and unopened mail.

Well, you have to start somewhere.

CHAPTER
SEVEN

A strange parcel arrived on the afternoon of my first day of work as a humble assistant at *Pandora* magazine.

I'd scoffed down an unsatisfying deli-bought thing called a 'Reuben', and I was just preparing a post-lunch coffee to have ready for Skye, when a courier arrived. (The editor appeared to be fuelled solely by caffeine. Really. My head would spin with that much java and tea-leaf.) I heard a little bell chime and watched the man enter, clothed in wet lycra and sweat, a heavy satchel around his neck. Morticia signed for the stack of goods he gave her and the moment the man walked out the door, she turned and nodded to me, her full arms extended. She held a stack of A4-sized parcels I could safely assume were rival magazines or back issues. And she also held one heavy-looking cube, wrapped in brown paper.

Strange.

It seemed I was having one of my odd feelings again. It was as if – as if whatever was in the cube-shaped parcel was quietly leaching the life from the air. I tried my best to ignore it, but it just wouldn't go away. I searched Morticia's face to see if she, too, sensed something weird about the parcel she was holding. Apparently she did not.

Morticia gave me a strange look and asked, 'You all right?'

'I'm fine,' I replied. I hesitated again, and then took hold of all the items, with the cube resting on top of the other parcels, finding that I was reluctant to let it make contact with my hands.

'What is this?' I asked Morticia.

'I dunno. Probably a product sample,' she explained. 'Skye gets sent a lot of stuff before it comes out so she can road-test it. The publicists send her everything. Actually, I think she's waiting on some new skin cream that's launching tomorrow. It's supposed to be better than a facelift, not that *we* need one yet, but boy is it looking like it will be popular! The big celebs have started using it overseas.'

'Really? Who?' I asked excitedly.

Morticia curled her lip. 'Dunno. Real famous ones.'

'Oh,' I said.

'I hope this is it, or heads will roll. We're doing some big promotion for it and she hasn't even got her coveted sample yet.'

Morticia leaned in and flipped the square parcel over to read the sender's address. 'Bingo! *BloodofYouth*. Thank the stars! We're running a big shoot with the brand ambassador as a tie-in — who is super hot by the way — and doing some giveaway and everything. When Skye didn't get her magic tub of the wonder cream...well...'

'I can imagine. *Get the woman her beauty cream*,' I said dramatically, as if it were a dose of lifesaving penicillin. I resisted calling our boss Medusa. Besides, it wasn't even the original Medusa's fault that she was a monster. A curse from the wrathful and jealous Athena turned her into the petrifying Gorgon, and I hardly thought Skye's ill temper was the result of a curse from the gods.

'Get the woman her beauty cream!' Morticia repeated, and we chuckled until the tension was gone.

'Funny,' I added. 'But my great-aunt looks really good for her age. Like, *weirdly good*. Maybe she's using this stuff,' I joked. Well, half joked.

'Maybe she's a vampire!' Morticia joked. She lifted her hands above her head like monster claws, went bug-eyed and mouthed '*Oooooo*' to complete the effect.

I thought of my nightmare about Celia, and bit my lip.

'Look, you'd better give this *BloodofYouth* sample to Skye the moment she comes back from lunch,' Morticia advised. 'It might put her in a better mood.' She looked at her watch – an amusingly retro plastic Swatch with eighties fluoro detail – and stuck out her lip a little. 'It's after one o'clock already. You'll want to have a skim chai latte ready for her and have all the mail waiting in a neat pile. She likes neat piles. She likes neat everything.'

I nodded. 'Understood.' I was lucky Morticia had experience with Skye and was willing to help me out. 'Wait,' I said. 'When she left for lunch I thought she told me she wanted a skim latte when she got back, not a skim *chai* latte?'

Morticia raised her eyebrows as if to say *Are you willing to risk it?*

Frankly, I was not.

I marched back into the main office and placed the courier packages in a stack on my desk. I proceeded to prepare a skim chai latte along with the already prepared skim latte in the little communal kitchenette a few feet from my cubicle. All the while, my eyes were constantly drawn back to the cube on my desk. The strange feeling was as strong as ever: the feeling that something wasn't right. It was so strong that I wondered how come no one else had noticed.

It's in your head. Stop being the weird girl.

I had to remember that I had an overactive imagination and that kind of imagination had no place here at work.

'Okay, editorial meeting in my office, five minutes!' came a shriek, and I dropped the spoon into the chai at the sound of the voice.

My boss had returned, and boy, did the entire office know it. The lively chatter died in an instant, and the area sprang into action. Within minutes the relevant people were crowded into Skye's office, clutching sketches and laptops and papers. I got myself together, pushed that feeling about the parcel out of my mind and approached the open office door. I knocked, and there was an alarming scream of 'What?!'

It was her. Skye.

'There is nothing costs less than civility,' Cervantes once said. Skye clearly disagreed. But I couldn't afford to. 'Before you begin,' I said with exaggerated politeness, 'was it chai or coffee you wanted?'

'Skim chai latte,' Skye demanded, and I smiled as if everything were just peachy. 'Here it is then.' I handed her the cup in my left hand. 'You also have some couriered parcels. Your sample of *Blood of Youth* has arrived, I believe.' I gave her the prized parcel. I was quite efficient for a worker on her first day, I thought. 'Have a good meeting, everyone.'

Skye stood with her chai in one hand and her eagerly awaited parcel in the other, and I thought an impressed 'Hmmm' escaped her thin pastel lips. She squinted at me for a fraction of a second before putting both items on the desk and getting on with the meeting. Not a thank you. Not even a polite goodbye.

I slipped away, but not before I witnessed a wiry blonde woman rip into the parcel and exclaim, 'Oh, good.'

'Garcia says the shoot with Athanasia last night came up really well,' the one male staff member said. 'Very *edgy*. Good cover options. He's uploading the pics now and apparently she is coming in herself for final shot approval this afternoon.'

'We've got a deadline, people...' was the last thing I heard before I shut the door of the office.

I took a seat at my cubicle.

And exhaled.

At five-thirty the winter sun set outside the windows of *Pandora* magazine's SoHo office. I watched the sky turn red and begin to darken. The office fluoros provided unnatural light, turning each of us wan. My first day of work in New York City had involved a lot of preparation of hot beverages (I was getting to be quite the barista) and monotonous and mind-numbing filing. Not quite what I had envisaged back in Gretchenville, but it was a job in the media and therefore exciting.

I'd spent half my day sorting little piles of stuff my predecessor had left behind. One pile was Samantha's unfinished filing, of which there was plenty (oh joy), one pile was garbage, and the third was miscellaneous items. I'd found the expected pens and pencils, paperclips, a hair band, a stray lipstick (not my colour), a few coins and a partially torn photograph of a young woman with a female relative. This last miscellaneous item was creased and curved to the shape of a wallet. I assumed it was an image of Samantha with her mother. The two women had similar features – curly blonde hair, wide blue eyes and round faces. They wore their hair in a similar style, just above the shoulders. If this was Samantha, she looked like a nice girl, and fashionable, of course, more fashionable than me – although that was changing now I had Celia's help. My predecessor looked to be about my age. I wondered what had happened to her.

I gathered my things, and stood. It was time for me to head home and thank Celia for her uncanny suggestion, and as my thoughts turned to Celia, I again wondered about the woman who had taken me into her home. Why had she invited me here? Why now? What was the secret of her youthful looks? What a strangely deserted place she lived in. Well, not *all* deserted. Would handsome Lieutenant Luke visit me for a third time? I found myself hoping he would.

'I am super excited about Athanasia coming in!' Morticia declared, hovering around my desk after clocking off. 'She'll be here any second now, I know it. I'm so excited I could spontaneously combust!'

I drew a blank. 'Athanasia?'

'Athanasia, the *supermodel*!'

Oh. So the supermodel's parents had given her a weird name too. Thanks to the books my mother left around the house, I knew a bit about ancient mythology and names. Athanasia was from the Greek, meaning 'Immortal'. It was better than Pandora, that was for sure. Morticia was clearly hanging around in the hopes of a glimpse of this Athanasia, her supermodel crush.

'I've always wondered about the term "supermodel",' I ventured. 'What special powers do supermodels have over non-super models?'

X-ray vision or the ability to shoot lasers out of their eyes, maybe?

Morticia shrugged. 'They are more beautiful and more famous, I guess.'

I nodded. 'I guess.'

I was mildly curious to see what impressive charms Morticia's supermodel might possess, if she ever did show up. The atmosphere in the office had become increasingly strained as the time grew later and their magazine cover model had not shown up to execute the required approvals. She sure had the office in a state. I did not know much about models and magazines and photo shoots, but it seemed to me that this model must be special to demand photo approval for her shoot. Or was it simply that she had a good agent? Perhaps this was her special super power?

Most of the other office staff were in for a late one, it seemed.

Oh...

There was a soft chime and everyone looked up at the same instant. All of the staff of *Pandora* magazine stopped their hurried work, their chatter, their business, and gaped at the tall visitor who had arrived. The energy in the office changed as dramatically as if a tiger had strolled in.

Good grief, she is gorgeous.

This was clearly the supermodel. I realise it is redundant and quite unnecessary to point out that a professional model is gorgeous. That's basically their sole job description. But this one really *was*. She appeared ageless, statuesque and as pale as snow. Her auburn hair was glossy and thick, and trailed around her shoulders with the soft movement of slithering serpents. Her lips were plump, red and inviting, her eyes were feline and set wide, giving her a striking, almost alien look. Her body was willowy and stretched, with a waspish waist even smaller than my own. A pair of fashionably skinny dark denim jeans showed off the shape of her long legs. She wore her jeans with tight, calf-height heeled leather boots and a slightly futuristic-looking black leather vest that showcased her feminine waist and slender arms. Some unusual jewellery shone around her neck.

Lordy me.

There was nothing vanilla about this girl. She had real presence.

'She's no wallflower,' my Aunt Georgia would have said, and I know it sounds crazy, but it was impossible to see those lips and not think about what kissing them might be like. Don't get me wrong, I like men. (A lot. Not that I'd known many back in little Gretchenville, mind you.) But there was something about her – and I could tell the whole office felt the same as I did.

I blinked a few times and tried to rein in my wild thoughts.

Morticia seemed to be silently vibrating next to me. I thought she might go weak at the knees and actually swoon.

'I am Athanasia,' we all heard her declare across the hushed room, and in seconds Morticia was running over to her and I was headed towards Skye's office to let her know that her cover model had finally arrived to complete the shot approval for the feature.

I knocked on Skye's door.

'What?'

'Athanasia is here,' I told her through the door.

The door opened without hesitation, the edge of it nearly beaning me in the head (which was perhaps what I needed to snap me out of my strange trance) and Skye breezed past me with an uncharacteristic smile painted on her face.

Looking at Athanasia across the room while she waited, arranged in a model pose with one hand on her hip, I imagined the shoot had indeed gone well, and this model would be on the cover of *Pandora* magazine and selling a whole lot of copies in a very short time. And perhaps this little bit of brand promotion with the magazine would sell a lot of beauty products, and keep Skye in *BloodofYouth* miracle cream in perpetuity. Was that how this stuff worked? Was that what was making Skye look so fresh this afternoon? I'd noticed her making herself up again in the bathroom after lunch and now it was evening and even under the unflattering fluoros her complexion was still flawless, despite the stress of the day. In fact, she looked noticeably better than she had when I first laid eyes on her. Was that possible?

Skye met with Athanasia at reception and walked the model to her office, glowing. Morticia trailed behind for a while, presumably just to be near Athanasia. Her normally animated face was slack with awe.

The supermodel passed me at my desk, and I felt a cold wall of disinterest. Then her nostrils flared, and she fixed me with a look, as if my scent had given her pause.

Death.

I froze. Those eyes seemed black — her gaze more deadly than the mythological basilisk, killing with a single glance. More deadly than the petrifying Medusa. *Death*, I thought again, and the thought came with terrible visions — blood running like ink. Screaming. Horror.

I shivered. Athanasia's penetrating gaze finally broke off, and she slipped into the office with Skye. The door closed behind them. Our eyes had met for only a matter of seconds, but I was wounded by the exchange. Shaken. I looked down at myself and saw my hands clenched so hard my knuckles were white. My nerves were on violent edge, like I had just narrowly avoided being hit by a car, or crushed by the jaws of some giant T-Rex. I couldn't believe that a mere sixty seconds earlier, I had felt like kissing this creature. I felt queasy and disoriented.

What was going on here?

'Holy crap, she looked at you,' Morticia whispered breathlessly at my side.

She sure did.

'Why are you so obsessed with her?' I snapped.

Poor Morticia recoiled like she'd been slapped. 'You don't think she is amazing?'

Amazing, yes. But…

'I think she is very beautiful,' I admitted cautiously. 'But doesn't she seem a bit…cold?' 'Cold' was severely inadequate to describe what I'd felt, but I couldn't think how else to describe it without seeming crazy.

'I don't care. She's awesome,' Morticia said defensively.

I left it at that. Why should I care if everyone was falling over some supermodel who had fixed me with a gaze fit to turn me to stone? I didn't even know why I found her so confronting. So, maybe she wasn't very nice. Who cared? Probably I was just jealous of her.

But…

There had been something else. The blood. The darkness. I realised I was talking myself out of what I had sensed, and whatever it was had been very, very powerful and menacing.

'I think I'll head home,' I said. 'Are you sticking around?' I found myself wishing she wouldn't. I found myself thinking that it would be better for Morticia if she left the office.

'I've got some, ah, things to do,' Morticia lied, not meeting my eyes. I could see that she wanted to be near Athanasia. I had probably insulted her by suggesting her model heroine was not worthy.

'Okay, well, take it easy,' I said, and gathered my briefcase. (Which still didn't have any writing assignments in it, but it *was* only my first day...) I'd been told to come in to work by nine thirty, which seemed civilised.

'See you tomorrow, Morticia,' I said. 'Thanks for everything today. You've been really nice to me. I hope you...have an early night.'

CHAPTER
EIGHT

*W*hen I left my new job I was tired enough and hungry enough to decide to hail the first available cab on the streets of SoHo, rather than attempt the walk uptown in the dark. The 'first available', however, took a long time to find. Living in Gretchenville I'd known nothing of rush hour and after a frustrating twenty minutes walking from street to street, during which time it started to rain, I became desperate to get back to the comfort of my new abode.

'Oh please, just one taxi,' I muttered, ready to give up.

Just then a yellow cab let out a passenger but two feet from where I stood. I barely waited for the other passenger to pay before I folded my dripping umbrella and slid into the back seat with my briefcase. 'Thanks,' I said gratefully, and belted myself in. The taxicab was pretty clean and it smelled of fake pine scent permeating from a tree-shaped deodoriser hanging from the rear-view mirror. It had a thick plexiglass divider between the front and back seats, and the driver was sitting on one of those fluffy seat protectors.

I said, 'Spektor, please.'

'Pardon me?' the driver responded with a slight accent. He was an older gentleman, and his bald spot was visible from the back seat, despite an ambitious comb-over. I had been led to believe there were a lot of cabbies in New York who weren't polite, but this one seemed to be, if perhaps a little hard of hearing.

'I need you to drive me to Spektor, please,' I repeated, noticing the driver's pale, washed-out eyes observing me in the rear-view mirror. They seemed to ask something. 'It's on the Upper West Side,' I explained. 'Only I think you have to head up the east side to take the tunnel through Central Park.' That was the way the chauffeur had driven, and the way I had walked.

In the rear-view mirror I saw a crease form between his bushy grey brows. 'I've never heard of no Spektor Street, lady,' he said. 'And I've been driving this cab for twenty-two years.'

I resisted rolling my eyes. 'Spektor is a suburb, not a street,' I corrected him, but there was still no recognition in his face. 'Just drive uptown, please. May I have your map?'

'There's no such suburb as Spektor in Manhattan, lady, I'm telling you,' the driver said, this time a bit more aggressively. We had not moved from the kerb.

'Nevertheless,' I said patiently, 'would you mind driving uptown and passing me your map, please?'

He slid open the little divide and chucked a heavy directory into the back seat with a thud. It flattened my hand.

Well that doesn't seem real polite, I thought.

I flipped through the directory and, to my dismay, I couldn't find Addams Avenue or Spektor. *Oh, come on*, I thought. I'd spent a long day in New York at a new and unexpected job, and I was starting to feel on edge about being out and about, alone after dark. I had been warned about it by Harold and Celia. What if I couldn't find Spektor on this map, as I hadn't been able to find it on my own map? Or what if this cabbie refused to take me there? Would I have to walk back to *Pandora* magazine and face Athanasia and my new boss in order to call another taxi? How embarrassing.

'It's got to be here... I know I'll see it,' I mumbled desperately.

And then I saw it. I breathed a tiny sigh of relief, and my shoulders relaxed. I marked the page and triumphantly passed the directory back through the opening in the divider. 'Just here, please,' I told the man as politely as I could, pointing at the spot on the map. 'Take me to Addams Avenue, Spektor.'

All that anxiety for nothing...

Without a word he placed the directory open on the seat beside him and pulled into the flow of traffic. Beside us I saw a long black car, a bit like Celia's chauffeur's one, and I thought of how many rich New Yorkers there were who could afford such luxuries.

When my taxi driver stopped at the next set of lights he picked up the map with a sigh. 'Let's see now,' he said, not sounding very convinced. But when he saw where I had been pointing he changed his tone. *'Well, I'll be.* Huh.'

He drove uptown, across Central Park and into the tunnel, and the city grew darker as we approached Spektor. Despite the occasional streetlight, the air seemed thicker, denser, and the taxi driver slowed down and leaned forward to examine the quiet buildings out his front windscreen. He didn't say anything, but I imagined he was wondering what I was doing living in such a neighbourhood. I had to admit it looked a bit spooky on this particular night. I was quite surprised to see Harold's Grocer was closed when we passed it. The lights were off in the shop, and it even had an abandoned air about it. I thought Harold had said he was always open? I had planned to drop in and pick up that cheese he'd said he would get in for me. I loved my cheese and crackers. Comfort food. I hoped nothing bad had happened that would force Harold to close. He'd seemed a nice, albeit green, fellow.

We pulled up at Celia's building, which had a small yellow carriage light glowing out the front, and the cabbie kindly waited for me to open the spiky iron gate and the heavy wooden door with my keys before he drove away. Then he drove *fast*.

If there was a trick to opening the heavy door of Celia's old gothic Victorian building, evidently I was learning it. After anticipating that it would be troublesome, I said a little encouragement to myself, pushed with all my might, and nearly fell into the lobby when it opened with ease. The door closed behind me with a puff of dust. Well that hadn't been so hard. I grinned triumphantly as I crossed the tiles of the entryway, anticipating the pleasure of sharing my good news about *Pandora* magazine with Celia. She would be well pleased that her advice had paid off so spectacularly. I barely registered the cobwebs and dust, the broken pieces of ironwork, the flicker of the once-majestic chandelier overhead. I was halfway to the caged lift when I stopped dead in my tracks.

There was a sound coming from *beneath* the floor.

My ears pricked and I fixed my eyes on the tiles below my feet, holding my breath, and gripping my briefcase with white knuckles. All the tiny hairs on the back of my neck stood on end.

What. Was. That?

Movement below. A tremor? Creaking? Shuffling? Chanting? What had I heard? It seemed indescribable in any language I knew, and while I couldn't identify it, the sound had set my nerves on edge. I thought the building was empty save for Celia, Freyja and myself? Were we on a fault line? I felt a cold sensation in the pit of my stomach.

K-k-k-r-a-a-c-k. S-s-s-h-h-h-k.

I continued to stare at the tiles, eyes wide, but the floor did not crack open and pull me into a fiery pit or dark abyss. Nothing happened at all. The building grew silent once more and I was left frozen in the lobby. Perhaps that had been the building 'settling'? Or there was someone in the basement? My imagination was getting the better of me. Surely it hadn't been so dastardly a sound. It was hardly surprising that an old building should creak. *You're nervous about your move to the big city*, I told myself, and continued to the elevator.

When I arrived at Celia's penthouse apartment I remembered to knock. I was relieved to be 'home' again. I'd shaken off the weird feeling I'd had about a supposed sound coming from beneath the lobby floor (imagined), the supermodel at *Pandora* magazine (just a not-so-nice supermodel; what did it matter?) and the weird parcel from the courier as well (my active imagination – again), and now all I could think about was how amazing it was that my great-aunt had known I should apply for a job at the magazine that shared my very name. On only my second day in New York I already had a job in the media. This more than made up for my rejection at *Mia*.

After knocking I waited a few beats, and then opened the door.

'Hi, Celia, I'm home,' I sang.

I stepped inside the penthouse smiling and saw that Celia was at her usual spot, under the halo of her reading lamp in the little alcove to one side of the lounge room. The curtains were drawn shut. This time she wore her veil as she read. Her shoes were off and her feet were up, ankles crossed elegantly. Freyja was curled next to her toes. She raised her head to acknowledge me with her pink opal eyes, and then went back to resting.

I couldn't wait even to ask her how her day was. 'Great-Aunt Celia, *how did you know?*' I queried. I took off my winter shawl, put my briefcase and umbrella down in the entryway and walked towards her, then remembered to take my shoes off. 'They hired me on the spot! I couldn't believe it!'

Celia placed a big feather bookmark in the novel she

was reading, and rested it on the arm of the leather chair. 'Things went well today, then?' she replied, and turned to grin at me through her veil.

'Did it ever!' I slid her Chanel jacket off, and folded it carefully over my arm. She remained seated, elegantly reclining in her chair. 'You are just *amazing*,' I marvelled. 'How did you know they needed someone so urgently?'

Great-Aunt Celia just smiled enigmatically.

'Thank you. Thank you,' I repeated. If she hadn't suggested the magazine, who knew how long it might have taken me to find a job? How many days of rejection would I have endured? How quickly would I have run through my measly savings in this town? The taxi home had cost more than two dinners out in Gretchenville.

'You're welcome, darling Pandora. Call it serendipity,' Celia told me.

'You were so right. I just can't believe my luck,' I said.

Not that my new job would be all easy, of course. Skye DeVille did seem a little difficult.

'I think their print deadline for the next issue is in a few days, so everyone's a bit stressed. Perhaps it's like that every month? I don't know. And I saw the cover model for the next issue,' I said, thinking of Athanasia. 'The model was...very interesting-looking.'

'Is that so?' Celia lifted her stockinged feet off the leather hassock, and sat forward.

I could see she wanted to know more, but what was I going to say? That a really hot fashion model gave me a dirty look?

'Um, Great-Aunt Celia, is there anyone else living here?' I asked to change the subject.

She cocked her head. 'No, Pandora, there is no one else living in this building,' she said. 'Just the three of us.' She nodded to Freyja, who looked lazily in my direction and rested her chin on her white paws.

'No one living in the basement or anything like that?' I had to double check.

I thought I detected a brief smile beneath the veil. 'Not a living soul, no. Why do you ask, Pandora?'

'Oh, no reason,' I replied quickly to cover my anxiety. 'I was just curious. Anyway, I can't believe the magazine hired me on the spot. Thanks for your advice.'

'I am happy for you, Pandora,' Celia said. 'And I think you'll be surprised at what you can achieve when you put your mind to it.'

CHAPTER
NINE

*T*he next morning I went back to *Pandora*'s offices. It felt exciting to return, even knowing it wasn't my ideal job. *Yet.* In my mind I was already plotting ways to showcase my writing ability and ditch my position as Skye's minion and personal barista.

To my surprise, the receptionist Morticia presented me with a slimline computer monitor and a wireless keyboard. She placed it on my desk with a clumsy *thunk*.

'Samantha used this for a while,' I was told. 'Before we got her the laptop.'

'Oh, good. A computer.'

'I kinda borrowed it when Samantha got the laptop,' Morticia admitted guiltily. 'Which she hasn't returned yet. Anyway, this should do. I've set up your email account, and here's the WiFi password.' She had written it down for me on a purple Post-it note with an illustrated spider web decorating one corner. It made me think of the cobwebs in Celia's building.

'You know how to use it?' she asked me.

I was pretty good with computers, and I tended to be

a quick study with new things. I'd had use of a computer in Aunt Georgia's study, though her bulky old second-hand monitor was the size of one of those old cathode-ray tube television sets. Her Internet was still *dial up*. I could read a book while I waited for websites to load, and often did. But dial up had been better than nothing, and the Internet had been my portal to bigger places; an escape from that little town. I had surfed the news sites, the fashion blogs and websites for my favourite authors and movies. This computer, on the other hand, was sleek and new. I was already excited about the possibility of looking up a few things online – vintage clothing trends for the article I planned to write, info on the supermodel Athanasia, and that miracle beauty cream she was the face of, among other things.

'I'll let you know if I have any questions,' I said. 'Thanks, Morticia. This is great. I appreciate you parting with it.'

'Yeah, right.' Morticia winked. 'Pleasure.'

'How were things last night?' I had to ask. 'With Athanasia?'

At this, Morticia took a deep breath. 'Oh, isn't she beautiful?' she gushed, more to the heavens than to me. 'Well, she sat in Skye's office for an eternity and picked out the shortlist of photos, I guess. Apparently all that's needed now is some text about the product launch and we are good to go with the feature. I knew she would come through on time.'

I smiled at her. 'Did you get to meet her?' I knew that had been her goal in hanging around.

Her crooked smiled dropped. 'No. Some creepy guy came to collect her and she left about an hour after you did.'

Maybe that was for the best. She didn't seem to me like a very nice person, and Morticia would doubtless have been disappointed if she'd actually met her idol.

The door chimed and Morticia jumped to attention.

It was Skye – boss, magazine editor and office dominatrix. It was nine-thirty on the dot as she sashayed through the empty reception and into the office, radiating confidence and, well, just *radiating*. She swanned past us, seeming unperturbed that Morticia was not at her post. This morning she was dressed in some expensive-looking silk beaded top and immaculate designer jeans and heels, a woolly winter coat thrown over her arm, and when I caught a glimpse of her face I thought she looked different from the day before. Her hair was the same; short and slicked back from her face. Her makeup didn't look especially different, but she looked sort of 'glowy' and fresh, like she had managed a peaceful twelve-hour sleep, though that seemed unlikely considering the publishing deadline.

Morticia watched Skye pass warily, and when the editor's door closed behind her, we both exhaled. The receptionist gave me a nervous little crooked smile, and walked away with her Doc Martens squeaking on the polished concrete floors.

Left to my own devices, I gratefully turned my attention to my new computer.

I fumbled around a bit and found a power switch at

the back of the computer, in a dome-shaped spot like a mosquito bite. Once it had powered up, I quickly familiarised myself with the set-up, logged on to the email program and sent my first message from my new account:

> *Dear Aunt Georgia,*
> *Having a great time here in New York. The city is amazing. Celia is a generous host, and very interesting. I already have a job at a magazine called* Pandora. *What a coincidence, hey??? I hope all is well with you and the kids at school are being good. Love, Pandora*
> *PS All the buildings here are enormous.*
> *PPS I'll send you my number when I get a cell phone.*

I clicked Send and found myself wishing I had some friends in Gretchenville to impress with an email from my new job in New York. But I didn't. I had always been considered a strange girl in a small town where strange was noticed every single day. I had had a bit of interest from boys, naturally, but had only had one real boyfriend, short-lived though that relationship had been. The gene pool was lacking, and I refused to be desperate about it. I had grown quite accustomed to being alone. Perhaps things would be better for me here in New York, where my differences seemed so much less pronounced.

The morning passed in a monotonous cycle of filing and beverage preparation. Skye was in a good mood, but nonetheless demanding. At noon, most of the office left for lunch, including Skye, and I stayed behind to take advantage of my new Internet capabilities to search out info for my article.

Vintage clothes.

Recycling.

Pre-loved fashion.

I took a few notes and thought again of Celia's insight into the difference between fashion and style. And then I thought of her unusual home, and something else she had said when I first arrived. Something about the building at Addams Avenue. I struggled for a moment to recall the name Celia had mentioned in the elevator. Edward, was it? No, it was *Edmund Barrett*, and as soon as I recalled the name correctly I got a number of relevant Google hits for the Victorian-era architect and scientist. It seemed that the man who designed Celia's unusual building in 1888 was not just any run-of-the-mill scientist dabbling in Gothic Revival architecture (as you do), but a founding member of something called the Global Society for Psychical Research. I didn't know what such a society would do, exactly, but it seemed important to his biographical information, as it was frequently mentioned.

Psychical research?

I cut and pasted the name of the society and was about to click on Search when I heard footsteps behind me. It was nearly one o'clock; time to get back to work and get Skye's post-lunch chai ready. I guiltily closed the search window on my screen and the email window quickly popped up. I turned and actually sighed with relief when I saw that it was Morticia. I should have recognised her squeaking Doc Martens.

'I can't believe Skye has fallen ill just like that! And only days before deadline. She must be steaming mad!'

'What?' I said with surprise. Skye had looked so well and relaxed only that morning. 'That's sudden. Is she okay? Is it a stomach bug or something?'

'I dunno. She just phoned to say she isn't coming back in this afternoon.' And at this next bit, Morticia lit up. 'And so… it looks like she can't attend the launch of the *BloodofYouth* beauty cream tonight. I wonder if they will let me go? It should be a real exciting night!'

I didn't think magazines normally sent receptionists to product launches, but then, what did I know?

Despite her enthusiasm, my mind was on one track. 'This is a probably a weird question, Morticia, but have you heard of something called "psychical research"?'

The receptionist frowned. 'Like research on crazy people?' Morticia cocked a pencilled eyebrow and thought about that. 'I saw *One Flew Over the Cuckoo's Nest*. Did you see that movie? They zapped them with electricity or something, because they were mental patients.'

'The Jack Nicholson film? Yeah, I've seen it,' I replied impatiently. 'I don't know what the term "psychical" means,' I repeated, this time to myself. *But it doesn't mean crazy.* 'Never mind. So, tell me about this launch tonight…' I wasn't really interested, but I thought I ought to at least be polite. Morticia was probably my only friend

in New York, apart from Celia. She was certainly my only
friend in the office.

'Uh-oh, here comes Pepper,' Morticia hissed, in a
slightly strained voice.

I turned around and found myself face to face with
Pepper Smith, the deputy editor. I took her title to mean
that she was second-in-command. Such was the level of
stress in the office and the lowliness of my status within
it, I had not been formally introduced to Pepper the day
before. In fact, I had not been introduced to anyone but
Skye and Morticia. Pepper, the deputy editor of *Pandora*,
was ice blonde and wiry, like a long-distance athlete. She
wore a cool T-shirt and jeans under a thigh-length suede
coat. I guessed her to be in her twenties.

Pepper surveyed my apparel – another 'vintage'
ensemble I'd borrowed from Celia, including a knee-
length wool skirt and short jacket with a scoop neck and
large round buttons. 'Vintage,' she stated more than
asked.

I nodded.

'You'll have to tell me where you shop,' she said.

I smiled. *Not a chance.*

'You can write?' she asked me.

I nodded vigorously. 'I am a writer. Yes.'

'Well, Pandora, we are on deadline, as you know, and
our editor has just fallen ill. She can't get to this launch
tonight. I need you to go.'

I heard an intake of breath from Morticia.

'Which launch? *The* launch?' I was too surprised to
answer with anything more intelligent.

'The *BloodofYouth* launch,' Pepper confirmed. 'We're covering it for this issue. All I need you to do is take a few notes. You *can* do that, can't you?'

'I can help,' Morticia chimed in before I could reply.

'There are only two invites and I didn't ask you,' Pepper informed her brusquely, and the receptionist seemed to actually deflate. Crestfallen, she drifted back to her reception desk, her shoulders slumped. I wondered if she would be angry at me for going to the launch she wanted so desperately to attend. If I could have, I would have invited her in a heartbeat.

'I can absolutely cover the launch,' I told the deputy editor in my most professional tone. 'What sort of piece do you want me to write?'

Pepper curled one side of her mouth in a smirk. 'No, Pandora. *I'll* be writing the piece. You just take some notes and get them to me tomorrow. Social stuff. Who was there, celebrities, any highlights. I'll be coming but I won't be able to stay long. I've got my hands full here.'

Now it was my turn to deflate a little.

'And *make sure* you get as many samples as you can,' she told me emphatically. 'They'll have gift bags or something.'

So Skye was hogging all the samples. 'I can do that,' I told Pepper confidently. 'Will we leave from here or…?'

Pepper looked at me as if I'd burped. 'I'm not going *with* you. Just get yourself there, take notes and give them to me tomorrow.' She placed the invitation for the *BloodofYouth* launch on my desk and started to walk away. 'Is Pandora your real name?' she asked over her shoulder.

'Sure is,' I replied cheerfully. 'Quite serendipitous…'

But Pepper had already stalked off to get back to whatever vital task she was busy with. I couldn't tell whether she was impressed by the serendipity or not.

CHAPTER
TEN

$\mathcal{W}$hen I arrived at the penthouse I again remembered to knock.

Celia was in her spot under her reading lamp. Her feet were up on the hassock, ankles crossed elegantly next to her cat. A pair of high, slip-on shoes were lined up next to the chair. Her veil was in place, as usual. Even as an older widow, that habit of hers seemed quite eccentric.

'Good evening, Great-Aunt Celia,' I said, and slipped my shoes off.

'Hello, darling Pandora. You are home early. How was your day?' Celia marked her page with the long feather, and closed the novel she was reading. She remained seated, and I walked over to her and put my briefcase down at my feet. My case was still empty, save for the new romance novel I'd bought. Freyja jumped down from her position on the hassock and padded up to me.

'Hi, Freyja,' I said in a singsong voice and gave her a nice pat. 'How are you?' She butted her head into my hand and purred. I stood and turned to Celia, excited. 'My day was good. I have a computer at work now – and

I have my first assignment. I'm covering a product launch tonight. Something called *BloodofYouth*.'

Celia's eyes flashed with recognition. Freyja stopped her purring progression around my ankles and sat at my feet, staring up at me.

'I have to be there in an hour,' I explained.

'Well, you ought to get ready, then. I'll organise my chauffeur to take you there,' Celia replied serenely.

'That's not necessary,' I said. 'I'll call a cab.'

'Call a cab? Nonsense. We don't have a phone. Cabs are simply impossible around here, and more importantly, darling, *how* you arrive at these things is half the trick. The other half is *when*. You must be late so you can make an entrance. You must make them wonder who you are. You must make them all curious about you, and jealous,' Celia said with a wicked look in her eye.

This was obviously how things had worked in the forties and fifties, when Celia was hanging with the Hollywood crowd, but I wasn't convinced in the least. I didn't want to make an *entrance*, as she put it. I wanted to write about the launch, that was all.

'I'll have the chauffeur ready for you in one hour,' Celia insisted, and I could see that there was no talking her out of it. 'And I suggest you wear the dress hanging on your wardrobe door,' she added.

I raised an eyebrow. Another outfit?

'I designed it for Lauren Bacall. I think you'll like it.'

I smiled and started towards my room. 'Celia, you said that Edmund Barrett designed this building?'

She smiled through the omnipresent dark mesh of

her veil. 'You've been doing a bit of research, clever girl.'

'A little, yes,' I replied. 'Just on the Internet. What was the Global Society for Psychical Research?' I asked.

Again, a veiled smile, doubly wicked now. 'We'll talk about that when you get home, shall we? You go and get ready now.'

So I went.

The dress hanging from the door of my wardrobe was ravishing. It was made of scarlet silk, and designed with a collar, delicate buttons down the front, and a tie waist. It was certainly the most stunning piece of clothing I had ever owned or borrowed, and tonight, I would wear it to the media launch of *BloodofYouth*, with a certain pair of ruby red Mary Jane shoes. I slipped it on and felt quite transformed. The silk hugged my figure, the collar adding formality and the tie emphasised my small waist. I seemed to fit all of Celia's clothes perfectly. *Uncanny.*

'Ta-da,' I said when I stepped into the lounge room forty-five minutes later, all showered, changed and freshly made-up.

Celia sauntered up to me. She looked me over and nodded. It seemed she approved. 'Just one more thing,' Celia said, seeming to derive pleasure from seeing her clothes on me.

She disappeared into her side of the flat, and I stood waiting for a spell. When she reappeared she held a beaded ruby red purse, which matched the shoes perfectly.

She also had a little brightly coloured enamel hair clip of red, blue and black. 'May I?' Celia asked, and carefully arranged my hair for me, her fingers cool and dexterous against my scalp. When she was done, she secured my hair with the little clip. I turned and looked in the mirror next to the door.

'You ought to show off your cheekbones and delicate jaw,' she explained. 'They are two of your best physical assets. And look how elegant and long your neck is.'

I'd never noticed. This new hairstyle did seem to flatter me. My hair was swept off my face, high at the crown, and clipped into place high behind my head. It cascaded down around my shoulders elegantly. I wasn't accustomed to looking this way, but I did look much more sophisticated. It seemed to shake the last of the 'small town' image off me.

'The red lipstick suits you, also. Yes...' she mused.

I had matched it to the shoes. 'Thank you,' I said.

Freyja appeared at the end of the hallway and sat down. She meowed.

'Go on, have a wonderful time,' Great-Aunt Celia said, and ushered me out the door. 'Vlad is waiting for you downstairs.'

Vlad? The chauffeur's name was Vlad?

'You didn't have to do that,' I told my great-aunt again.

'It's impossible to get a cab out this way, darling,' she repeated. '*Really*. Trust me. And you shouldn't be walking across town in those shoes, nor in that dress.'

True enough.

'Okay, but I'll take a cab home. And I'll be paying you back for this driver.'

'As you wish,' Celia responded, with a knowing smile. 'As you wish.' The expression on her face told me I was a stubborn girl, but I didn't mind that tag one bit, and my great-aunt seemed almost to respect it.

CHAPTER
ELEVEN

There is nothing comfortable about social events for me. I don't have a lot of experience of crowds – and crowds of beautiful people? Well, the thought was a little terrifying as well as exciting.

According to the invitation Pepper had given me, the launch of *BloodofYouth* was being held at a trendy restaurant called Elizabett in the Meatpacking District. The address was printed on the beautifully produced invitation, along with the dress code 'cocktail' and a vampish image of the face of *BloodofYouth* slung over a chaise longue in a clinging blood red dress, her skin luminous, lips glistening. I tried not to dwell on Athanasia's image, disturbed as I'd been by our brief encounter at *Pandora*.

Celia's driver Vlad knew where to go. As I had with Celia, I insisted that I would make my own way home after the launch. Vlad only nodded silently in response. (He either didn't speak English or didn't speak, I decided.) The silence in the car gave me time to steel myself for my first big social outing.

Before long the big black car pulled up at the kerb

outside the venue. I must have been nervous because I actually got out on the wrong side of the car while Vlad was coming around to open the door for me. I found myself standing on the cobblestone street with cars whipping past, clothed in Celia's beautiful red dress and clutching the invite like an oversized bus ticket. I turned towards the restaurant and froze.

Oh. Of course.

Spotlights were set up outside along a red carpet. The hot lights illuminated the entrance like an interrogator's lamp, and swarming around this blast of light was a nest of photographers snapping guests as they entered. Every few seconds the night was brightened with another strobe-like flash. It was enough to send a person into epileptic fits. I'd seen scenes like this during coverage of the Oscars. Logically, this had to be a on a much smaller scale, but it didn't seem it just at the moment. Why couldn't I have at least arrived with Pepper? Why had she insisted on arriving separately? I didn't have a great impression of her so far, but at least I would not have felt so lost.

I bid Vlad goodnight with an awkward stutter, and walked around the car. There was no moisture in my mouth, I noticed. My tongue felt like a dried-out husk. My hands were clammy. I took a breath, and stepped on to the red carpet in Celia's ruby shoes.

Please don't trip.

'Hey!' a photographer yelled, and then another. I strode quickly up the red carpet with my head down, smiling nervously. A few flashes went off around me (for someone else, I hoped) and after a tense thirty seconds that felt like much longer, I was inside the doors of the restaurant and catching my breath. I had managed to dodge my way inside without falling over my shoes or otherwise embarrassing myself. This was a small triumph, I felt, under the circumstances.

'What's your name?' someone asked.

I whirled around. 'Oh. Pandora. Pandora English,' I said.

It was a petite young woman in a black T-shirt emblazoned with the product name. She checked her clipboard. 'Pandora...Ah, *Pandora* magazine. Enjoy *BloodofYouth*,' she told me, before walking away to quiz the next guest.

Phew.

The main room of Elizabett was already buzzing with important people by the time I stepped inside. Of course, I didn't know *who* the important people were, which could pose a problem. I looked around to see if I could spot Pepper, but there was no sign of her. I noticed the organisers had cleared away the tables and had erected a small stage with a microphone stand. A display poster for *BloodofYouth* had been placed to one side, with a larger-than-life image of the product's chillingly beautiful muse. There was a pyramid built of the product itself taking up centre stage. They even had a red curtain set up behind it. (I thought it unlikely that the waiters normally emerged with steaming hot food through such a glittering red entrance.) As I looked at the stacked pile of little cellophane-wrapped boxes of product I had some of the same odd feeling that I'd had about the parcel the

courier had brought to the office. Again, I had the strange
sensation that the considerable energy of the whole room
was being sucked into that product display. It was most
unsettling.

I moved self-consciously to the back of the room,
feeling eyes on me. I was sure that some of the guests
were checking me out, as they seemed constantly to be
checking out each other. The surreal circumstances of my
presence at this event, and wearing Celia's clothes, made
me feel quite unlike myself. I wasn't in Gretchenville
anymore, that was for certain.

I found a piece of wall to stand against, retrieved my
notepad and pencil out of Celia's beaded purse, and set
to work observing the room.

Who's who in this who's who? I haven't a clue.

(But I ought to stop rhyming in my head, if I was to
find out.)

I think I've mentioned that my social skills are not
up to scratch? Well, if I was aware of that fact back in
Gretchenville, I was approximately thirty times more
aware of it in this Manhattan restaurant. It was a little
painful to stand alone at the back of such a charged
room of cool, beautiful, important people. The women,
and many of the men, seemed to me to be impossibly
groomed. Really. *Impossibly groomed.* Not a hair was out of
place. Every single fingernail was manicured to perfection.
Skin was tanned, despite the season. I looked down at my
own (clammy) hands, holding the notepad, and noticed
my clean, unvarnished nails and pale skin. I just wasn't
like these people. But if I was ever to rid myself of the

outsider status bestowed upon me by the good people of Gretchenville, it would be through the pursuit of that ephemeral, elusive thing called *cool*. And what could be cooler than writing about glamorous people for a glossy fashion magazine?

Here I was, fresh off the plane from Gretchenville and already in a room full of important people in arguably the biggest and most glamorous city in the world. No more dreaming about it. This was my opportunity and I knew I had better make the most of it. I had to write a piece on this skincare product launch that would somehow be so clever, witty and interesting that Skye would simply have to run it under my by-line. Who's who and highlights? *Pah.* That was child's play. I would deliver a *real* story. A story about how the product worked, how it was being promoted and what it could or couldn't do for *Pandora*'s readers.

Okay, it wasn't the sort of 'real story' that would change the world exactly, but it was better than my brief.

There was activity near the stage. It seemed that *BloodofYouth* had hired a small-screen actress to act as MC at the event. The woman moved behind the microphone, her grin revealing ultra-white teeth.

'Hi, my name is Toni Howard, and I am so excited to be helping to launch this revolutionary skincare product tonight,' she gushed. Toni was resplendent in sequins. I don't watch a lot of television, admittedly, but I was pretty sure from a glance that I recognised her from one of the long-running soaps. She was vaguely familiar.

'*BloodofYouth* saved my life!' Toni declared breathlessly

into the microphone, and tossed her teased blonde mane.

I frowned. Had I heard that properly?

'Now I am over forty and *fabulous*. I have never looked better,' she continued, and again flashed her dazzling, bleached smile. 'My wrinkles have all but vanished, along with my uneven skin tones and the dark circles under my eyes.'

Looking at this attractive blonde woman, I found it hard to believe she might have been plagued with such things before. She made it sound like she used to be hideous, and I knew that could not be true. She was quite radiant, which made me think of how Skye had looked the morning after her sample of *BloodofYouth* had arrived.

A movement near the door caught my eye. It was Pepper, arriving just in time. She had made herself up and she looked pretty good, I had to admit. She wore a sharp-looking jacket with a nipped waist and exaggerated shoulder pads, and her hair was pulled back. I waved and then realised that was uncool and lowered my hand again. She seemed not to have noticed me.

Back on stage the MC was carrying on with her spiel. 'And all this, ladies and gentlemen,' the actress explained, 'because of *BloodofYouth*. And how long have I been using this miracle product, I hear you ask?' No one had asked, but I was curious to know. 'Three days. That's right. I have only been using *BloodofYouth* for three days.' There were a few surprised murmurs in the crowd, and the people at the front seemed ready to surge forward and snatch the product samples from the display table. 'And that is why I am here to tell you tonight that this is *the best beauty product* available in this country. It sold out in stores across America today, faster than they could get new stock. It may be expensive, but ladies – and gentlemen too – it is well worth every single penny!'

I thought the MC was laying it on a bit thick, but the crowd appeared to be eating it up. Perhaps that's what was done at these launches?

'Hi,' came a man's voice, just near my ear.

I flinched, startled, and turned to see an enormously tall, rather good-looking man wearing a leather jacket. He was standing quite close to me, smiling.

'Hello,' I responded.

'My name's Jay,' the man said. 'Jay Rockwell, *Men Only* magazine.' He extended a hand.

Oh my. It was the guy from the elevator. The guy who'd thought I belonged in the law offices. The guy I'd had that strange fantasy about. I'd seen with vivid clarity this man's muscled torso and my own hand sliding up his chest. I'd felt his warm kiss. And now I felt a ripple of distaste on recalling the tacky cover of *Men Only* magazine.

'Yes, I remember you,' I said, my cheeks feeling a little warmer. 'Pandora English.' We shook hands.

'You know me?' he asked, evidently surprised.

'Of course,' I assured him, smiling.

He seemed confused. 'I'm sorry, where have we met?'

This stumped me. I thought he'd come up to me to be polite because we had met before, but it seemed he didn't remember the incident at all.

'Sixteenth floor, right? We met in the elevator,' I explained.

'Yeah, sixteenth floor,' he agreed, but I could tell by his face that he didn't remember the encounter in the slightest. 'The elevator?' He somehow made it sound possible that we'd got up to no good in the elevator, and he had subsequently forgotten me.

'I was going to a job interview with *Mia* magazine, and you thought I was working in the law offices. I flicked my jacket in your eye, as I recall.'

The penny finally dropped. Jay's attractive hazel eyes widened. (Neither of them red. Thankfully I hadn't caused any permanent damage.) He looked me over approvingly. 'Oh, wow. You look so... *different.*' He wasn't leering, exactly, but I did feel a little exposed by the intensity of his appraisal. 'You look really great,' he told me, and I could tell from his tone that he meant it.

'Thank you,' I said. *And thank you, Celia.* Her red Lauren Bacall dress was having quite an effect.

By now a promotional video for *BloodofYouth* was playing on a big screen. After a flash of Athanasia's beautiful, sultry, terrifying face, the picture flashed to a grey-haired man looking authoritative in a white lab coat. He was evidently explaining the revolutionary qualities of the new skincare product. He was subtitled in English. I couldn't make out his voice because of the din of the crowd. His name, according to a caption, was Dr E. Toth.

'So you got the job,' Jay said.

'Well, no,' I explained. 'Not at *Mia*. But I got a job at *Pandora*. I'm covering the launch for the next issue.'

I liked the way that sounded, and it was the truth, even if it was only because of Skye's mysterious illness that the invitation had come my way. And even if Pepper was ignoring me. I flicked my eyes in her direction and saw that she was shaking hands with a couple of well-dressed women. They gestured to a short, balding man next to them and Pepper shook his hand too. There was a lot of smiling and nodding. She was evidently networking.

'Are you covering the launch for *Men Only*?' I asked Jay. 'I can't imagine your magazine would be the right demographic.'

I pictured fishermen, lumberjacks, truckers. I imagined manly men flicking through bikini photos before heading to the hardware shop.

'Have you been living under a rock?' Jay exclaimed, coming fairly close to accurately describing my hometown. 'This product is hot stuff. The buzz these past weeks has been huge. It hit the shelves this morning and Macy's sold out after one hour. A lot of readers are dying to get their hands on it. Especially if it really does turn back the clock like it claims to.'

There was movement on the stage, and Toni announced, 'And now, I'd like to introduce you to the face of *BloodofYouth* . . . Athanasia!'

I stiffened at the model's name, and looked around to find her. Somehow it made me nervous to think of her being in the same room as me. Then a deep red curtain to the right of the stage was pulled back, and the model of the moment emerged under a spotlight. Her entrance was magnificent. Celia, I supposed, would be impressed. Athanasia wore a slinky scarlet fishtail dress, the colour of which popped against her pale, luminous skin. In fact, it was the very same colour I was wearing. But she sure wore it differently. She glided to the stage as if floating, the backless, low-cut dress shimmering under the spotlight. Her spine moved like a serpent.

I easily resisted gaping at the model this time, but I may have been the only one. Every eye seemed to follow her, and I felt the collective desire in the room pulsing around us like an electric current. Athanasia was beautiful, but now I could clearly see that part of her magnetic appeal was in her promise of − what was it? *Danger. Thanatos. Death.* She was alluring to the point of black magic. Inexplicably, the model seemed to have the whole room spellbound, and I wondered what it was about her that made such a thing possible. These were cynical big city folk. These were fashion types. They'd seen a thousand stunning faces. How was it that Athanasia could command their attention so completely? How was it that everyone in *Pandora* magazine had fallen under her spell, including me, before I was shocked out of it by her sudden and jarring death stare?

Athanasia placed a hand on her hip, and her dark eyes scanned her adoring public, flickering over each face.

Oh no.

Incredibly, she spotted me and did a double take − little insignificant me, even though I was at the back of the room. I thought perhaps I was imagining it, but I could swear her eyes burrowed into me from across the room. I felt my heart stop for a moment under her gaze. I actually felt fear.

And then, just like that, she went back to her sultry pouting for the masses, and I was grateful to be out of her gaze. I physically shook myself to lose the jolt of terror I'd felt. Surely I had imagined that?

I turned to my new friend Jay, wondering if he'd noticed my reaction to Athanasia, but the man was simply staring at her on the stage, mesmerised. We watched as Athanasia slid up to the microphone and pulled it close.

'Thank you,' she whispered with faux intimacy, and paused for a minute while hundreds of flashbulbs went off. 'I am Athanasia,' she declared once the photographers had paused. 'Please enjoy this miracle product, *BloodofYouth*. I know you are dying to get your hands on some...' And with that statement, she stepped away from the microphone and moved to the display table. She took a couple of the samples of the product and literally threw them into the baying crowd. I thought there would be a riot. Well-to-do socialites, business people and fashion types clawed at each other to catch one. One man made an acrobatic attempt to secure one in the air, and ended up on the floor. I could only gape in horror at the spectacle around me. Athanasia threw a few more samples, struck a final, vampish pose for the photographers, then vanished behind the red curtain again. The crowd surged forward, and the display table was empty before the curtains even slid closed.

'Holy...wow,' I exclaimed. 'Are product launches usually so...heated?'

Jay laughed softly. 'Not exactly.' He frowned, his brows knitting together. 'She really knows how to work a room,' he remarked.

I laughed nervously. 'Indeed.'

'Funny that no one from *BloodofYouth* spoke,' Jay said. 'There's always a CEO or a director of public relations or something to bore us to death with a long speech about the company while we all try to grab the gift bags and leave.'

In all the excitement, I hadn't noticed. 'Could I ask you a big favour, please? Would you be able to give me the names of some of the important people here? The VIPs and celebrities? I have no idea who anyone is.'

'Sure. If you'll consider giving me your number,' he replied.

I raised an eyebrow. *Cheeky.* 'I don't have a number,' I told him honestly.

Jay seemed to take my answer another way. '*Of course* you don't,' he said sarcastically. 'I understand. It's okay, I'm not afraid to work for it.'

So he thought I was playing hard to get?

He leaned in and whispered conspiratorially, 'Now see that man over there? The one with the bald spot? He is one of New York's richest men. And the woman next to him? She is not his wife...'

For the next thirty minutes, Jay Rockwell named the VIPs at the *BloodofYouth* launch for me, giving amusing biographies for each. He seemed to quite enjoy the process, and I did too. I found his attention flattering, and his cologne a little intoxicating as well. After he had identified almost everyone in the room (Jay seemed well connected, I thought), I decided I ought to go in search of Pepper, and also Toni, the actress, to interview her. I thanked Jay, and left his side with some reluctance. I noticed that he watched me cross the room before starting up a conversation with some of the guests he knew.

Pepper was no longer near the doorway networking but I nearly ran into the MC. 'Excuse me, Toni?'

She was standing next to the display table, which had been picked clean like a tray of ribs in a lion's enclosure. Pepper might want to kill me for not fighting the throng to secure her some free samples, but I wasn't about to kill myself trying to get them for her.

'Excuse me,' I repeated. 'May I interview you?'

At this the actor whirled around, smiling so broadly I thought I could count each of her bright teeth, top and bottom. Her blonde mane slid into place a second after she stopped moving.

'Helloooo,' she said in response, and she shook my hand.

'I'm Pandora English, of *Pandora* magazine. I was wondering if I could ask you a few questions?'

'Certainly.' She pulled a card from her handbag and passed it to me. 'Here's my contact info and website.' I read her card with interest before pocketing it, and the woman Toni had been talking to took the hint to drift away into the crowd while Toni was interviewed.

'Thank you,' I said, once we were alone. 'First up, I'm curious. Why did you decide to endorse this particular skincare product?'

'*Why?*' She seemed a little shocked by the question. 'Well, it works. Can't you see?' she said, and flicked her fingers towards her luminous face.

I nodded. 'Yes. You look fantastic,' I told her truthfully. I decided to rephrase my question. 'How were you approached to take part in the product launch? Was it through your agent?'

'No, actually,' she said a little guiltily. 'My agent and I parted ways after that hubbub over *Dancing with the Stars*. I'm looking for a new agent as a matter of fact. Do you know anyone?'

I shook my head. 'Sorry. I'm new to New York,' I explained. 'But about the launch…?'

'I was sent some samples,' Toni told me, and shrugged.

'And you liked the product?'

'Obviously. And I was promised more, so…'

I thought I'd got the gist. 'So you will be getting *BloodofYouth* product for a while? Lucky you,' I said, smiling. 'In exchange for being MC?'

'A year's worth, I'm told.'

I nodded. A good deal for everyone, by the sounds of it. But was that how things normally worked? I couldn't imagine, say, Cate Blanchett being paid only in that skincare stuff she spruiked, no matter how much she might like it. 'And who is your contact at *BloodofYouth* then?'

'It was through the promotions company, actually,' she said, and gestured towards one of the women in the black T-shirts. 'Henrietta Woods.'

I took a note to meet Henrietta.

'You don't know the CEO from *BloodofYouth*, or anyone

else from the company itself?' I asked, thinking of Jay's comment.

'I've met the model.' She swept a hand theatrically towards the red curtains. 'She doesn't like to do interviews, though, apparently.'

Athanasia did seem a woman of few words.

'Thanks, Toni. Um, just one more question. What do you think is in *BloodofYouth* that makes the cream so effective? What's the secret ingredient?' I wanted to be able to include it in my article.

She pouted. 'I don't know. The secret ingredient is a secret, I suppose.'

'Thanks again, Toni,' I said, when it was clear she wouldn't be able to shed any more light on the product.

She smiled, this time less dazzlingly, and turned to greet someone else.

I found Henrietta with no difficulty. She was the petite one with the clipboard who had grilled me when I'd entered the restaurant. 'Have you enjoyed the launch?' she asked me as I approached.

'Very much, thank you. Would you be able to answer a few questions for *Pandora* magazine?'

'Me? I'm pretty busy tonight,' she said. 'But I can tell you this is the best beauty product we've launched. I'm sure you'll see for yourself when you try it.'

'Are there any samples left?' I asked hopefully.

'You didn't get one?'

'No,' I told her.

She shrugged. 'Tough luck.' I guess that was it. No more free samples.

'Well,' I said, forcing a smile. 'Would I be able to get a copy of that promotional DVD?'

'Sure. *Pandora* is running a cover feature, right?' she asked. 'When is that coming out?'

I nodded. 'Yes. The issue comes out next Friday. The shoot came up really well, I understand. Who is your contact at *BloodofYouth*?' I asked, pen poised.

'Oh, we've had correspondence from Europe,' she said. 'Anyway, look, I'm sorry but I have to see to our other guests.' She tapped on the shoulder of one of the other women in a black T-shirt. 'Josephine, can you give Pandora here a copy of the promo DVD?'

'Do you have contact details for Dr Toth? Is he here tonight?' I asked as Henrietta tried again to escape me.

'He's Hungarian, or something. We're just handling the Manhattan launch.'

'So you haven't met anyone from the company yet?'

'In person? No,' she said. I could see my probing was beginning to annoy her. She broke away from me and this time I let her go.

'Thanks for your time,' I said to her back.

Josephine handed me a DVD, and a gift bag. 'Thanks,' I said sincerely, and eagerly opened the gift bag – then frowned. It only contained a bunch of *BloodofYouth* brochures, and a gift voucher offering ten per cent off if I bought the stuff at a department store. No cream.

Pepper was not going to be pleased. Where was she? Perhaps she had already left? Perhaps she had returned to the office to pull an all-nighter? I stood considering my next move for a moment. I had enough notes to satisfy

Pepper's expectations, but I didn't have her cream. My eyes flicked to the red curtain. *I could always just check...* I moved through the crowd, passing Toni, who took no notice of me this time. I caught the eye of Jay Rockwell, who offered a smile and an eyebrow raise from across the room, despite being engaged in deep discussion with a man whom he'd described as 'a philanderer and movie critic'. I reached the red curtains just beyond the empty display table, and walked through them into a tiled hallway leading to the bathrooms in one direction, and the kitchen in the other. There was a door at the far end, and I saw a flash of red there before the door swung shut. I rushed in the direction of the door, toting my gift bag, notepad and Celia's beaded purse.

I stepped out through the back entrance of the restaurant.

Oh.

I was standing alone in front of the supermodel Athanasia. In a back alley. Well, not quite alone. She was with two men who looked for all the world like undertakers. Undertakers who lifted a lot of heavy weights.

Gulp.

I took a sharp breath.

'You,' Athanasia said, turning to meet me. She was wearing tight leather designer jeans and a T-shirt, and her red dress was draped over her arm. It was the flash of colour I'd seen. Behind her was a long, black stretch limousine. Headlights flickered over the vehicle, and I saw the silhouette of someone in the back – a woman with a high collar. I sensed something powerful and very important about this woman. Beside the limo was a second car without anyone inside. It was yellow and low to the ground. It was branded with little Neptune forks on a round crest, which seemed to indicate it cost as much as a small apartment. Or two. *Fancy.*

This was a back alley creep convention with fancy cars.

'Who are you?' Athanasia asked me coldly, holding her arms so the dress fell across her middle like a toga. 'Why are you not like the others?'

I decided I was not going to be intimidated by some mean model, super or not. I stood tall, and raised my chin. 'I'm a writer,' I said proudly, as if it might be as significant a statement as, say, *I'm the sheriff of these woods.* 'And I'm not like the others...' *Because I am from a small town* wasn't going to cut it, so I left it there. The wind blew my dress open at the hem and I pushed it back down.

Athanasia's eyes narrowed to slits. There was something truly awful in them. It marred her beautiful features so completely that in that moment I thought I might be looking at a bat. *'You see me,'* she said angrily. 'Why is it that you see me?'

See me? I thought of Lieutenant Luke and his question about whether or not I could see him. Why was everyone so amazed that I saw them?

I stood my ground and didn't answer her. This seemed to enrage the woman.

'Who sent you?' she demanded, dark eyes blazing.

She looked around to see if I was alone. I was.

'*Pandora* magazine,' I said coolly. I brought the tip of my pencil to the notepad. 'I have a few questions...'

'I'm not telling you a thing,' she said. 'And I had nothing to do with the disappearance of your little friend,' she added.

My what?

'She left the shoot and I didn't see her again.'

I was stunned. Samantha? Was she talking about Samantha?

The model turned her back on me and strode towards the limo, the red dress she was holding whipping around in the winter wind. She said something to the men, something in a foreign language. One of them spoke back to her and she handed him the dress. He got into the driver's seat, put the dress on the seat beside him, and started up the limo. The long car pulled away.

The woman in the back seat. She was more important than Athanasia. And more powerful, too.

I watched the limo leave, trying to get a handle on the significance of what I was seeing. Athanasia stalked over to her car, and stood by the driver's side door.

'You write anything about me, and you'll be sorry,' she threatened.

My curiosity was more than aroused. My 'little friend'?

I heard the back door of the restaurant open and I turned. It was Jay.

'Hey there,' he said, and strode up to me, acting familiar. He took me gently by the elbow. 'Honey, we ought to get going.'

I saw what he was doing, and I linked my arm through his. 'Of course.'

I smiled at the model. 'Nice to meet you *Anastasia*,' I said.

I don't know what made me do it. I had purposely mispronounced her name.

Her black eyes flared in response and she gave me another of her death stares. 'Athanasia. My name is Athanasia,' she hissed.

Charming woman.

'Goodnight,' Jay said, and pulled me back towards the restaurant.

'I didn't need saving, you know,' I told him once we were inside.

'I missed you. I was wondering where you'd gone. You really pissed off that model. What happened?'

'That's what I hope to find out,' I replied.

'Well, it's all over in there,' he said of the launch. 'Let me drive you home. I won't bite. Honest.' He smiled.

Well, I have to admit I was tempted. But let a complete stranger drive me home in New York? No, I wasn't comfortable with that. 'I have some things to do. I'll just grab a cab. Thanks for the offer though,' I told him.

'Can I have your number, Pandora?'

He took my hesitation the wrong way. 'It's okay. I understand,' he said, looking a little deflated. 'I won't pressure you. I just thought you might like a friend in this town.' His offer seemed sincere.

'Thanks,' I said, and smiled. 'It was really nice to meet

you properly, Jay. I should get going. And thanks for your help. I won't forget it.'

I felt the urge to wrap my arms around this big handsome man. But of course I couldn't. I barely knew him. 'Bye,' I said, and walked away.

Something inside me didn't like walking away.

Elizabett was still buzzing with people, though the crowd was a little smaller. As I exited I passed a row of six young women in matching *BloodofYouth* T-shirts and short black skirts holding out little product bags. I thanked the girl who offered me one, and after a few steps I peeked in the bag.

Darn it.

This one was also filled with nothing but *BloodofYouth* brochures, and a discount voucher. No miracle *BloodofYouth* cream. Pepper would not be pleased. I'd failed. I could only hope that she had scored one herself before departing, if that's what she'd done.

I felt eager to escape the glamorous crowd and the odd, oppressive feeling of dread that *BloodofYouth* and Athanasia seemed to arouse in me. Head down, I walked the empty red carpet with the determined stride of someone who knew where they were going. But I stopped short when I noticed the growing line of finely dressed people waiting for taxis, limousines and valet parking out the front of the restaurant.

Perhaps I should not have insisted on making my own way home.

I joined the end of a long queue behind a short socialite with teased platinum hair. The woman, who appeared dwarfed by her fur coat, was gesticulating to her companion with fat fingers covered in big diamond rings. The flash of her expensive jewellery momentarily distracted me. Then I noticed the designer handbag she had slung under her arm. It was overflowing with samples of *BloodofYouth*. She must have been right at the front of the crowd when Athanasia started throwing samples and everyone had scrambled for the stuff. I could see four jars of the coveted cream, right in front of me. This guest had greedily snaffled a handbag full of those jars, and she looked like she could more than afford to buy the stuff!

'I just need *one*,' I whispered under my breath.

Barely had I uttered the words when, incredibly, a jar of *BloodofYouth* tumbled out of the top of the woman's open purse. I thought the jar would break when it hit the pavement but it landed on the end of the soft red carpet, and rolled to my feet.

I blinked and looked around. No one had seen it but me.

'Thanks,' I murmured as I bent down and scooped up the jar. 'Thank you.' I didn't feel the slightest bit guilty as I put it in my gift bag.

Phew.

By now more guests were filing out of the restaurant, the valet cars and limos were a confused tangle on the street and cabs seemed in short supply. After our conversation, I would have been a little embarrassed if Jay walked out and saw me waiting in that slow line for a cab, so despite Celia's warning not to wander alone around New York at night, I was going to do precisely that. I broke from the queue and walked past. A couple of guests turned their heads and I felt eyes on me. One swarthy man with slicked-back hair and a white suit and shoes actually winked at me as his Porsche showed up. (No one had ever winked at me back home. Was it Celia's outfit, or was it a New York thing?) I walked past at a brisk pace, away from the glamorous people and the taxis and the fancy cars, and right down the sidewalk. I still felt I was being watched as I walked away, and I hoped I looked confident, though I was not sure where I was headed.

About a block away from the restaurant, my adrenaline subsided and I noticed that under it all I was pretty peckish. I hadn't eaten dinner before the launch and I'd passed up the odd-looking hors d'oeuvres they were serving. I found myself walking in the direction of an illuminated sign for a convenience store two blocks away, and by the time I got there, I noticed my feet were beginning to hurt in Celia's shoes, and my stomach was hollow.

'Hi there,' I said cheerily to the man behind the counter as I entered the shop.

He looked a little startled and didn't respond.

Figuring Harold's Grocer might be closed, I bought myself a packet of penne pasta, a jar of pasta sauce, a wedge of parmesan sealed in plastic, a couple of slightly wrinkled 'fresh' tomatoes and a head of garlic. (When I asked if he carried fresh basil, the man looked at me like I was insane.) The unfriendly man rang the items through, mumbled the cost and I paid him with the cash I had.

I stepped out into the night with my bag of groceries just as a yellow cab was passing on its way to the line of people waiting outside the restaurant.

'Hey!' I called and threw my arm in the air. The cabbie saw me and screeched to a halt.

Amazingly, this taxi driver also needed to be convinced that Spektor actually existed.

It seemed these New York cabbies didn't know their town very well.

CHAPTER
TWELVE

*I*t was just before nine when I stepped inside Celia's building. The sky had turned inky, and the lobby was even darker. I found a light switch just inside the doorway and flicked it on, and the dusty chandelier came to life.

I crossed the floor with my footsteps echoing and my grocery bag rustling. The lift was waiting, and it began its ascent with the customary rattles and clicks. I watched the vacant floors pass. Click click. Rattle rattle. Ho hum. I planned to have a quick pasta dinner then spend the rest of the evening working on my piece for *Pandora* about the launch of *BloodofYouth*.

I stiffened when, from the corner of my eye, I caught movement on the third-floor landing.

What was that?

I did a double take.

Standing near the cobwebbed doorway on the landing was a young woman – a *naked* young woman. I was so startled that I cried out. In an instant, she was gone. The lift continued its ascent, and I dropped the groceries and crouched on the floor to peer through the ironwork, but I didn't catch another glimpse of the nude figure I was sure I'd seen. The lift doors opened on Celia's floor and the building grew quiet again. I stood frozen with indecision for a moment, heedless of the garlic and tomatoes rolling out of the plastic bag and across the floor of the lift.

Celia's warning not to go wandering through the other levels of the building replayed in my mind, yet I touched the round button for level three, unable to simply walk away from what I'd seen.

Oh boy...

The doors closed again and the old lift rattled its way back down to the floor below. The doors opened and I stepped out cautiously. Alert to noise and movement, like an animal investigating dangerous new territory, I stood stock-still on the landing, my eyes darting in all directions. The elevator rattled closed behind me and then grew still.

'Hello?' I called out tentatively.

There was no reply.

I tried to recall precisely what I'd seen. There'd been a young woman, nude. She'd had light hair, I thought. Blonde and wavy. Her body had appeared pale. I thought there'd been something dark on her arm. An arm band? A tattoo? A mark?

'Is anyone there?' I called. I walked to the door of the apartment and tried the handle. It was cold to the touch, and it was locked.

I knocked. 'Hello?' All was silent.

I gave it a little push. Then a shove. No, it was definitely locked. And the cobwebs were undisturbed, suggesting that it hadn't been opened in a long time. Yet I thought the woman had gone inside. Where else could she have gone? It wasn't possible that she had gone *through* the door, was it?

I shivered.

Maybe she was a ghost. Like Lieutenant Luke. But then, he was just a dream... wasn't he?

The elevator sprang to life behind me. I was startled and I ran towards it with desperate speed, as if I could somehow stop the momentum, but of course it was too late. I pressed the lift button helplessly and watched my groceries head up to the penthouse. I suddenly felt unaccountably terrified of being alone down here. And I was almost as scared of the fact that Great-Aunt Celia had probably just summoned the lift from above. What would she say if she saw me here on the third floor after she had expressly told me not to explore the other floors?

Great.

The following minute passed agonisingly slowly. I considered hiding, but where? And my shopping was on the floor of the lift. There was no getting around it – I had been caught out.

Through the panicked adrenaline pulsing in my ears, I heard the lift doors open at the floor above, then close. I heard the lift begin to descend. I braced myself to face Celia.

Sorry, Great-Aunt Celia, I thought I might π*have seen a tattooed naked chick floating around and I just had to investigate...*

The lift arrived on the third floor. The doors opened and I drew in my breath to say—

It was *empty.*

Well, it was empty except for my groceries, of course. I leapt in, and pressed the button for level four. I felt relieved, of course, and guilty that I'd disobeyed Celia's wishes, but also a little cowardly for having been scared – not to mention confused. I really thought I'd seen someone...or something. Was it my imagination, again? I knew what my father would have said: *I've had enough of your tall tales, young lady. Now grow up.*

I gathered my spilled groceries and stepped out of the lift.

I knocked carefully on Celia's door and entered. 'Celia, I'm home,' I said from the doorway. I bit my lip. I hadn't seen any naked woman on the third floor. Everything was fine, I told myself.

My great-aunt was in her reading chair. I could see her feet from where I stood.

'You're home early,' she declared. She unlaced her ankles and placed her feet on the floor. 'How was the launch? Did you meet anyone special?'

I thought of Jay and smiled. 'I met some nice people,' I said.

'And the model, Athanasia?'

'She was not one of them.'

There was a light chuckle in response. 'Yes,' she said. I heard a creak of the leather chair and saw Celia's feet swing off the hassock.

'I'm starved, so I'll just put some pasta on. Can I get you anything?'

'Oh, no, darling. Thank you,' she said. 'You're such a sweet girl.'

I slipped off Celia's ruby shoes, and walked into the kitchen. I laid my groceries across the counter, got out a chopping board and knife and filled a pot with water. I turned the knob of one of the gas stove elements until the flame was nice and high. The water on the bottom of the pot sizzled for a moment as I placed it on top.

'I'll just go change out of this lovely dress,' I called out. 'Thank you so much for lending it to me! It was a real hit!'

I hung Celia's scarlet dress carefully on a hanger on the front of the tall wardrobe. I hadn't spilled anything on it, and the slight wrinkles that had formed along the hem in the taxi would fall out in a few hours, I figured. I was amazed by the attention it had garnered. Jay Rockwell hadn't even recognised me as the girl he'd met in the elevator only a couple of days before. *Clothes do not make the woman, but they do seem to get her noticed*, I thought.

'Oh!' came a strangled voice outside my room. There was a thud, and the tinkle of breaking glass.

Startled, I ran towards the sound, dressed only in my underwear, and found my Great-Aunt Celia cowering against the wall in the hallway outside the kitchen. She had knocked over the vase in the hall, and the hardwood floor was covered in petals, water and shattered crystal.

'Don't move or you could cut yourself,' I cried. 'I'll clean up the glass.' I ran back into my room, threw a robe around myself and found the dustpan and broom in a kitchen cupboard. In a flash I was kneeling at her feet.

It was then I noticed that she was wearing shoes, so was in little danger of cutting her feet. 'Great-Aunt Celia?'

It seemed she wasn't cowering because of the glass. There was something else. Something in the kitchen.

'Get it out!' Celia half growled, half screamed in a voice I did not recognise.

The sound brought me to my feet instantly, my mouth agape.

Finally Celia's body animated again and she ran from the hallway, covering her nose and mouth with her hands.

I looked around, confused. My groceries were on the counter. The water was just starting to come to the boil on the stove. I could see nothing wrong. 'Get what out?'

My great-aunt paused in the doorway of her bedroom. 'The garlic! Get it out!'

She slammed the door.

CHAPTER THIRTEEN

It was a full thirty minutes later when Great-Aunt Celia reappeared in the hall, now unruffled. I'd cleaned up the mess and started boiling the water again. Celia's crystal vase couldn't be saved. She must have hit the table hard to knock it over.

'Darling Pandora?' she asked.

'I got rid of the garlic,' I responded stiffly, still utterly confused by the incident. Aunt Georgia had warned me that my great-aunt would be old, frail and possibly even a little senile, but I had not witnessed so much as a single moment of senility or even fragility from Celia until half an hour before. 'I threw it away. It's in the dumpster outside.'

Satisfied that the offending vegetable was gone from the apartment, she began to move slowly down the hallway, sniffing the air delicately. 'Oh, it does linger a bit, doesn't it?' she complained. I had only bought one head of garlic and had not managed to cook so much as a single clove. It was absurd to imagine anyone could smell it lingering in the apartment.

Celia let out a sigh, and approached me. Her black veil was in place, and through the fine netting I could see that the usual serenity had returned to her features.

'I'm sorry if I gave you a bit of a fright,' she said. 'I should have warned you that I am severely allergic to garlic.'

'Oh, no. I'm the one who is sorry,' I replied, trying to hide my puzzlement. I was no expert, but weren't food allergies normally restricted to eating, not smell? 'Are you okay? You didn't cut yourself?'

'I'm fine. Could you be a dear and open the kitchen window?' she said.

I opened the window as she requested, and was hit with cold night air. When I came back to where she was standing my great-aunt gave me a reassuring pat. 'I should have warned you,' she repeated. 'But never mind. Now you know.' Then she looked down at my right hand and her eyes narrowed. Beneath the mesh of her veil I saw a strange, wild look come over her. I followed her eyes down and noticed that I had cut my index finger on the broken crystal. The tiniest smear of blood marred my pale fingertip.

I flinched instinctively and hid my hand behind my back.

'Darling,' Great-Aunt Celia said, her smile fixed. 'You'd better fix that cut.'

'Ah . . . I hadn't realised.'

'You'll want a Band-Aid for that, sweetheart. They are in the spare bathroom. Top shelf,' she said smoothly.

I heard the water boil over on the stove behind me. I

ran over and turned down the heat. I had been so hungry, and now my appetite was quite gone.

'Take a seat,' Celia suggested when I returned from the stove. She gestured to the hassock. I sat on it, with my hands folded nervously in my lap. I pressed my cut finger hard against my palm. I'd get a Band-Aid later, if I needed one. 'You asked me earlier about the Global Society for Psychical Research. Has anyone ever told you that you have the mind of an investigative journalist?'

I perked up a little at the compliment. Perhaps one day I really could be an investigative journalist. Perhaps I could report on important events in the world rather than skin cream launches.

'Why don't I tell you a bit about this building?' Celia suggested, and it suddenly occurred to me that she was trying to distract me from the strange incident with the garlic.

'Oh, good,' I said a little cautiously. 'I've been really curious about it.'

'The Society for Psychical Research was first formed in Britain in Victorian days to study psychic or paranormal events.'

Paranormal.

Psychic.

My 'public denial' was so hard-wired that I felt myself freeze up at the mention. My hands clenched.

'The society was established in London by a group of prominent thinkers, academics, researchers and scientists of the time,' Celia explained. 'And similar societies started popping up overseas. Edmund Barrett, the man who designed this building, was part of a local group. Of course, back then there were many scandalous reports of telepathy, psychic ability, ghosts and hauntings. Séances were quite popular in Victorian days. As I understand it, they formed the society to research these things and try to discover the truth. Everything has changed since, of course. The existence of paranormal activity is simply not accepted in our mainstream culture. If the society wasn't fringe then, it certainly is now.'

'It still exists?' I was shocked.

'Oh yes. The SPR does exist. They have been publishing a journal since the 1880s.'

I was so enthralled by her story that my concerns about her strange behaviour began to dissipate.

'But it seems Edmund Barrett may have had some different ideas to his friends,' Celia continued. 'He was more aggressive with his experiments. Now keep in mind, he came from a very wealthy and prominent family,' she said, leaning forward. 'So naturally he wasn't challenged for a while.' She looked into the shadows thoughtfully. 'But he ended up causing a bit of a scandal, and he fell out with the society he had founded. Some say he was banished from the group for his activities, and some say he left them over differences of opinion. Either way, it was around then that Barrett started conducting his own research here.'

Here?

By now my heart was pounding like a hammer, and my palms had begun to sweat.

'Barrett conducted paranormal research experiments in this building?' I gasped.

'Well yes, darling Pandora. He did. While he was living here,' Celia replied soberly. 'The entire building we are sitting in right now was both his home and his paranormal testing laboratory, as I understand it. Only later was the mansion divided into separate apartments.'

I blinked, speechless. There were so many rooms. Of course a wealthy man could afford such a palatial abode. But the research laboratory? Where was that? What did he do there?

'Barrett, as an architect, believed that he could effectively create a structure which would encourage psychical ability in his subjects. His architectural ideas were like science projects, really. He believed that the right environment could enhance and magnify the strength of paranormal activity, and act as a sort of super-conductor for the spirits, telepathy, psychic ability and so on. He designed this building specially.' She eyed me carefully, perhaps to gauge my response to her revelations. 'The building we live in is a magnet of sorts for certain energies. Certain activity. Or according to Barrett it was. There are strong forces here.'

I felt the hair on the back of my neck prickle and my flesh shiver with goose pimples.

'Of course, most people regarded him as having lost his mind,' she added, as if to soften the blow of these disclosures. 'History did not judge Barrett kindly.'

'What kind of experiments did he conduct here?' I dared to ask.

Great-Aunt Celia looked thoughtful. She laced her elegant fingers. 'It is hard to know for certain. His personal journals weren't found after the fire.'

Again, my heart skipped.

'There was a fire?' What little I'd seen of the building looked original and reasonably undamaged, apart from the wear and tear of age.

'Barrett died in an unusual fire in...when was it? I think it was 1908. A case of supposed "spontaneous combustion".'

I'd only ever heard the term used humorously. Hadn't Morticia joked about spontaneously combusting?

'His body was ashes, along with what they believe were his journals. The rest of the room, and the building, was untouched, they say. And his feet, also untouched. Still in his shoes.'

I felt sick.

'But surely spontaneous human combustion is impossible,' I said warily. 'People don't just burst into flames.'

'Perhaps.'

I was quiet for some time after that. I just didn't know how to respond to all this talk of paranormal research and telepathy and spirits and spontaneous combustion. It was tempting to imagine that my Great-Aunt Celia was as batty as an old lady could get, despite her deceivingly youthful appearance. (I still had no explanation for that, I remembered. Had I only imagined her fresh, unwrinkled face?)

'What about his family? Did he have children?'

'Ah, that is a sad piece of history,' Celia said. 'They had no children, but his widow hanged herself a year to the day after the fire. In the lobby, I believe. Quite a scandal. Taking your own life is a gruesome thing, really, don't you think?'

I nodded.

'Have you perhaps had any unusual experiences while you've been here?' my great-aunt asked. Her eyes were studying me; steadily, calmly. They were not at all the eyes of a crazy old woman. My mind was still so fixated on the image of the sad widow hanging herself in the lobby that it took a moment for my handsome soldier to pop into my head.

Lieutenant Luke. And the woman on level three.

I broke Celia's gaze, and looked at my hands. *Does she know about Luke?* I wondered. But how could she? He was only make-believe.

'I have certain gifts, but I am not visited by the spirits of the dead,' Celia told me with what sounded like mild regret. '*Are you, Pandora?*'

Was Celia suggesting my imaginings were real?

'I don't believe in that stuff,' I responded weakly, not meeting Celia's eyes. I sounded all wrong in my own ears because I knew I was lying. Or was I? I still didn't know what I believed, or what I'd seen. But the thing was, I'd always seen *something*. Always. My imaginings had started at an early age, and though they had diminished until recently, I had never successfully blocked them out entirely, not even at Aunt Georgia's — and let me tell you, Aunt Georgia is the *last* person on earth you would want to broach the subject of ghosts and psychic visions with. When I was thirteen I'd thought my dead mother was visiting me. We chatted a lot that year. She even taught me a bit about archaeology. I'd figured it was a stage of grief.

My thoughts were interrupted when Celia stood up from her leather reading chair, and smoothed out her dress. She slipped her shoes on with a series of delicate movements. 'I'm sorry to have to run off like this,' she declared.

I could see the conversation was over. I wondered if my resistance to what she had been telling me was to blame.

'But I have a date,' she finished.

This was perhaps the most surprising thing she'd said all evening.

'Oh.' I did my best to conceal my surprise, lest I insult her, um, *date-ability*. 'Well, that's wonderful. I, um, I hope you have a good time,' I managed.

She grinned. 'Oh, *I will*. Now don't worry, we'll talk more about all this later, Pandora, dear. Think about what I've said. I know you will have a lot of questions. I'm glad I've told you about this building, anyway. I hope things begin to make more sense. Goodnight – don't wait up,' she said, and walked to the door. She slipped a fox stole around her shoulders and unlocked the door. I noticed she didn't bother with the mahogany cane, which was now leaning against the umbrella stand, discarded.

'Oh, by the way, what's your favourite number?'

I blinked. 'Favourite number? Uh...seven,' I replied.

Celia smiled knowingly. 'Yes. Seven.'

I was truly confused now.

'Do look after that cut, won't you?' Celia said calmly and stepped out. I still hadn't put a Band-Aid on it, though the bleeding had stopped. 'And don't get up to no good.'

She knew about the third floor! I opened my mouth to apologise but the door had already clicked shut behind her.

CHAPTER
FOURTEEN

T tried to be good. I really did.

I ate a small plate of pasta, *sans* garlic, and bathed in the claw-foot tub. For hours afterwards I sat in my room, in my nightie, with my feet snug under the blankets. I tried to read my book, but I couldn't get into it. I started to make notes on the article I wanted to write about the *Blood of Youth* launch, but I couldn't concentrate. Instead I stared at the ceiling cornices and replayed Great-Aunt Celia's every word.

Spontaneous combustion. Psychical research. Hauntings.

Could my great-aunt be confirming my lifetime of imaginings as real? For nineteen years I'd been told that I was weird and different and unnatural and *wrong*. I had an overactive imagination, I was told. And yet, if I'd understood her correctly, my aunt seemed to be suggesting that all that time it was my accusers who had been wrong, and not me. It was a staggering idea.

Level three. Go back down to level three.

If my imaginings were real, I had to know for sure. What was the thing on the third floor? Was it a ghost?

Was I really psychic? A medium of some kind? The new explorer in me simply had to go down there and test this theory. If there was another ghost down there, a ghost like Lieutenant Luke, then what harm could it do to meet her? And since I was definitely awake, I positively knew I wasn't dreaming; if I saw something, I would be sure I hadn't imagined it. That would settle it, I decided.

I pulled off my nightie, and put on my favourite pair of jeans and a T-shirt, wrapped my warm winter shawl around me and left the penthouse, armed with a kitchen knife (well, it was New York) and a confidence buoyed by a lifetime of curiosity.

'Sorry, Celia,' I said aloud as I got into the lift and pressed the button for level three.

The gothic machinery began to rattle downwards. It didn't have far to go, but by the time the doors opened again, my heart was in my throat.

I stepped out. 'Hello? Is anyone there?' I stood still on the landing just outside the lift, which closed behind me with its customary rattle. 'Hellooooo?'

I paced from one end of the landing to the other. The doors were still locked of course. I stood against the railing, and then leaned, listening intently. But there was nothing.

After perhaps the longest ten minutes of my life I decided this attempt at communicating with the dead was utterly ridiculous. Just because I thought I'd seen a nude woman hanging around earlier, didn't mean she would be here now. And just because I had a new, revolutionary perspective on my visions, that didn't mean they would walk up and welcome me into this new understanding.

Fool.

I turned to walk back to the lift – then stopped.

A pale figure was folded into the corner at the opposite end of the landing, holding her knees to her chest. It was the woman I'd seen earlier.

I hadn't imagined her. She was there. She was real – or as real as a ghost could be. That's what she had to be. A ghost. Like the butcher all those years ago. Like Luke.

'Hello,' I said, steeling myself. 'I am Pandora English. I come in peace.' *What is this, an alien movie?* 'I mean to say, I won't harm you,' I told the figure. 'I'm going to approach you now.' I carefully placed the kitchen knife on the floor between my feet.

I walked slowly towards the crouching figure, finding myself barely able to breathe. This was by no means the first ghost I had encountered, but now that Celia had encouraged me to believe that what I was seeing was real, it felt very different. I stopped a safe distance away – perhaps two metres.

'Hello. What's your name?' I asked, both terrified and fascinated.

'Why am I here?' the woman asked me, looking over my head, and from side to side. She ran bloodless fingers over her young face and began to rock back and forth. 'Why am I here? Where am I?' she pleaded.

I bit my lip. 'Oh, I'm sorry. You're asking the wrong psychic, if that's what I am. I don't know how this stuff works yet,' I apologised.

I moved closer and offered her my hand. She took it

in hers, and to my surprise she felt as real as any human I'd touched, only much, much cooler. She stood up and I blushed. She was nude, after all. Not to mention deceased and evidently a little puzzled about it.

'Here, why don't you cover yourself?' I suggested, offering her my shawl.

She took it and wrapped it around herself.

'Thank you,' she said vaguely, then stood listlessly in the corner, silent.

I wondered what I could say to help her with her questions. 'Well, my Great-Aunt Celia and I just had a very interesting talk tonight – she owns the building, you see, and she says this place was designed to strengthen paranormal activity. That could be why you are here, now that you are, um...' *Dead.*

This particular ghost did not appear edified by my explanation of the building's unusual qualities.

'I've already met one other ghost here,' I added quietly, thinking of Luke. The ghost before me had a very different quality about her, though; she seemed much more 'real' than the lieutenant, if very pale. I hadn't seen her go all nebulous yet. And her hand had felt quite real when I'd taken it in mine. 'Do you remember this place?' I asked her. 'Did you live here?'

She shook her head. 'I don't know. I don't recognise things...well, maybe a little.' She looked around her, seeming unsure. 'You are the only person I've seen who will talk to me.'

This made me feel better, like I was doing an afterlife public service of some kind.

'It's okay. Just stay calm. I know we will figure this out.' And then what? I'll send her to heaven? I was possibly a medium, but I wasn't God. 'Have you been here long?' I asked the nude ghost.

She shook her head again. 'I don't think so.' Her lower lip trembled. Was hers the death I had sensed when I first entered the building? Was that possible? The ghost woman turned and leaned against the wall. She began to cry.

'Did you say ghost? I'm dead?'

I nodded. 'I'm afraid so,' I replied, for lack of less morbid answer.

At this she became hysterical. 'I'm dead!' she screamed. 'I'm dead! I'm dead!'

I bit my lip again, and put my hands on her shoulders, trying to calm her. She threw her arms in the air, pushing me away. 'I'm dead! Oh, I'm dead!'

'Oh no! Oh, I'm sorry! It's just that I thought...' Well, I had thought it was a rhetorical question, actually. 'You don't remember anything? You don't remember what happened to you?' I asked her.

Another head shake. She was calming now. Her face grew slack and her arms fell to her sides. 'I was on the shoot, and then... and then I can't remember anything.'

'On the shoot?' I repeated, puzzled. Then a thought struck me.

Was it possible?

'Is your name Samantha?' I asked, shocked. I held my breath, waiting for her reply.

'*Samantha*,' she repeated dreamily. 'Yes, Samantha. I am Samantha.'

I could hardly believe it. This was my predecessor at *Pandora*! I recognised her from the photograph in her desk, I realised now. But how did she come to be dead and haunting Celia's building? That was a pretty big coincidence. And it was just a coincidence . . . wasn't it?

'You don't know why you are here?' I queried.

'No. I don't think I know this place. Or, maybe I do, but I can't recall.'

I thought about that. 'Well, maybe it's me then? Because I got your job?' I seemed to be the only link.

Will I be haunted by all the previous employees of Pandora *magazine?* I wondered fleetingly. *Because I could see that being a full-time job.*

'What happened to you?' I asked. I brought my hands to her face, imploring her to remember. (She certainly felt awfully 'firm' under my hands. Not at all like the misty Civil War soldier.) 'Did someone harm you?' I cocked my head. 'What's that on your neck?' I pulled my hands away, and my fingers raked across the seam of my jeans.

'What? What?' she asked, trying to look at her own neck, which was of course impossible.

My goodness.

'Those look like . . . bite marks. Bite marks on your neck.' I backed away slowly, my legs trembling like the earth was giving way beneath me.

Could it be? Bite marks? *Fang* marks?

Oh my goodness. My sweet, generous, helpful, far-too-young-looking, light-avoiding, garlic-hating Great-Aunt

Celia is a vampire and she killed this poor girl so I could get her job!

I covered my mouth with my hand to stop myself screaming.

'What is it?' dead Samantha asked, still tilting her head to try to catch a glimpse of her neck.

'Nothing. I take that back. Forget I said anything.' Oh, this was bad. This was very, very bad. Had my nice great-aunt sucked this woman dry to get me a job? *Really?* No. I couldn't convict Celia solely on the possible presence of bite marks on the neck of an apparition living downstairs from her. That just wouldn't be right. Would it? I needed a second opinion. But from whom?

I broke off from musing when I realised that dead Samantha seemed to be undergoing some kind of change. Her eyes turned as dark as jet, and she was staring fixedly at my hand with a glittering gaze. It took me a moment to understand that she was focusing on the end of my finger. My cut was bleeding. I even had a little blood on the seam of my jeans.

Dead Samantha opened her mouth into a hideous snarl and this time I couldn't repress my scream. This nice, confused young dead woman had fangs!

What the hell? She lunged and I backed away as fast as I could.

'Whoa! Wait!' I yelped.

She wasn't dead. She was undead. Big difference.

I thought of the garlic I'd tossed out on account of Celia. Just my luck it was in the dumpster downstairs instead of in a bag beside me as it had been when I'd first seen her. Perhaps that was the reason she had run.

Oh!

Quite out of nowhere, there was a crushing blow between us, and the young fanged woman was thrown back two metres. She fell to the floor of the landing with a thud, and lay there, looking even more confused than before. All the aggression went out of her.

'I'm sorry. What happened?' she murmured from the floor. 'Where am I?'

I felt quite cold suddenly, and not only because the creature on the floor was wearing my shawl. The air around me was moist and cool, like a cloud. In front of me the figure of Lieutenant Luke Thomas formed, slowly at first, and then quite quickly. He placed his arms around me protectively.

'Let's get you back upstairs,' he said urgently.

I had no objection to the plan.

My dead soldier friend guided me into the lift, and when we got out I let us into the apartment, though I suspected he didn't need me to open the door for him.

Celia wasn't home yet, I was relieved to see. I led Luke into my room, closed the door and sat on the edge of my bed, doing my best to hold myself together.

'I didn't need you to rescue me,' I said for the second time that night. This time, however, it probably wasn't true.

Lieutenant Luke held his cap in his hand. 'Really? Because it sure seemed like you needed—'

'Okay, okay. Maybe I did need you to rescue me a little,' I admitted. 'I thought she was a ghost, like you! No

ghost has ever hurt me. I didn't realise that there are...'
I trailed off.

'Vampires?' he said.

'Exactly. *Those.*'

'There are a lot of things in Spektor,' Lieutenant Luke
informed me. 'It is best not to go out alone after dark
here.'

That fact was finally sinking in.

'It's this building,' he said. 'It is the nucleus of the
whole neighbourhood, and it has changed everything
increasingly, year by year, since it was erected. Though
from what I've heard the rest of New York is not much
safer at night,' he said, perhaps trying to lighten the
mood.

Spektor had seemed strange, I'll grant, but then I
hadn't been around much. Who was I to judge what was
strange after growing up in a town like Gretchenville?
We'd had plenty of bizarre deaths and scandals there,
even a little boy who was abducted by a paedophile. With
such monsters around, were vampires so hard to believe?
Ghosts?

'That girl is new here,' Luke said. 'I've not seen her
before. I think she is a very new vampire.'

That explained her air of confusion, anyway.

'I'd be careful of her. The new ones are unpredictable.'
And the older ones aren't? I wondered. 'You won't leave now,
will you, Miss Pandora?'

'Leave the apartment? Not tonight!'

'No, Miss Pandora. I mean, you won't leave Spektor,
will you?'

I thought about that and shrugged. 'I don't know. I'm afraid that Celia might be...well, *dangerous*.'

'Oh no,' Luke said. 'No.' He moved closer. 'May I sit?'

I nodded and he sat next to me, barely making an indent in the bed. He put an arm around my shoulder. It felt cool and wonderful. 'Don't be afraid of Ms Celia. She would never hurt you. You are safe up here in the penthouse. No one will hurt you here. And she tried to warn you not to go out at night,' he reasoned.

So had Harold. 'I know but...' *But I think she may have made someone 'undead' in order to get me a job. That's just taking the friendship too far, even if she'd done it with my best interests at heart.*

'Miss Pandora, please don't leave,' Luke begged. His bright blue eyes implored me to stay. 'I haven't had anyone to talk to in so long. I really like you, Miss Pandora.'

'I like you, too,' I found myself saying.

Our eyes met. And then our lips met.

What a sensation.

Luke's lips were soft as pillows, and he held me with a passion I had never before experienced. Okay, I hadn't been kissed a lot, but *wow*, this was quite a different kind of kiss to those of the boys back in my hometown. My only 'steady' back in Gretchenville had been Ben Roberts, whom I'd known since we were six, but we were just learning about kissing four years ago. After he moved away with his family at sixteen, there were some other boys, the usual embarrassing fumblings from time to time – a badly manoeuvred tongue in my ear while watching DVDs downstairs at Aunt Georgia's, that sort of thing. Ultimately, the local boys didn't interest me. I think I could count the boys I'd kissed on one hand. And they sure didn't know how to do what dead Lieutenant Luke Thomas was doing to me right now.

Oh, the bliss. Oh my, the bliss of kissing a beautiful ghost...

The soldier pushed me gently to the bed, and I wrapped my arms around his strong, cool back. His ghost body felt simultaneously firm and misty, as if he were totally real on one level, but on another was just a dream. Our tongues intermingled, and I saw flashes of white light. I felt myself lifting.

'Oh, Luke...' I murmured with pleasure.

He pulled away. 'Oh, Miss Pandora. I am so sorry.'

I sat up on my elbows on the bed. 'Sorry? Don't be sorry,' I said, and meant it. I didn't want him to stop.

'I got carried away, Miss. You've been traumatised tonight. I can't take advantage of that.' He took his cap in his hand and stood with his head bowed. 'You should go to sleep now, Miss Pandora.'

Being taken advantage of by a ghost? Now that was a thought.

I looked at the clock. It was past one. It had been rather a big night. 'I do have to go to work in the morning,' I managed, my body slowly returning to normal. The warm tingling began to settle. Goodness, had I really been kissing a ghost?

I slipped under my covers and pulled my jeans off. I threw them on the floor next to the bed. Somehow, because he was dead, I felt comfortable in his presence.

'If you get scared or anything you just call for me,

okay?' Luke said, placing a cool hand on my forehead.

I nodded sleepily.

'Sleep, Miss Pandora. Sleep. You are safe now,' he assured me, and he gave me one last, cool kiss.

I felt my eyelids grow heavy, and soon Luke had disappeared to go wherever it was that ghosts went when they weren't visiting the living.

My ghost friend had disappeared, but I no longer felt alone.

CHAPTER
FIFTEEN

Sleep would have been too easy.

When I woke again it was still dark. I was in bed in my T-shirt and underwear, my bra pinching under my arms. The clock told me it was a quarter to three.

What a night.

Really, how could I sleep soundly after the night I'd just had? (Could you? I think not.)

It didn't take long for me to decide to get up, to test another theory. I was fairly sure Celia had not yet returned home from her 'date'. (Was she out there somewhere, sucking someone dry? I wondered darkly.) I'd been exhausted, but I had not slept deeply enough to miss the sound of her arrival, I thought. I got up and tiptoed through the apartment in my T-shirt. Her fox stole was not hanging by the door. I crept down the hall and listened at her locked door. There was not a sound.

I had somehow found a second wind, and was wired on a new rush of adrenaline, I spent the next twenty minutes arranging the apartment and myself for Celia's return. I then settled myself in Celia's leather reading chair. And I waited.

And waited.

I may have drifted off a few times before, finally, there was a tinkle of keys and the front door opened. I heard footsteps.

Celia.

It was past four in the morning, my eyes were burning, and I felt as strung out and tense as I'd ever been in my life. *Edmund Barrett? Psychics? Hauntings? Vampires? Ghost kisses?* These things had cycled through my head enough times to drive me half mad.

Despite the hour, Celia entered the penthouse looking as fresh as when she had left the house.

Now for the truth, Celia.

In what felt like a surreal role reversal, I switched the reading light on, and she saw me waiting in her leather chair. I was wearing a crucifix, a piece of costume jewellery I'd bought for a retro eighties school dance back in Gretchenville. The cross was oversized and made of plastic, and it sat heavily on my chest. (No, I wasn't wearing the BOY TOY belt buckle that had gone with it.) I had moved the mirror to a strategic position, to see if Celia had a reflection. I'd only stopped short of fetching the garlic from the dumpster outside because I was too frightened to leave the apartment after my run-in with a fanged Samantha.

'Hello, Pandora. You're up late,' Celia said calmly upon noticing me. She hung up her stole and paused in the entryway, looking elegant.

'I am,' I said, as steadily as I could. 'I was wondering if I could ask you about something?' I stood up from the leather chair and indicated that I wished for her to sit.

Beneath the omnipresent veil, I thought I saw a slight smirk. 'Certainly. There is much to discuss,' she agreed. 'It can wait till morning though, I trust?'

'I never see you in the morning,' I said flatly.

There was an uncomfortable silence.

'True,' she conceded. Now she smiled through her veil with closed lips. 'All right then. I guess this is as good a time as any.'

My great-aunt glided across the apartment and stood in front of me in the lounge. Her eyes drifted down to my choice of pendant and back up again. She didn't flinch, let alone burst into flames. Her entirely normal form was reflected in the mirror behind her. I felt ridiculous. I was only just coming to terms with the idea that I was really able to see dead people. I obviously had a lot to learn about the whole 'undead' thing.

Ever graceful, Celia took a seat in her leather chair. It creaked lightly as it took her weight. She tilted her head in my direction, her veil casting a shadowy web across her perfect alabaster skin.

My heart was beating far too fast, and I willed it to slow to a normal pace. I sat on the hassock opposite her, and took a breath. 'Celia, how old are you?' I asked her outright.

She blinked slowly. Her expression did not change. She crossed her arms. 'Darling, your mother should have taught you that it's rude to ask a lady her age.'

'You *are* my great-aunt, though, yes? My mother's mother's sister?'

'Of course I am, darling,' she assured me. 'Is this what you wanted to ask me? About our family tree? You look awfully tired. You ought to get some sleep. We can discuss all this another—'

'*Then why are you so young?*' I demanded.

Great-Aunt Celia pursed her lips and let out a delicate sigh. 'I see. There's no putting you off tonight, is there?' The words sounded heavy as they came from her lips. She took my hands in hers – her skin felt much cooler than mine – and said in a grave voice, 'I wondered when we would need to have this little chat. I'd hoped it would be a while yet. I am quite sure you already have some theories about the reason for my youth . . .'

At that moment I realised how desperately I wanted everything to be okay, how desperately I wanted to stay in this place and not have to go back to Aunt Georgia and to live in boring little Gretchenville for the rest of my life. Even after all I'd seen that night I was ready for any lie. Herbs. The fountain of youth. An amazing plastic surgeon. Buckets of *BloodofYouth* skin cream. Anything.

'Do I?' I asked.

'Yes,' she said calmly and squeezed my hands affection- ately. With one hand she lifted the black veil she always wore, and pinned it back into her hair. Some of the fear ran out of me as I found myself face to face with the woman I had already become so fond of. She had been generous to me, so welcoming, helpful and caring. Her face was serenely beautiful and I could see no venom in her, nothing sinister at all, just a grandmotherly warmth, wrapped in a too-perfect, too-young package. I found it impossible to imagine this woman killing someone, but still, I wondered if I could forgive her if she had.

'Look, it's not all as scary as people make out. You mustn't believe what you read about...'

'About?' I waited apprehensively for her to finish her sentence. I couldn't be the one to say it. It was too absurd.

'Really, it's not such a big deal.'

It's true then. 'You're a VAMPIRE!' I blurted out, and pulled away, nearly falling off the edge of the hassock. My hands flew to my mouth but it was too late, I'd already let it slip.

Celia let out a throaty laugh in response. She leaned back in her chair and tilted her face to the ceiling, chuckling delicately.

'Did you really do that to Samantha so I would get her job?' I probed. 'Did you? My god! That's terrible!'

'What?' Celia stopped laughing. 'I've done what to whom? Please, darling, do *relax*. You don't know what you're talking about.'

'Oh, I think I *do*,' I contradicted her.

At this fresh accusation she only started laughing again.

'What? It's not funny! Why are you laughing at me?' I wanted to know.

'No, darling.' She smiled broadly, pulling her lips

back to show her teeth. 'I'm no vamp. See? No fangs.' And indeed, her teeth were completely normal and human. There wasn't one pointy incisor in there. Not like Samantha.

I thought about the books I'd been reading about vampires – all this time I'd *thought* they were fiction. But didn't most of them say that vampires could hide their fangs, only to have them come out like cat's claws when needed? Or when they were, um, excited? 'But you might be...keeping them in,' I argued. 'That doesn't mean you don't have fangs.'

My great-aunt chuckled at me again. 'Is that what this big Madonna crucifix is about?'

I felt too ridiculous to go on accusing her. I slumped forward, feeling like a royal idiot. 'Then what? What's not so bad?' I had to know.

She sighed and examined me patiently. 'Oh, your mother taught you nothing, did she?'

'What? What was she supposed to teach me?'

'Oh, Oriel.' She said my mother's name with a little exasperation. 'Darling Pandora, you are a supernatural girl living in a supernatural world,' she said, making a theatrical gesture with one hand.

I blinked. I was ready for anything that would help my life make more sense but this variation on a Madonna lyric was not it.

'Let me start at the beginning before we get into all this other business about immortals and so on,' Celia said, and then leaned in and wagged her finger at me. 'And you shouldn't have gone wandering around the building after dark. I told you not to, and look at the result. You're practically hysterical.'

I ducked my head guiltily.

'And you can take off that silly crucifix. It's cheap, and it won't do a thing to any real undead. And it doesn't do a thing for you, either.'

I took it off, humiliated.

'Now, the most important thing you should know, and I really wish your mother had helped you with this...' She took my hands in hers again. 'You have *the gift*,' she said finally. 'Pandora, it is in your name, in your heritage. You are gifted. All the Lucasta women are gifted.' Lucasta was my mother's maiden name. Celia was a Lucasta, too, and I would have been, if child naming were not so invariably patriarchal. 'You have abilities. And you... well... You are a very *special* Lucasta girl.' She looked at me with something significant behind her eyes, something I wasn't sure she would share. *Special?* 'Surely you are already aware of this?'

Celia studied my face and frowned. She shook her head. 'Oh dear. It was that man she married,' she said, evidently cross. 'Sorry, darling.' She had obviously recalled that she was talking about my father. She patted my hand. 'It's just that she *insisted* on marrying your father against her better judgment. He stifled her abilities. She had such talent, such potential. It was a terrible waste in my opinion. I suppose he was a good man, and he made your mother happy, I think. But...' She crossed her arms. 'Well, your father and I never quite saw eye to eye.'

That was pretty clear.

'Pandora, your great-great-grandmother was Madame Aurora.' Celia announced this proudly, as if I would recognise the name. I must have looked a little blank. 'Madame Aurora was with the travelling shows at the turn of the century. She was Barnum and Bailey's most famous and gifted psychic.' She sighed. 'I suppose Oriel neglected to tell you that as well?'

'I guess so,' I said. I'd not heard a word about my great-great-grandmother or a Madame Aurora.

Celia shook her head gently, clearly disappointed.

'So, you're not a vampire,' I said softly, ashamed of myself for even considering the possibility.

'No, darling. But that model of yours, well...'

'*What?*'

Celia stood. 'Now I've said too much. Look, it's late. You need to go to bed, darling Pandora. You are too tired to take all this in.' I could tell from her tone that there would be no further discussion. And indeed I was beginning to shake from exhaustion. Once upright I could feel the weight of my intense fatigue. It was half past four after a rather eventful day and I could barely stand.

'You're not a vampire? You don't have fangs?' I babbled. I felt overtired and confused, but I just couldn't stop my big mouth. 'You're not going to kill me?'

Celia looked at me soberly. 'Sweetheart, no. I'm not going to kill you.' She helped me up and walked me to my room. 'You have an important day ahead of you at work. Investigations to be done for your writing, and so on. You won't even make it to the office if we keep you up much longer. We'll talk more tomorrow,' she promised.

Just before I plunged into sleep I heard her mumble, 'That Bram Stoker has a lot to answer for...'

CHAPTER
SIXTEEN

J arrived at Pandora magazine at nine twenty-five in the morning sporting my first-ever serious eye baggage. My eyes were bloodshot, puffy and underscored with dark rings. Sleeplessness and being freaked out evidently made quite an impression on my face. Morticia noticed my altered appearance immediately.

'Oh, you must have had fun at the launch,' she declared, bravely trying not to sound jealous about my little coup.

It had been a big night. But not the kind of big night I could confide in the receptionist about. I only nodded wearily in response. 'Is Pepper here?' I wondered if she'd come back to the office after she slipped away from the launch.

Morticia shook her head. 'Not yet.'

I looked around. The office seemed a little quiet. 'Is Skye still sick?' I asked.

'Yeah. And the issue goes to print in, like, three days. I've never known her to call in sick before. I mean, she went ballistic when Samantha quit just before deadline,

and she's not even here herself now. Can you believe it?'
She studied my face. 'You aren't coming down with what
she has, are you?' she asked with concern.

'No, I'm not sick – it's just lack of sleep,' I assured
her, without getting into details. Where would I begin?
The bit where I French-kissed a ghost? Or the bit where
a vampire tried to neck me?

'Morticia, can you tell me what happened with the
other girl, Samantha?' I ventured cautiously. This could
be a normal question, I reasoned. I was new in the office
and maybe I was just curious about why she'd quit. 'Um,
did she have a run-in with Skye or something?' I tried
to seem casual about it, although under my tired visage
I was desperate for answers. 'I don't want to make the
same mistakes.'

'Oh, no,' Morticia replied. 'Skye blows up all the
time, but she calms down eventually.' She shrugged. 'I
don't really know what happened. The night before you
arrived, Samantha was on the cover shoot with Athanasia,
to be sort of an assistant if they needed anything.' She
took a deep breath and looked away for a moment, and I
detected that Morticia was put out that she had not been
invited to perform the task herself. Again, I felt a touch
guilty that she hadn't been asked to accompany Pepper
or myself to the launch. 'And she checked in with Skye
to say that everything was going well, and they were on
schedule, then hours later she left a message on the office
line saying she quit and she wouldn't be coming in again.
Just like that, she quit in a phone message! I didn't find
out until I got in that morning. She didn't even clean

out her desk.' Morticia saw my expression and said, 'Oh yeah, *as you know*, right? And that was it. Not a word from her yesterday. Weird. If she hadn't quit, Skye would have fired her ass for that.'

True enough.

'I did wonder if maybe something had happened at the shoot,' Morticia said. 'But that's ridiculous, right? She'd probably been planning to quit for ages.'

That was an interesting instinct.

'Did something happen, do you think?' Perhaps it was Athanasia who had got to her? Would that explain the strange feeling I'd had about the model? Was she a vamp, like Samantha? Admittedly, of all the new information I had to grapple with, the idea that Athanasia was an evil blood-sucker was not exactly the biggest stretch. Hadn't Celia alluded to something like that? I wish I hadn't been so tired when we spoke. I could barely remember what was said, and I wanted nothing more than to go over Celia's every word.

Morticia shrugged. 'The photographer didn't seem to think so. It all went fine, apparently. It's not like Samantha had been here long, anyway. They don't always last, you know.'

Thinking of Skye/Medusa, I could imagine that was the case.

The flame-haired receptionist was lost in thought for a moment, then she became animated again. 'But Skye nearly had a conniption, it being less than a week off deadline and not being given any notice at all! I put an ad on the usual recruitment websites. If I didn't fill her position fast, I was going to get throttled, I think.' She made a fake strangled sound and crossed her eyes.

'Good thing I showed up,' I said.

'Oh! Good thing!' she agreed. 'And like only an hour after I put the ad out. Like magic!'

Magic.

Morticia looked down for a moment. 'And Samantha was all right, but I like you better. I hope you don't quit.' Morticia looked up and smiled her adorable crooked smile at me, and I felt kind of touched.

'Thanks, Morticia. I'm not planning on quitting,' I assured her.

I thought of the picture I'd found in the desk drawer. 'I was wondering if you'd heard from Samantha because I found a picture in her desk that might be important to her,' I explained. I went over to my cubicle, put my briefcase and coat down, and returned to reception with the creased photograph.

That's when I saw the tattoo on her arm. I'd seen it in the photograph before, but not really noticed it. Now it registered – now it *really* registered, and I was totally sure.

'Yeah, that's her,' Morticia said, and nodded. 'You may as well throw it away. I don't think she's coming back for it.'

You're probably right about that, I thought. *But if she does come back, you won't want to hang around...*

So what do you do on your first day of knowing that the world is not at all what you thought it was? That vampires exist? That you've been communicating with the dead... and the undead?

You work, apparently. You work really, really hard.

With few scientific answers available to account for my recent discoveries (rational thinking would have been my dad's approach), I decided to bury myself in research for the article I planned to present to Pepper. She arrived late, looking a whole lot more rested than I did, but she seemed preoccupied and she didn't hassle me for my notes from the launch. That suited me just fine, especially as every question about *BloodofYouth* I sought answers for only led to further questions.

I played the *BloodofYouth* DVD and read every subtitled word of Dr Toth's speech. Strangely, there did not seem to be any revolutionary new ingredients in this apparently revolutionary new cream. I called the actor, Toni, to ask her if she knew that the patent for the product was only made up of things like methylparaben, butylparaben, ethylparaben, isobutylparaben, propyl-paraben, simethicone and some perfume – all common ingredients in skin creams, apparently, and nothing that could logically cause the dramatic results she claimed. But Toni didn't answer the phone. I sent her an email and hoped for a speedy response so I could include her quote in the piece I presented to Pepper. I sent a similar email to Henrietta at the PR company, but expected a more cautious response from her, if any.

Weirdly, my Internet searches for *BloodofYouth* resulted in a lot of hits about the buzz surrounding the product, but very little information. The product website was basic. The company was based in Eastern Europe as far as I could tell, and it was not attached to any major cosmetic company, as I imagined most big products were. *BloodofYouth* seemed to have brought America to a fever pitch in a remarkably short period of time, and for no obvious pharmaceutical reason. I was intrigued, and even more so when Dr Toth, the doctor behind the 'revolutionary' product, came up only in searches related to *BloodofYouth*. He did not seem to be attached to any university, scientific institution or major company. Who was he? I was determined to click on every single link referencing him online.

At noon I stepped out to pick up some takeaway and when I returned with a tray of sushi, I noticed a bouquet of flowers sitting on my desk. It was so big I could see it clearly from across the room and I am ashamed to admit that the sight of them made my heart skip a beat. *Long-stemmed red roses? For me?* It took a moment before the obvious dawned on me, and my hopes fell in a heap. Naturally they would be for *Skye*, not for me. Doubtless it was something from her boyfriend or an admirer. A get-well card would be attached. Who had I imagined would send me flowers? I'd never been sent flowers in my life.

Silly.

Morticia was eating a bagel for lunch. She had her Doc Martens up on the reception desk, and she gave me a wink. 'You sure made an impression on someone at the launch...'

'The flowers?' I looked at them again. 'They're for *me*?' *Can ghosts send flowers?* I wondered fleetingly, and was glad the idea didn't escape my lips.

'Yup,' Morticia said. 'They arrived just after you left.'

'Oh...' I hurried towards my desk, and Morticia trailed behind, still chewing. When she stood waiting next to me, I flashed her a look.

'Oh, come on,' she said. 'It's no secret, is it? Who are they from?'

I raised an eyebrow at her and she got my drift.

'Okay, fine,' she said reluctantly. 'If you don't want to tell me who your boyfriend is, that's fine.' She slunk away, disappointed, and plonked herself at reception with an exaggerated flop.

I took off my coat and sat in my chair. *Oh boy...* The flowers were completely gorgeous; plump red and long-stemmed. They didn't have any scent, but they were exquisite to look at. And there were so *many* of them. It was quite a romantic gesture – but from whom? I found a small white envelope stuck to the side of the bouquet with a pin. I took a breath, pulled the pin out and opened the envelope. I slid the little rectangular card out with my eyes closed.

I held the card in my hand, and opened my tired eyes.

Dear Pandora,
It was lovely to see you last night. Please give me your number.

I'd like to show you New York.
Jay

My heart fluttered and I put the card down on my desk. Inside the envelope was a second card, this one a little less romantic. It was Jay's business card for *Men Only* magazine. It had his email address and cell number on it.

Oh boy...

CHAPTER
SEVENTEEN

$\mathcal{I}$ got home, remembered to knock, and slipped inside Celia's penthouse bursting with questions. 'Good evening, Great-Aunt Celia.'

'Hello, darling Pandora,' she replied, and closed her book. 'Oh dear, you do look a bit fatigued.'

I nodded. 'I know, I know. But I don't care – I'm a genius!' I cried.

'Oh, I see,' she replied, ever understated.

I held up a printout of an email I had received from an actor in Romania – an actor who had a website listing his appearance in a commercial for *BloodofYouth* among his credits. He had responded eagerly to my enquiry, probably because he didn't mind getting famous if there was a scandal. This was gold. Absolute gold.

'I've got them! There is no Dr Toth – they had an actor play him. He's a fabrication!' I waved the piece of paper triumphantly.

'Well, it seems you've had an interesting day.'

'Oh, there will be a scandal when this breaks,' I told

Celia excitedly. 'Pepper gave me until tomorrow morning. I think she'll be *well* impressed.' How could she resist running the story? It was huge.

'And what about everyone else? Will they be impressed?' Celia asked. She didn't seem as overjoyed as I was.

'Who? The public?' I asked. 'They will be amazed and rather cross to discover they are being sold an expensive lie about a beauty product that's no more revolutionary than the hand cream they buy at the local supermarket! There is no secret ingredient. It's hogwash!' I declared.

I'd heard stories about this kind of thing − how marketing basic products with fancy labels and beautiful advertising campaigns could earn a fortune under false pretences − and now I'd found a classic example, from what appeared to be a fraudulent company to boot. This beat the heck out of my idea for an article about vintage clothing. Yet Great-Aunt Celia did not seem as excited as I'd expected.

'*There is no secret ingredient?*' she repeated slowly, and raised an eyebrow. There was something very odd about the way she said the words. It was as if she already knew the answer, and was asking the question solely for my benefit.

'No,' I confirmed. I frowned. 'The listed ingredients are all found in other products.' That's what I'd discovered, and easily too. There was nothing new about it, and the manufacturers must have thought they could get away with their claim to be revolutionary because so many products had got away with similarly exaggerated claims before. They were crazy if they thought it wouldn't catch up with them.

'Hmm,' Celia said, not sounding convinced.

I frowned again. In my enthusiasm, it seemed I had missed what she was trying to tell me, but I couldn't imagine what that might be.

'Well, good luck with the article, darling.' Celia looked down, and crossed her ankles. 'Now, have you thought any more about what we were talking about last night?' she asked, smoothly changing the subject.

'We were talking last night about your age. And about...' *Vampires.*

'Oh yes, my age – my favourite subject,' she said.

'I've been thinking about our conversation,' I said, although in truth I'd been so caught up in my *BloodofYouth* research that I hadn't given it much thought since my conversation with Morticia about poor, deadly, undead Samantha. I tried to recall one of the many questions that had been buzzing around my brain as I'd walked to work that morning. 'You said Lucasta women have gifts. So is your special gift immortality?'

Celia sighed. 'Well, no,' she said patiently. 'Please sit down.'

I did, taking my usual place on the edge of the hassock while my host reclined glamorously. I was still vibrating with excitement about my article on *BloodofYouth*. I began tapping my foot impatiently, caught myself and stopped.

'Darling, the Lucasta women have all had gifts, different gifts, different strengths, but none of the Lucasta women has ever been immortal,' my great-aunt explained. Then she pinched her brows together. 'Well, none that I am aware of. I suppose some of them may have become *undead*, but if so they never dropped me a line. I think that would be rude, don't you?'

Celia's face was as elegantly deadpan as ever.

Undead was a significant new word in my big-city vocabulary, it seemed, along with *psychic* and *spontaneous combustion*. I knew I'd have a lot to learn when I left Gretchenville.

'I can see you are a clever girl with an inquiring mind, Pandora. I know you aren't going to give this up, this business about my age and identity. But if I tell you, you have to promise not to tell anyone. Okay? Really. Not Georgia, and not any of your friends at work.'

I nodded vigorously. 'I promise.'

'I'll make you keep this promise,' she warned me. 'And I have ways of making sure this promise is kept.'

Somehow I believed her.

Could I really promise though? What if Celia told me she was a mass-murdering impostor? Of course, I didn't believe that, but still, what if?

Celia smiled, almost as if she'd heard my thoughts. 'Be patient, and you will have all the knowledge you want,' she told me. 'First of all, I think you should see this.' Celia reached behind her and pulled a large photo album into her lap. 'This should settle any qualms you have about identity.'

The book she handed me was heavy, and a little dusty. It was filled with yellowing photographs and newspaper clippings from Celia's past life as a high-flying designer for the stars. Here she was with Lauren Bacall – whom she'd designed that knockout red dress for – and Humphrey Bogart, Frank Sinatra, Ava Gardner.

My eyes grew wide. 'Oh wow! Celia, this is amazing.' I pored over the images, finding myself quite star-struck. I even recognised one of the photographs as one my mother used to have on her vanity. This was indeed Celia.

'This was on the set of *Ziegfeld Girl*,' Celia explained. 'That's Judy Garland.' She turned the page over to show a black and white image of two women standing in front of racks of elaborate costumes. I saw feathers, sequins, furs. 'That's Lana Turner with Judy. Such a lovely-looking woman, don't you think?'

I paused when I came to a photo of two women who looked very alike. One of the women was Celia, I could tell, though her face was a little rounder then. The woman she was with looked like she could be Celia's older sister. 'Who is *this*?'

'That's Hedy Lamarr.'

I squinted. I knew the name, though not well.

'I fell in with Hedwig for a while,' Celia mused, tapping the image with her fingernail. 'She was known as Hedy by all the Hollywood types, but I called her Hedwig, her real name. She was a very troubled woman, but so very intelligent, with a body for fashion and a head for science. She was quite mathematical. And she knew all kinds of things too. She had "gifts", a bit like you, Pandora. She could have been a Lucasta.'

I gazed at the woman's face in the photograph. There

was something quite extraordinary about her eyes. I recognised something about her. She had been quite famous in her day, but of course those days had been the 1930s and 40s. Most people would have forgotten her by now.

'Did you know that she coinvented spread-spectrum communications technology with the composer George Antheil?' Celia asked.

I shook my head. 'Really?'

'Yes. She took me under her wing for a while when I was young and new to Hollywood,' Celia explained. 'She was the first to get me interested in science. Frequencies and so on. She had escaped her awful husband, an arms manufacturer in Vienna, and come to Hollywood armed with all kinds of political and military knowledge. By the time we met her film career was at its peak. Only a few years later, things became difficult for her.' She looked at the photograph thoughtfully. 'On a trip to New York we found this place. It was very rundown, but she could see that it was unusual, and I could too... Pandora, your abilities will shine here. Mine did. Moving here changed everything for me.'

She closed the album and sighed delicately. 'So, can you see now that I am your great-aunt? That I am not an impostor?'

I nodded. None of this explained her youthful appearance, but I could not doubt her identity. 'What happened to Hedy?' I asked.

'Oh, Hedwig. After I bought this place we drifted apart. It was the distance from Hollywood. Back then you didn't just jet back and forth on a whim, like the stars do now. She was getting older and she went a little mad after her looks began to fade and Hollywood turned its back on her. By 1951, it was practically over for her. Hollywood eats up beautiful women and spits them out.' Celia pursed her lips angrily. 'They always have. She was only in her mid-thirties by then. Can you imagine? And she was not exactly the type to fade away quietly. That beautiful mind of hers was too much of a burden for her, I guess. She ended up in the headlines later in life for stealing underwear from a department store. She wound up in Florida, quite poor. She wrote me a letter once saying that she'd probably earned and spent nearly thirty million dollars, and then found she hadn't enough to buy a sandwich. Her friends tried to help her out, but she was a proud woman. And who could blame her? I just wish she'd stayed in New York. She might have been present when Deus first called on me. He would have liked her a lot, I think.'

This, I could tell, was getting to the really interesting part of the story.

'Pandora,' she began, leaning forward. 'I have a special friend. His name is Deus. He is ... *Sanguine*.'

Sanguine? 'You mean he is cheerfully optimistic?' I asked. I knew the word from reading the dictionary, something I did a lot of in Gretchenville. Sanguine also meant ruddy of complexion, if memory served, but I doubted Celia would think that worth telling me.

My great-aunt chuckled. 'No, darling. Not cheerful. He is, you know, *Sanguineus*.'

I frowned. I had the word filed away somewhere. *Sanguineus* . . . I thought of museums, textbooks. It was used in the Latin names for things. I thought of snapper, the fish. Scarlet snapper. *Red.*

'*Sanguineus*: of blood,' I said triumphantly as soon as it came to me. And then I thought immediately of the other familiar term: *exsanguinate*, to drain of blood, and my complexion did a little exsanguination of its own. 'Do you mean he's a vampire?'

Celia's serene face tensed, and her cherry lips curled in distaste. 'Darling, you really should know that we don't use that word. It's rude. I should have made that clear last night. Beings like Deus are Sanguine.' Right. Cheerful vampires. That was better than melancholic, I supposed.

'Vampire is a terribly pejorative term,' Celia continued. 'Well, *vamp* is sort of okay. Some of them use it in jest, or with irony, I suppose, the way African-American rappers use that horrible N word which I can't bring myself to say.' She wrinkled her nose. 'In any event, I wouldn't count on getting away with using the V word around a Sanguine. They are not likely to take it in good humour. But whatever you do don't go calling them *Nosferatu*. It's an old Slavonic expression meaning "plague carrier".'

Oh god. Vampires. Sanguine. It's real.

Hearing her say it aloud made me exhale suddenly. I went a little limp, and I felt Great-Aunt Celia's icy hands hold me firmly by the upper arms. I'd been holding my breath.

'Just take a breath now,' she instructed me.

I did.

'Do you need to? Breathe?' I asked.

'Of course. I told you, darling, I am not undead.'

Oh good. Celia is alive. I am not living with the undead. That's nice.

'Technically Deus doesn't need to breathe, but, darling, no one will force you to meet him – though if you do meet him you'll find he's quite a gentleman, so don't excite yourself. As I was saying, you mustn't believe the things you read in those silly books of yours.' She was speaking about her vampire friend casually now, in a tone one might use to discuss a friend who was a vegetarian or Scientologist. I felt a little freakout coming on, but I suppressed it. Who was I to say what was strange, or who my great-aunt could consort with? As the 'weird girl' who'd talked to the dead Gretchenville butcher, I was in no position to judge.

I nodded. 'Okay, so Bram Stoker was wrong.'

'About many things, yes.' She thought for a moment. 'And Sanguine don't sparkle in the daylight, like those silly books everyone's reading at the moment.'

'... And there are no "vegetarian" Sanguine.'

Gulp. Right.

'But vampires are immortal, right?'

Celia shook her head. 'Only the gods are truly immortal,' she said. 'And even they are rumoured to have fallen. Everything passes, young Pandora, though some creatures don't age or decay. Some creatures live so long it makes our short lives seem as insignificant as the fleeting lifetime of a butterfly.'

I didn't quite understand what she was driving at. 'But how are you so young then, if you're not...Sanguine yourself?'

'There are ways,' she said significantly, and then winked. 'I found myself growing old a few decades back. Naturally. And frankly, darling, it's not all it's cracked up to be, as poor Hedy can attest. Now, thanks to my special friend, I am stronger and more beautiful than I ever was before,' Celia declared.

'But are you...happier, Great-Aunt Celia?' I asked pointedly.

If I was expecting her to be wrestling with some kind of profound moral or spiritual dilemma, I was wrong. 'Happier? Well, *obviously*,' she answered without hesitation. 'Why do you think "sanguine" came to mean cheerful all those years ago? Think about it.'

Oh, boy. Was that possible? What about Hippocrates and his 'four humours'? Did he know about all this?

'Of course I'm happier,' my great-aunt scoffed, bringing me back from 400 BC. 'Do you realise how frail I would be by now? So I'm allergic to garlic and a little light-sensitive. So what? It's a small price to pay.'

I blinked.

'It's the dilated pupils,' she explained, with some regret. 'Great for night vision but a real pain during the day.'

Dilated pupils. Night vision. Exsanguination.

Buffeted by this flood of wild truths, I was struggling to keep up. If I understood the situation correctly, I was some kind of psychic medium living with my great-aunt whose friend the blood-sucking Sanguine kept her young. Somehow.

'So your friend, Deus. He is one of these Sanguines...'

Celia smiled as if recalling a lover. 'Indeed he is, darling. And a magnificent one. An ancient.'

Ancient. Oh boy. 'So, he sucks the blood out of people and kills them?'

'Kills them? Oh, no, darling. Why would he need to kill? Really, there are plenty of young women who are willing. And men too, of course, though that isn't particularly to his *taste*.'

I gathered she meant 'taste' literally.

'But he hasn't made you...Sanguine?' I said, to be sure.

'No.'

'And you don't suck blood?'

'No,' she confirmed, to my relief.

'So how come you aren't ageing? I don't get it.'

She sighed. 'Oh, darling Pandora, *use your imagination*,' she suggested.

'My imagination is getting quite a workout lately,' I replied flatly. 'I only just found out that I really can see ghosts.'

'Really? You only just found out? Be honest with yourself, dear.'

I thought about that. Of course she was right; I had known – and yet I had not known. 'My parents – especially my dad – insisted such things didn't exist.'

'Oh, they were so short-sighted,' Celia said regretfully. 'Do try to get all of that out of your head now. It won't help you here.' She leaned forward. 'Pandora, your mother must have known. I can't believe she wouldn't know about the beings beyond us. There are Sanguine all around the world, some of them quite culturally advanced, and some quite primitive and ferocious. I am sure she heard about those. Some of the cultures she studied are much more in touch with the undead than we are here in New York. The Otgiruru of Namibia and the Russian Erestun, for example.' She watched my face and saw that these creatures weren't ringing any bells. 'Or the Draugs of Northern Europe. Oh, and the flesh-eating Craqueuhhe. Now that's one nasty revenant. Give me a Sanguine any day,' she mused.

'I just thought they were only in books and movies,' I replied quietly.

'Well *vampires* are in books and movies, but like any good fictional cliché, they are based on at least a few truths. Some of the misconceptions about these Sanguine are just mistakes that caught on, a bit like "Chinese whispers", as they call it. Others are rumours planted to make them look bad.'

'Who would plant rumours?'

'The Church. The ... others,' she said vaguely. *Others.* 'Beings who are naturally opposed to the Sanguine,' she clarified.

I thought of the book I'd been reading. 'You mean *werewolves*?'

Celia laughed out loud. 'Do you really think a mortal, half-crazed hairy dog-man would be a match for an "immortal" being? Please.'

Oh.

'So there is, like, a supernatural eco-system?' I said, trying not to think about what other beings might be out there.

'Oh yes. Now you are getting it. We are all part of the eco-system. Only we humans choose to believe the supernatural doesn't exist, and that makes it easier to assure us we are right. In the human brain, perceptions and belief – what you wish to perceive – has much to do with what you actually see. It works out better for everyone, really. People who can't handle the existence of the supernatural usually don't have to worry about it. Things happen to them and they just figure it's coincidence, luck, or instinct, or their imagination.'

'I see. So they aren't about to come out of the closet – and drink synthetic blood?'

She sighed. 'No. Nobody wants the crusades all over again, Pandora. Spektor, for instance, has been invisible to most common people since Barrett erected this building. It is a magnet for the spirit world, and it repels the consciousness of humans who reject the supernatural, like a blind spot. I find it quite remarkable, don't you?'

I nodded emphatically. 'I noticed that cabbies don't really know about it.'

'You have a genetic predisposition to sensitivity to the supernatural, just as I have. Just as your mother did.'

I had so many questions, I didn't really know where to begin so I started with the most urgent question. 'Celia, could your friend...' I hesitated, careful not to sound hysterical. 'Could he turn *you* into a vamp—' I quickly corrected myself. 'Could he make you Sanguine?' I imagined opening my eyes in the middle of the night to find sweet Great-Aunt Celia leaning over me with giant fangs and a demonic look in her eye.

'Of course. But he wouldn't. He doesn't want me as his child.'

'What about me?'

'*You?*' Her eyebrows raised in an expression of genuine shock. 'Darling, your Aunt Georgia would be *so* upset.'

That was true.

'Not until you are at least twenty-one,' Celia said firmly. 'And only if you're sure that's what you really want. An immortal's lifetime is awfully long. I know I wouldn't want it.'

I could become immortal at twenty-one if I was really sure about it. And this was a real discussion, I could see. Well, Celia was very different from Aunt Georgia, that much was clear. I couldn't help but like that. 'Great-Aunt Celia, there is a young lady downstairs in this building named Samantha. She has fangs. Did Deus make her?'

Celia shook her head, seeming more than a little offended by the suggestion. 'Oh no. Deus doesn't like to propagate and he is much too ancient and powerful to make children by accident.' *Children?* That was the second time she'd used the word in reference to someone being turned into a vamp. 'Samantha was made by someone else.'

I had been afraid of that.

'What do your instincts tell you?' she asked, and regarded me shrewdly.

Athanasia is responsible, I thought. *Athanasia is a vampire.*

'I've been told not to trust my instincts,' I responded cautiously.

Celia rolled her eyes. 'You aren't in *Gretchenville* anymore, darling. Put all that nonsense behind you. And *think*,' she pressed. '*Feel*. I can tell you have a name there. Trust it.'

I did as she said. 'Well, I am sure that the woman down there is Samantha, my predecessor at *Pandora* magazine. And I'm sure she has been turned into...' Celia nodded, encouraging me to continue. 'And she was last seen at the photo shoot with Athanasia.'

'Yes?'

'So the face of *BloodofYouth* is a vampire?' I asked. 'I mean, a Sanguine?' It would take a while to get used to the term.

'Just Sanguine. That's how you say it. He is Sanguine, she is Sanguine, they are Sanguine.' Celia continued to regard me intently, silently urging me to continue my deductions.

'So, how does a...um...creature like that hide its nature from its employers? I suppose by only meeting people after dark, only ever doing photo shoots and launches after dark. Unless she doesn't have to?' I concluded, thinking of the woman in the back of the limousine. The woman with the high collar. 'Because her employers are *also*...' Could it be true? Could *BloodofYouth* really be run by a bunch of entrepreneurial vampires?

'Exactly,' Celia concluded.

'Oh.'

I fell silent.

'Well then,' Celia said briskly, and stood. 'Cup of tea?' she suggested, and sauntered to the kitchen to put the kettle on.

I sat on the hassock, my mind reeling. 'Poor Samantha,' I said finally. I was glad that Morticia hadn't had a moment alone with her supermodel crush. I followed Celia to the kitchen. 'Why is Samantha downstairs?'

'She is most likely an abandoned Fledgling,' Celia explained, scooping aromatic leaves of English Breakfast tea into a teapot. What a time of day for breakfast tea, I thought. 'Such behaviour is quite frowned upon in the supernatural community,' Celia continued. 'As you can imagine. The poor girl won't know what she's doing there.'

'We'll have to help her,' I said.

Celia frowned, but didn't say anything. The kettle came to the boil and she warmed two cups with hot water and let the tea steep in the pot.

'You wish to help this Samantha?' she asked at last.

'Yes,' I heard myself saying. Sure, she had tried to eat me, but she was so confused, I didn't think she'd meant it. If the poor thing didn't know where she was, or why she was so thirsty, she needed someone to help her.

'You are a generous soul,' Celia stated, and smiled as if this both pleased and bewildered her. 'Well, if I can't stop you from going down there, I ought to at least go with you,' she suggested.

'Oh, would you?'

'All right. But let's drink our tea first.'

CHAPTER
EIGHTEEN

$\mathcal{I}$ left the penthouse with my Great Aunt Celia around nine. Celia knew how to make one wicked pot of tea and I was as hopped up as I'd ever been. She insisted I change into something casual in case 'things got messy', as she put it. Obediently, I put on jeans, a T-shirt and an old sweater, though I noticed she still looked impossibly glamorous in a silk dress, silk stockings, Mary Jane shoes, buckled leather gloves, her fox stole and ubiquitous black veil. We each carried a torch and, strangely, she was carrying a small bag of rice.

'Do you really think it's safe to go down there?' I asked, as we descended in the old lift.

'Safe as it ever is, darling.'

I found this to be a less-than-comforting reply, under the circumstances.

'Why the rice?' I had to ask.

'Here, you hold it,' Celia said, and passed the bag to me.

It weighed more than I'd thought, and I made a brief exhalation of air upon receiving it. The doors opened on the third floor. The lights were on, but most of the gilded wall sconces were broken or lacking bulbs. The area was only dimly lit, and the whole landing seemed draped in dust.

'There are two important things you should know about these particular creatures,' Celia explained. She switched her torch on and I did the same. 'Number one: they need to be invited to enter a home.'

I had heard that before, but then I'd also heard that crucifixes made them burst into flames, and that they could not be photographed. What did I know?

'Okay,' I said.

'So, for the lady of the house, obviously, it is easy to repeal that invitation if it suits,' Celia said, looking around for signs of the undead. She stepped out of the lift before the doors closed again, and I followed her. 'If anyone acts out, I cast them out. Not that I've had to. They know better than that.'

Handy, I thought.

We stood on the landing just outside the lift, and shone our torches over the floor. Celia also shone hers across the high ceiling above her, as if looking for spiders. I found it strangely unsettling.

'So, Samantha had to ask your permission to come in here?' I said. Celia had known she was here all along? Did she know she was from *Pandora* magazine? Was that how she knew there was a job opening?

'Well, no. This Samantha was able to come in here of her own will – or she was brought here once she was turned, or even about to be turned, we can't be sure. It's a deal I have with Deus and his, um, bosses. The undead aren't allowed on the penthouse level without an explicit invitation, but they can use the rest of the building as a kind of safe house.' She gestured with her leather-gloved hand in that casual way of hers, as if what she was telling me was perfectly mundane. 'Those are the rules. So there will be Fledglings like Samantha from time to time, if someone turns them and then turns them out. Though that's a pretty naughty thing to do.'

'Right,' I said, and tried to comprehend the implications of such a deal. Was the whole place crawling with vampires after dark? I felt the small hairs on the back of my neck stand up. 'And what is the second thing?' I asked, now nervously casting my eyes about.

'The second thing is about the rice,' she told me, and gestured to the bag I was holding. 'It is a peculiar fascination... If you spill rice or seeds, for instance, these creatures will be distracted, especially the new ones, the Fledglings. They will be compelled to count every grain. The Chinese have long known this. It is said the Poles favour carrot seeds, but I prefer rice.' She paused. 'Let's go this way first.'

I followed in silence, deeply puzzled.

Rice? Carrot seeds? This was possibly the most preposterous thing I had ever heard. At least I could see some thread of a reason for the violent allergy to garlic, as garlic is supposedly a blood purifier. But was I now to believe the undead were obsessive-compulsive counters, suffering some kind of special, undead arithmomania? *Inconceivable.* But then I thought of that old childhood favourite, Count von Count from *Sesame Street*. *The makers of* Sesame Street *knew this?*

No way.

It occurred to me that I ought to be taking notes. I'd have to record all these rules and facts – invitations, rice, garlic – when I was feeling less on edge. As it was, we were searching for a newbie vamp with an awful thirst – one that had already attacked me once. And if I understood what Celia was suggesting, the place could be crawling with them.

Ah.

We found Samantha curled up in the far corner of the third-floor landing, asleep or quite possibly unconscious. She still had my woolly shawl wrapped around her, and she was not far from where I had seen her last. Her knees were folded up into her chest, and her head had lolled to one side at a slightly unnatural angle. Samantha looked truly awful. Her pale complexion had turned sickly, and she looked much thinner than when I'd last seen her. Her cheekbones were already jutting out sharply.

'Oh, would you look at that? Bloody Fledglings...' Great-Aunt Celia cursed quietly, fixing her eyes on the wooden railing nearest to her. It had been chewed like the end of a pencil, as if by a teething puppy. 'Damn.' She moved in dangerously close to the woman, kneeled for a moment and looked at her mouth. 'Fledgling teeth,' she confirmed. 'Hmm. You stay with her, darling. I'll get a cat or something.'

'A cat?' Was this to be some kind of ritual?

'She has to eat something, poor thing...'

A cat? I couldn't let her do that.

I stood stiffly on the third level holding the bag of rice while Celia walked back to the old elevator and made her way downstairs. I heard the lift stop at street level, followed by the *click, click, click* of Celia's heels on the tiles. When the heavy entry door closed, the building was quiet again, and I felt very, very alone with this sleeping vampire next to me. Alone and uneasy. I found myself wondering if I would be safer back in the penthouse, just until Celia returned. I looked at my bag of rice, and then looked at the sleeping (dead?) vampire.

Hmmm.

I couldn't help myself. I had to see if it was true. 'Oh boy...' I muttered, and spilled a small heap of rice grains at Samantha's feet.

I waited. She didn't stir.

'Oh, I'm an idiot,' I told myself, and looked nervously around me. Every shadow seemed to hide another bloodthirsty creature, each more deadly than the last. I held the bag of rice like a weapon. I bit my lip. 'Oh, boy. I really don't want to be alone right now...'

In moments I felt a chill descend, and in front of the railing a white, nebulous shape materialised.

Lieutenant Luke!

He formed before me, slowly at first, and then with some speed. I tilted my head up slightly to look into his face. 'Hi,' I said, beaming, and dropped the bag of rice.

'Miss Pandora, are you okay?' he asked anxiously.

He took off his dark blue cap and held it in his hands respectfully.

I nodded. 'I'm okay. Hi,' I said again, stupidly. 'It is really nice to see you.'

Luke put a cool, misty arm around me. 'I don't want anything to happen to you.'

I found myself grinning. I leaned into him, and found his attractive form comforting. 'I missed you. I sure wish you weren't dead,' I remarked.

I explained why we were looking for Samantha, and he said, 'You have a good heart.'

The return of my great-aunt was announced by her echoing footsteps downstairs and the rattle of the ascending lift. Luke and I stopped talking, so I wouldn't seem to be talking to myself. Celia approached us with two small hessian sacks. The sacks didn't appear large enough to be holding fully grown cats. I couldn't be sure, but I thought the sacks were moving.

Kittens? I thought with horror. *No!*

'Oh, darling, I'm not about to feed her kittens. Relax,' my great-aunt said. She sounded amused. 'Harold can get anything when you need it most. He's such a dear.'

Wait, did she just read my mind?

'What's this?' she asked, pointing at the small pile of rice on the floor.

I blushed.

Luke bent his head to see what she was pointing at.

'Um,' I began, embarrassed. My cheeks grew warmer by the heartbeat. 'I wanted to see...'

'Darling, it's a lot more effective when they're conscious,' Celia said, then paused. She cocked her head and looked at me. 'Is your friend here?' She turned left then right. 'He is, isn't he? How sweet.'

I looked at Lieutenant Luke, who returned my gaze with his piercing blue eyes. I turned back to my great-aunt, who grinned at me naughtily. 'Is he very handsome?' she asked with one sculpted eyebrow raised.

I nodded in the affirmative.

'Ah, I wish I could see him, but it's not my gift,' she said wistfully, and sighed. I wondered how she knew about my phantom friend, but before I could ask, she bent over Samantha. 'Now, darling, you have been made Sanguine, but only if you drink,' she explained to the young undead woman.

Samantha still had her eyes closed. She wasn't moving, not even to breathe.

Celia opened a sack, and, to my mingled repulsion and relief, it held two very plump and fairly disgusting rats. 'This ought to wake you up,' she murmured and held the wriggling rodents out by their long, scaly tails, one in each gloved hand. Somehow, she managed this gesture elegantly, as a high priestess would feed a prized snake.

What happened next was something I would never forget. Samantha opened her eyes with a start and snatched at the air with her mouth, fangs extended. She caught hold of the rats with a hand bent like claws, clamped her mouth down and began drinking from them eagerly, one and then the other, like a child sucking the juice out of an orange. It was an altogether bestial, inhuman act, and it happened in the blink of an eye. So fast. So animal.

I swallowed. My mouth was dry.

Samantha was soon strangely transformed by this brief, orgiastic feed. 'Oh,' she remarked, and licked her lips clean. Almost immediately I thought I noticed a new pinkness under her skin.

'Darling, you must feed,' Celia explained to her. 'You are Sanguine.'

'A vampire,' I added helpfully, because I couldn't imagine the young woman could know what Sanguine meant.

Celia gave me a sharp look.

Samantha licked her lips again. Her eyes were wild as they fixed upon Celia and me. She seemed not to be aware of Luke. Then she spied the small pile of grains at her feet. 'Oh!' she gasped and bent towards the rice eagerly. 'One, two, three, four, five, six, seven...'

I couldn't believe what I was witnessing.

Celia let out a little sigh of resignation. 'Well, this will take a while. Thank goodness you didn't spill the whole bag.' She leaned against the railing and waited.

I flushed.

After an agonising few minutes, Samantha stopped counting the sixty-nine grains of rice.

'As I was saying, my dear, you must drink blood now, if you wish to survive. You are no longer human,' my great-aunt explained to her.

'I am not...human?'

'Who did this to you?' I pressed. 'Samantha, was it at the photo shoot? Or afterwards? Who was it?'

The young vampire furrowed her pale brow. 'Uh...' She seemed to concentrate. 'I remember that I was with that beautiful model... after the photo shoot for *Pandora*. We went for a drink. I really liked her. She was so nice to me...'

She was nice? That sounded highly suspicious.

'And then I... I found myself here.' Her delicate eyebrows pinched together again. 'I don't know how I got here.'

I do, I thought. *Athanasia.*

'What happened to your clothes? And your wallet and things?'

She shook her head. 'I don't know.'

'I am going to give you some of my clothes,' I declared, and Celia raised an eyebrow. 'I don't need my clothes from Gretchenville anymore.' I would keep my jeans and T-shirts, but that grey suit had to go, I decided. I found the idea of a vampire lurking around in it strangely irresistible.

'You can stay here,' Celia offered. 'We'll get a coffin for you, if you like.'

'Oh, thank you. I feel much better now,' Samantha said, and smiled. 'Thank you so much.'

Her smile, though sweet, was a little unnerving. Perhaps it was the Fledgling fangs.

CHAPTER
NINETEEN

I had it. I had a fantastic story.

Of course I could only write *one tenth* of the interesting things I'd learned since landing in New York, but the article I had for Pepper Smith was sure to get Skye's attention without getting me thrown into a mental institution in the way that, say, an article titled 'The Truth About *BloodofYouth*'s Vampire Model' might. Not that I didn't have a lot to say on the issue. I mean how unethical was it to model a beauty product on a creature that couldn't age?

'*BloodofYouth exposed*', was the none-too-subtle title of my 'note' for Pepper about the *BloodofYouth* launch.

Serious questions have been raised about the safety of BloodofYouth, *the most hyped beauty product in New York this year*, I wrote. I covered a lot of interesting points, not least of which was that the *BloodofYouth* laboratories in Eastern Europe could not be contacted, or even located:

> *A search of business listings across Eastern Europe revealed that no business of that name has been trademarked there, and*

Dr E. Toth, the Hungarian scientist credited with coming up with the revolutionary formula, appears not to exist. Romanian actor Charles Shultvitz, who plays Dr Toth in the BloodofYouth promotional video, claims he was simply paid to read from the script and has no knowledge of any real Dr Toth.

'I had no idea where the video would ultimately be used,' he told Pandora. *He also claimed that he was only paid five hundred dollars for the shoot that is now being used to establish the 'credibility' of the BloodofYouth product.*

Actress Toni Howard, who helped launch the product at Elizabett restaurant earlier this week, admits she was paid in product for her role as master of ceremonies, and that she never met anyone claiming to directly represent the company.

'The buzz about it was so good. And I looked great when I first started using it. I had no idea there might be something amiss with BloodofYouth,' she told Pandora. *'But after only a few days I started to break out. I've never had an allergic reaction like this before? I can't get out of bed.'*

No one interviewed seemed to have met anyone directly linked to the brand, except the product's muse. Naturally, I had to be most diplomatic when writing about Athanasia, because although I suspected a lot of things about her, I had no scientific evidence, and I suspected the world was not yet ready for the idea of vampire supermodels.

Supermodel Athanasia, the stunning public face of BloodofYouth, was not available for comment at the time of printing. Little is known about the model, no contact details for her have been found and, though Pandora *contacted all the model agencies in New York, not one claimed representation of the supermodel or knowledge of her exact origins, thought to be Eastern Europe.*

But perhaps most disturbing is the mystery surrounding the product itself. Officially the product contains a standard concoction of ingredients found in many other inexpensive creams, but Pandora *knows of at least two clients falling mysteriously ill shortly after using the product, including a magazine staff member. Is it a coincidence, or is the FDA's approval as non-existent as Dr Toth and the rest of the BloodofYouth company? And if BloodofYouth and Dr Toth prove not to exist, who will be accountable if the product does contain a dangerous unapproved ingredient?*

At the time of printing, Pandora *is recommending a reevaluation of BloodofYouth through the FDA. Buyer beware…*

I proudly presented my article to Pepper.

From the look on her face I could see that she didn't expect much. She took it into Skye's office and closed the door. Skye was evidently on the mend (though arguably less 'radiant'), yet her deputy editor sure seemed at home in that office, I thought. She was not going to enjoy relinquishing her new power.

It took all of six minutes for Pepper to come over to my desk. I could feel her presence behind me. 'You did all this yourself?' she asked, incredulous.

I turned and nodded. 'I did.'

'And this is true? Dr Toth is played by an actor?'

Again, I nodded. 'I found him online. I have his words on email.'

'You have evidence of these conversations? The stuff about Dr Toth and the company being non-existent? I'll need all of your notes.'

I was prepared for this reaction. No one wanted to get sued. I handed the deputy editor the results of my research, the contact details and the notes. 'The FDA has to take a look at this,' I said emphatically. '*BloodofYouth* is at best a fraudulent company, and at worst... I don't know. It could even be a dangerous product.'

'Mmm,' Pepper said. I could see her mind ticking over. 'I'll have to speak with Henrietta about this.' The woman from the PR company. 'Perhaps she can shed some light on the company.'

'Good luck with that,' I said. Henrietta had not returned any of my calls. Unsurprisingly.

Pepper looked pretty impressed, I thought. This was sure to get my work noticed.

It would soon be print time for the next issue of *Pandora* magazine. Perhaps I really could make an impact in this town.

CHAPTER
TWENTY

*I*t is a true measure of how unhappy I had been in Gretchenville that things at home in Spektor began to feel normal for me.

As eccentric as she was, I had a real connection with my Great-Aunt Celia – something I'd always lacked with my Aunt Georgia. Celia was like a fairy godmother to me. (Or perhaps a vampire godmother, minus the troublesome teeth.) She gave me tips on sartorial elegance, shared stories about her life as a designer, and answered some of my questions about my family history. Bit by bit she was helping me piece together the puzzle of my existence. It would be a slow process, I could tell, but I was finally coming to terms with my 'gift' of communicating with the dead, and that seemed to hold some important key to my identity.

Harold's Grocer did indeed seem to be open day and night, as the unusual-looking Harold had promised, and he insisted that he was always open, despite what I'd seen that night from the cab. I got the cheese he promised, and ordered some of the crackers I'd liked back home, and he also sourced for me the satchel I'd seen on the cover of *Mia* magazine, which I thought was pretty cool.

The vampire Samantha did not attempt to lunge at my throat again. We were even becoming friends, although I showed more caution traversing the building after dark, just in case she – or another like her – had another moment of blind thirst. But though I sensed there were many other residents in Spektor, the little suburb remained quiet to me, as if they had not yet decided to trust me or introduce themselves.

At *Pandora* I worked quietly on my piece about vintage clothing (between fetching beverages and whatever other tasks I was given), but I admit my mind was fairly caught up with considering the more important new things I'd learned. *Fangs. Blood. Spirits of the dead.* I did some research on Edmund Barrett but, amazingly, not one article mentioned Spektor or the building that was my new home. This 'safe house' for the undead was, quite literally, off the grid. I suppose I shouldn't have been surprised. It did surprise me, though, that Pepper had no further questions about the article I had given her.

Lieutenant Luke didn't visit me, and I found I really wanted to see him again. I missed him something terrible. But where could it all go? He was dead. Jay Rockwell, however, was not dead. He and I exchanged emails and though I wouldn't give him my number – because I didn't have one – it was by email that I finally I agreed to have dinner with him. I'd heard that Little Italy was nice, so he agreed to show me a place there.

It was quarter to six on a Friday evening when I left the

Pandora magazine offices for my first date in New York. It had already been a strange day, and though I didn't know it yet, it was scheduled to get a whole lot stranger...

I carried my new black leather satchel on my shoulder. I wore one of Celia's nicest silk dresses under a warm camel-coloured cashmere winter coat. I had on my great-aunt's ruby red shoes, which gave my calves a nice shape, and I'd dabbed on some perfume, applied a slick of fresh red lipstick and brushed out my light brown hair.

'So, who is he?' Morticia pressed. She was leaving the office at the same time, so we were walking out together.

Thanks to my date preparations and Celia's lovely clothes, I looked pretty good, but I was feeling quiet after the day I'd had. (More on that later.) Possibly against my better judgment, I'd admitted to Morticia that I was going on a date, so naturally she wouldn't stop asking me about it. Due to my mood, I remained vague and a little sullen, though I couldn't tell her why. Besides, I figured I ought to see how it went before I started sharing my thoughts and feelings about Jay Rockwell. I didn't want to put too much pressure on things, and I didn't need the whole office knowing the details of my personal life, right? (Ghosts and all...) Needless to say, my uncharacteristically unresponsive attitude had made things awkward by the time Morticia and I stepped onto the chilly streets of SoHo outside.

Vlad.

Celia's tight-lipped chauffeur was waiting for me at the kerb. I hadn't expected that. He was looking as formidable and expressionless as ever, standing by the door of his black, polished car, in the pose of a bodyguard from a Hollywood movie: feet shoulder-width apart and hands clasped behind his back. His pressed black suit, impressive stature, and the fact that he always wore dark sunglasses – even now with the sun about to set – combined to add weight to the illusion that he was either CIA or hired muscle. New York traffic flew past on the street behind him in a clamorous blur, seeming like a totally separate, noisy, fast-moving dimension set against his static, silent figure in the foreground.

I hadn't counted on Vlad picking me up, though I should have guessed Celia would send him. (I'd told her about my date, too. It seems I couldn't keep my mouth shut about it.) With Vlad and his car waiting outside *Pandora*, I felt a vague, immature desire to have Pepper or Skye there to witness little me, office peasant, getting into the fancy chauffeured car. The idea surfaced as a little shameful bubble of vanity. 'The illusion of importance', and all that. As it was, the only witness was Morticia.

'Well, this is me. Have a good weekend,' I told her, without having answered any of her previous questions about my date.

I got into the back of the big sleek car, put my seat belt on and held my leather satchel in my lap. Silent Vlad closed the door behind me, and I saw through the window that Morticia's eyes were as big as saucers. She stood on the sidewalk and stared, red hair flying around her pale face in the winter wind. The car pulled away, and part of me felt bad that she would be taking the subway home while I was being driven off in a luxurious car. There were bound to be a lot of questions on Monday.

Although I couldn't remember telling Celia where I had agreed to meet Jay, Vlad already had the address for my date it seemed, and, typically, he drove me there without a word. When he slowed and pulled up at the kerb I saw the name of the restaurant in glowing neon outside, and my heart sped up. *Giovanni's*, the sign said. I hopped out before he could come around to open my door.

I took a few steps along the cobblestone street then turned. 'Thanks, Vlad,' I said. 'Have a good weekend.'

Vlad was standing beside his door again, and he nodded silently in response. Since he never seemed to speak, I fancied this nod to mean 'Have a good time' or something similar. He watched me walk up the path in front of the restaurant before he climbed into his car. When I was safely inside he would drive off to some mysterious destination at which silent men named 'Vlad' spent their evenings. Where was that exactly?

This was my first visit to the area of Manhattan called Little Italy, and I was excited. I'd wanted to see it ever since I saw *The Godfather: Part II*. The sun was setting in soft oranges and reds, and the darkening streets were already filled with glowing white fairy lights. The winter evenings in New York could be bitterly cold, I'd found, but here warmth radiated from the many outdoor heaters set up on the sidewalks. Restaurants were nestled side by side, decorated with traditional décor and Italian flags. Patrons already sat under the heat lamps enjoying bottles of wine, their collars pulled up around their throats and their smiles wide. My nostrils filled with the delicious smells of Italian cooking. All around me I could hear laughter, music and the clanging of plates.

Wonderful.

I had insisted to Jay that I didn't want anything fancy, and after some consideration he'd suggested a casual 'Ma and Pa pasta joint' that had a good reputation. Though I suspected Jay had a lot of connections with the maître d's at the bigger restaurants in trendier places, he evidently didn't at this one. Their only opening for us was at six-fifteen. That had seemed fine by me, though it necessitated bringing a change of clothes to work and leaving directly from the office – via Vlad, apparently.

I negotiated the uneven cobblestones in Celia's beautiful ruby red shoes, stepped up to the door, ran a hand over my hair to smooth it down again, and pushed my way inside.

Here we go...

I was hit with a wall of chatter and a pleasant blast of warm air, infused with the smells of Italian cooking. The place was almost filled to capacity already, each little table set with the traditional red and white checked tablecloth, wine glasses, cutlery and a basket of bread. A few couples were already eating from overflowing plates of spaghetti. I quickly located my attractive date, waiting for me at an intimate window table in one corner. He stood – all six-foot-hunky-six of him –

and I moved towards him through the crowd of tables.
Some of the patrons stopped what they were doing to
watch us. (I still wasn't used to the way people in this
town always checked each other out. Was it a New York
thing? Or a big-city thing?) Jay looked good enough to
eat in a black collared shirt and blue jeans. His sleeves
were rolled partway up his forearms and I noticed the
masculine veins and sinewy muscle with some pleasure.
As we weren't on kissing terms, he gave me a friendly
hug as a greeting, and the closeness gave me a rush of
excitement.

'Hi,' we said simultaneously.

Jay helped me with Celia's cashmere coat, and in a
flash a thin young Italian waiter had taken it from us.
He offered me a complimentary nod of approval. '*Bella*,'
he murmured. 'I hang up your coat, beautiful lady.' He
made an animated gesture with his fingers at his lips, as
if to blow me a kiss.

The amorous waiter left us and my date pulled out
my chair for me.

'You have a chauffeur?' Jay Rockwell remarked,
seeming surprised and possibly a little impressed. I took
my seat, and he sat opposite. Our chairs squealed when
we moved them forward. Jay leaned in attentively, his
hazel eyes alive with mischief. 'I thought you didn't like
things too fancy?' he said teasingly.

'I don't. And I don't,' I replied in answer to both
questions. 'That's Celia's driver. She insisted he pick me
up,' I explained. 'And I don't need you taking me to some
swish, overpriced restaurant.' Truthfully, I didn't want the

pressure of a fancy restaurant. The idea of a room full of rich New Yorkers was terrifying to me. I'm sure I would have used the wrong fork or something.

'You sure are an unusual lady,' Jay remarked with a shake of his head, and in a flash I had a vision of him impressing other women by taking them out to expensive Manhattan restaurants and buying them fifty-dollar cocktails and exorbitant meals. The idea made me a touch jealous.

'I'd like to meet your great-aunt one day,' he added. 'She sounds like an extraordinary woman.'

'She is,' I told him. I nervously smoothed down my silk dress, and shifted my heavy satchel to one side under our table with my foot. 'I hope you don't mind that I came straight from work.'

'I came straight from work, too,' he said. 'I should have mentioned you look gorgeous tonight. You are the best-dressed person here.'

I felt myself blush, though I doubted what he said was really true. 'Thanks.'

A period of awkward silence descended on us, and we opened our menus to cover the lack of conversation.

'So, did you end up writing that piece on the *BloodofYouth* launch? How did it go?' he asked me.

I stiffened.

The question, I'm sure, was an innocent one. I'd last seen him in person at the launch, after all. Jay had no idea about the detective work I'd done in the interim, or the bizarre things I'd uncovered. I hadn't mentioned a word of it in our email exchange. Pepper had been quite clear that I wasn't to tell anyone because it was an exclusive for our magazine. Thus, unless he happened to pick up the first copy of *Pandora* hot off the press today, Jay probably knew nothing of my accusations about *BloodofYouth*, and certainly no one knew about my outrageous suspicions regarding the *BloodofYouth* model, Athanasia, or what I believed she had done to my predecessor, Samantha. After a lifetime of repressing the urge to tell my parents – and later Aunt Georgia – about every strange imagining or visitation I experienced, it seemed I was getting pretty good at keeping extraordinary secrets. And that was doubtless a good thing in this case. Who could I confide in about these otherworldly conundrums? Who would believe me? *No one.* Except Celia. Or perhaps the Sanguine Samantha, and my friend Second Lieutenant Luke Thomas, who had died a century and a half ago.

'Didn't the new issue come out today?' my date added, unknowingly pursuing an unwelcome topic.

'Um, yes. I can't talk about it right now,' I responded cryptically.

A copy of the new issue of *Pandora* magazine was in fact sitting in the satchel at my feet. Though I was eagerly awaiting this new issue, no one had said anything about it to me at the office, not even Morticia. Through the day I'd had a creeping suspicion that the deputy editor, Pepper, was avoiding me. Skye was on the mend after her mysterious illness, but she hadn't come in, or called me about my piece. Finally I'd seen the magazine during my afternoon coffee break and grabbed it. When I read the cover piece, the atmosphere in the office became all too clear. (I'd had to fix my eye makeup in the hall bathroom before returning to work.) No one had wanted to be the one to let me down. Pepper had avoided me for good reason.

I didn't want to show the magazine to Jay. I couldn't discuss it. Awkwardly, I changed the subject. 'So how are things at *Men Only*?'

Jay noted my evasive response, and looked at me quizzically for a moment, his hazel eyes searching mine. Then he said, 'Things are good. I have a couple of big new clients. The advertising base is growing.'

Jay managed the advertising accounts for *Men Only*.

'Oh, good,' I said vaguely, still stewing about what Pepper had done with the article I'd written.

My date sensed something was amiss, and leaned in. He took my hand gently in his and said, 'Who cares about all that work stuff? I'm not here to talk shop with you. I'm here to enjoy your company.'

I managed a smile.

CHAPTER
TWENTY-ONE

*I*t was after nine when we finished up with a lovely thing called tiramisu, a dessert I'd never tried before.

Jay insisted on paying. I wanted to pay my half but the bill came and he put his credit card down and wouldn't let me contribute.

'Am I allowed to have your number now?' my date asked, and grinned. We'd enjoyed a nice meal together and were experiencing a moment of feeling relaxed with each other, but in response to his question I looked to my hands. What should I say? That I was too poor to get one yet, but I was working on it? That my eccentric great-aunt was allergic to phones, as well as garlic?

After a few beats, when I didn't respond to his request, Jay nodded and made an amused sound. 'I've met girls who've played hard to get, but you really are impressive.' There didn't seem to be any bitterness in his voice. If anything, he seemed to admire my reticence.

Not that I had been aloof. Over the previous couple of hours Jay had gently grilled me about my life, and

I'd more or less done the same. I tried to tell him a bit
about Gretchenville without going into too much detail,
but he'd got me talking about the shacks along the creek,
where it wasn't safe to go. The local redneck bullies
who were impossible to avoid. The fact that so many
locals thought there was nothing to do but get drunk
every weekend. How Gretchenville had one rundown
cinema and no Starbucks or Wal-Mart, and no diversity
to speak of, apart from one African-American family
who were descended from slaves. They lived in a big old
house on the outskirts of town, and doubtless dreamed
of leaving. No wonder I'd lived with my face buried in
books, or surfing the net, right? If I didn't want Jay to
think I was some naive small town hick I had doubtless
said too much. Perhaps it was such a relief to finally talk
about Gretchenville behind Gretchenville's back that I
just couldn't help myself.

Jay Rockwell, on the other hand, was a college
graduate and ex-rower, which explained the very
impressive build. His father, an apparently quite wealthy,
three-times divorced bachelor, knew the owner of *Men
Only* magazine, and I figured that connection had got him
the job. His mother had passed away from breast cancer
when he was seventeen, which still affected him deeply,
I could tell. I explained that my parents had both died
in an accident in Egypt, but I didn't elaborate, and he
offered condolences but didn't press. There had been one
particularly awkward moment when Jay, who was twenty-
five years old (exactly Lieutenant Luke's 'age', oddly
enough), ordered a bottle of wine and then remembered

that I was still underage. I'm not particularly interested in drinking, but at that moment I badly wished we were in Europe or Canada or Australia, just so I could have said, 'Thank you, but I don't drink,' and it could have been an issue of choice, not age. As it was he cancelled the bottle of wine and we both drank soda. I found myself longing for age.

A slip of paper came back with Jay's credit card, and he signed it.

'Pandora, I was wondering if you would accompany me to an event tomorrow night?' he asked me.

This was unexpected. I had imagined he was one of those guys who played by those dull dating 'rules' I'd heard about. 'Don't call for three days' and all that. I guess I was wrong.

'Um, what kind of event?' I ventured.

'A fashion show. It's not quite New York Fashion Week, but it's kind of a big deal. A lot of celebrities will be there. I thought you might like it.'

I tried to disguise my delight, but I wasn't overly successful. 'Oh, I'd love to!' I blurted, and then shut my mouth tight and nodded. I wondered if Pepper would be there, and see that I was there too, and I wondered if I could write about it, and then I realised these were selfish thoughts and had nothing to do with the man who was asking me, and I felt a bit guilty. 'Is it sort of a work thing for you?'

He nodded. 'But it would be fun with you.'

I beamed. We'd both be mixing work and pleasure, so that made it okay, right?

'Is there anywhere else you'd like to go tonight?' Jay asked me.

I thought for a moment then shrugged. 'I don't really know New York that well yet. I've only been here for a couple of weeks.'

He raised an eyebrow. 'Really?'

'I met you shortly after I arrived,' I explained. 'Well, I saw you in the elevator the day after I got here.' Not that he remembered, I reminded myself. I shouldn't have mentioned it.

'All the better for me,' Jay responded smoothly, and I took it to mean that he was glad I hadn't met anyone else.

'I think I'll just head home, if you don't mind,' I said finally. The bars were off-limits to me for another couple of years, and I didn't want to risk the embarrassment of being carded somewhere. Most importantly, though, I didn't want him to think I would go home with him. I had a feeling there were plenty of girls who did go home with him on the first date.

Jay touched me gently on the hand. 'I'll drive you home then. We'll see each other tomorrow.'

'Thank you,' I said, relieved at the lack of pressure. We both stood up. The waiter arrived with my coat before we had to ask, and he tried to help me with it before Jay took over the job with what I thought was a bit of a possessive snarl. The young waiter backed off quickly.

Jay opened the door, and we stepped onto the streets of Little Italy. The air felt refreshingly cool at first, then downright cold. 'Will you be warm enough? You could wait inside,' Jay offered, seeming a little concerned about leaving me with my new waiter friend.

'This coat is warm enough. Thank you,' I told him, although the flesh on my calves had turned to goosebumps.

He put an arm around me, which I didn't mind in the slightest, and as we stood in the chill wind waiting for the valet to bring his car around, another silence descended on us. Our conversation had flowed at times through the evening, but at other times there were these awkward silences. Was that normal? I hadn't been on enough dates to know. Actually, as I stood there I realised this was my first 'proper' date, and not just in New York, either. The pickings were slim enough in Gretchenville to keep me largely single by choice, and things had been pretty relaxed with Ben, my high school sweetheart. We hadn't gone on any dates and we certainly never went to a restaurant together.

'Here it is,' I heard Jay remark. He'd grown impatient with the valet, I could tell, though I didn't think it had taken too long.

Oh boy.

The car that pulled up made me gape. It was silver, very expensive and impossibly low to the ground.

'Thanks,' Jay said when the valet handed him his keys. He slipped the valet a large bill, I noticed, and I thought of the rich father he had mentioned over dinner. I guessed that Jay didn't need to worry about things like money, and perhaps he never had. The issue of money would be a very big difference between us. Where I came from, that tip was big money, and as for the car – well, the very existence of such a vehicle in Gretchenville was an impossibility.

The door on my side opened upwards, like the entry hatch of a spacecraft. I was taken aback. I vaguely recognised this kind of vehicle from the movies, but I couldn't say what sort of car it was, except that it was worth more than Aunt Georgia's entire house. With a creeping sense of embarrassment I felt the eyes of the patrons inside the restaurant again. We were being watched. *Oh goodness*, I thought. *This is different.* Part of me wished he drove a pickup, like I was used to everyone driving back in Gretchenville, and the other part of me...well the other part of me sort of loved the madness of it all.

Jay held my elbow while I scrambled inelegantly into the passenger side of his low-slung car. Celia's silk dress was knee-length and elegantly designed in two halves that wrapped at the waist, and as I got into the car it split open in the centre to flash an expanse of my thighs. I quickly corrected the fall of the fabric, and Jay smiled, but was too polite to comment. I liked him for that. He passed me my heavy satchel and I held it awkwardly in my lap. The automatic door couldn't close fast enough, as far as I was concerned, and I was happy when we pulled away from Giovanni's and the patrons went back to focusing on their meals.

I spotted a name on the steering wheel. It said *Ferrari.*

'I live on Addams Avenue in Spektor,' I informed my date while I tried to find a comfortable position in my seat.

'Spektor?' Jay repeated. 'Where's that?'

'Oh, it's uptown,' I told him. 'I can direct you.'

'So it's definitely in Manhattan?' he asked, uncertain. I nodded. 'Yes.'

Jay seemed doubtful about a suburb called 'Spektor' on Manhattan Island, but he followed my directions without complaint. I thought of Celia's comment about it being a 'blind spot' and realised I might have made a mistake in letting him drive me home. I didn't really understand how it all worked. We moved slowly through the Friday night traffic in Little Italy to Bowery and Third, and gradually made our way uptown. I indicated the northern road that cut through Central Park, and as we drove through the dark expanse of green, the Ferrari's headlights illuminated a pair of dog walkers on a night stroll.

'I hope you don't go walking through Central Park at night,' he remarked.

I took this to mean that Jay figured I was 'fresh off the farm'. I had clearly been too open about what my little hometown had been like, and now I was paying for it. It made my hackles rise.

'I may be new here,' I told him sharply. 'But I'm not that green.' Celia had warned me not to wander around New York at night, and I knew better than to jog through Central Park after dark on my own, or in any park in any city at night. 'I'm not crazy,' I added, and wondered if that was entirely true.

'Manhattan is not Gretchenville, you know,' he continued unwisely.

'Really?' I replied, and thought, *You don't know the half of it.*

Jay sped up a touch and heaved a sigh of regret at my response. 'Okay, I deserve your sarcasm. Sorry. It's just... I care about you, and I want to make sure you are safe,' he said with his eyes firmly on the road. 'I worry about you, being so new here. New York is not always the most friendly place.' We passed what appeared to be a homeless person sleeping on a bench, as if to prove his point.

'I can look after myself,' I told him firmly.

'Okay. I won't say another word about it. You don't live in Harlem or something, do you?'

'No,' I told him.

Jay concentrated on his driving, and it seemed another of our silences was upon us.

I had been oversensitive to his touch of condescension and had barely noticed that he'd said, 'I care about you.' Jay and I had only met a couple of times (well, three times, but he didn't remember the elevator encounter so that hardly counted) and we certainly didn't have common backgrounds, or circumstances (example: he drove a Ferrari and I couldn't even afford my own cell phone) but there was a mutual attraction there, undeniably. But did he 'care' for me? Had he meant that? I didn't even know how I felt. On our date, I'd thought of Luke a couple of times, a touch guiltily. I saw his face (not literally, thank goodness) and recalled the way he looked at me with his beautiful blue eyes. He seemed so full of longing. But of course, Luke was an apparition and it made things... well, it made things between us a *dead end*. Jay Rockwell had beautiful eyes too; big, hazel, *living* eyes. He was real, and human, and interested, and available – though I'd have to clarify that last bit. I had a strong feeling that Jay had a lot of other attractive women in his circle, though I didn't know in what capacity. Did he have girlfriends? Casual lovers? I wasn't sure, and the question niggled at the back of my mind. The smoothness of his manners had been learned through experience, that much I could tell.

'Are you seeing anyone at the moment, Jay?' I dared to ask.

My question hung in the air for a moment.

'Um, I'm seeing you right now,' he replied a little too casually, and offered me a charming smile instead of an answer.

'Do you have a lot of girlfriends?' I wanted to know. I didn't want to mess around with a player, if that's what he was.

'No one serious,' he told me, and I believed him.

I nodded. 'Me neither,' I said, supposing my ghost didn't count. Did he?

I directed us down the tunnel at the end of Central Park, and we came out the other side in an oppressive opaque mist.

'What a funny fog,' Jay remarked, frowning and looking around. He slowed down and drove his Ferrari carefully through it.

I wondered again about Spektor. The cabbie had got me here, as had Jay. So how did it work? I had so many questions. After a moment I noticed we were on Addams

Avenue. There were no people on the street, and no other cars. I indicated Celia's large corner building and Jay pulled the car up to the empty kerb. 'What an ... unusual place,' he said, leaning forward and looking out the car window.

'I like it,' I said, smiling broadly. I did, I had discovered. I really did.

'Well, if you like it then I like it,' Jay offered, still sounding unsure. We looked at each other and there was an awkward pause, where we both wondered what to do next. Finally his hand ventured across the seat and clasped mine for a moment, and he said, 'Well, I guess I'll walk you to your door.'

He got out of the car and walked around to my side. I got out before he arrived, and we walked up to the iron gates of the building together, our shoulders close.

Jay was still distracted by his surrounds. 'Is it a safe neighbourhood? It seems kind of deserted?'

'Oh no,' I replied. 'It's not deserted at all. Just quiet. I think most of the residents are older. They've been here for a while.'

That was certainly true.

'So what time should I pick you up tomorrow?' Jay asked. 'The event starts at eight.'

'Whatever you think. Seven? Or seven thirty?' I began, and then stopped myself. Maybe it wasn't such a good idea, him coming here to get me. I cast a glance in the direction of Harold's Grocer, and sure enough it was closed. It was only ever closed when I had company, I realised – company from outside Spektor. *Right.* This place didn't like visitors. 'Actually, I'll be downtown, so perhaps I can meet you there, or somewhere nearby?' I suggested.

Jay seemed a little surprised, but he agreed and gave me an address. 'Seven thirty then. We'll have a drink first. The dress code is cocktail. Just dress like ... well like you did at the launch the other night.'

It seemed he had really liked that red dress. Well, everyone had. 'Okay,' I agreed.

I fished my key out of my satchel and put it in the gate, and when I turned to wish my date goodnight, his lips found mine before I could speak. His kiss took me by surprise, and I pulled back from him a touch. He stopped and looked down at me thoughtfully, perhaps worried he'd come on too strong. But I was smiling, and he relaxed when he saw that. His mouth trembled and then curled up at the corners. I stretched up and threw my arms around him, locking my hands behind his muscly neck, and we searched each other's eyes silently for a moment before our lips met again. *Oh, screw it.* I leaned into him for more and we kissed deeper this time, my breasts pressing against his ribs. I opened to him a little more this time, enjoying the warmth and sweetness of his lips. And boy, did he know how to kiss a girl. I had never been kissed like that before. Well, not by a living man anyway.

After a wonderful moment we pulled apart, both breathing a little fast. 'Well...' I began. I dared to lean my forehead into his big shoulder for a moment while I caught my breath. 'Um, thanks for tonight. I should go inside,' I managed and prised myself out of his arms.

'Does this mean I can have your number now?' Jay asked, still not realising I didn't have one. We both laughed. I was not in the mood to explain. 'Thank you, Pandora,' he said after a moment. 'I had a wonderful time. See you tomorrow, then?'

'Yes. Goodnight,' I said dreamily.

I stepped through the heavy wooden door, which opened easily and slammed shut behind me with the usual puff of dust. One day I ought to get a duster and broom down here and tidy things up, I thought absently. It was the least I could do for Celia. *Boy oh boy, that Jay Rockwell is some kisser*, I thought next, with somewhat more interest and intensity.

Boy oh boy.

Then I registered that the lobby chandelier was glowing, and I was not alone.

'Oh!' I exclaimed, startled.

Lieutenant Luke, former Civil War soldier, was standing stiffly in the lobby, only a few feet away from me. His hands were clenched and he looked extremely distraught.

'Oh, Luke, for goodness' sake!' I exclaimed. 'Don't look at me like that! You know I really like you, but you're dead.' I immediately regretted what I'd said, of course, but I still meant it. I couldn't have Casper the Possessive Ghost waiting around for me every time I went on a date. What if I had invited Jay inside? Would Luke stand over us, radiating invisible, otherworldly jealousy while I tried to pretend that he wasn't there? Talk about awkward.

Perhaps he could even see through the door, and had watched us kissing? I was so confused about Luke, I didn't know what to think.

'*Look out!*' Luke called to me.

'What—' I began in response, and was hit from behind with the force of a linebacker. I tumbled forward and struck the hard tiled floor with a slap, my hands barely breaking my fall in time. My satchel was flung forward and went skittering across the floor ahead of me.

'*I'm going to enjoy sucking you dry, virgin,*' came a low, demonic voice, sounding far too close for comfort.

Was this Samantha? Surely not.

'Consider yourself lucky I got to you before my mistress, Báthory. She really likes to take her time...' continued the abhorrent voice. Then it clicked. I thought of the woman in the back of the limousine. The woman with the high collar. I had sensed something powerful about her. Powerful and evil. 'You'll make a tasty little trophy. I'll bring her your head.'

Athanasia. I've ruined her career, and she isn't taking it well.

The sharp heel of a designer boot jabbed into my back. 'You dumb virgin bitch!' she yelled, and I was not at all impressed with her language, or her focus on the whole virgin issue, which frankly was none of her cotton-picking business. Her hand found the back of my head and yanked my hair upwards, stinging my scalp and straining my neck back as far as it would stretch. I tucked my head in and curled into the foetal position with all the speed and strength I possessed, losing a small clump of hair in the process but throwing her boot off me. I was repaid with a swift kick to the spine. I protected my neck and head with my arms, and swung a leg out to kick, my eyes darting about to find my attacker.

I sure hope I'm wrong about her being a homicidal, bloodsucking...

I noticed with alarm that Lieutenant Luke, standing at the foot of the staircase, looked totally helpless. He was semi-transparent, and seemed unable to move forward. 'She hexed me or something! I can't get within ten feet of her,' he exclaimed, and his magnificent jaw was flexing like mad. I thought he might explode from tension. Well, he wouldn't be helping anyone out this time.

Right.

Without hesitation, I jumped up and assumed my ninja pose, ignoring the stabbing pain in my lower back. I had seen a lot of movies, and it was the best fight stance I knew.

Bang.

Another blow, this time to the back of the head. Goodness, she was a nasty little supermodel. And agile. I hadn't caught more than a blur of her yet. Her latest strike was powerful and smarted like hell, and I stumbled forward awkwardly, but still had the presence of mind to kick into the air behind me like an angry mule. My shoe made forceful contact with something before I went down on one knee.

I whirled around to look for my attacker, but she was no longer there.

I looked up.

Things had gone from bad to worse. Athanasia was crouched directly above me on all fours *upside down* on the high, cobwebbed ceiling, clinging to it effortlessly like some scary-as-hell gravity-defying lizard. Her neck was twisted round at an unnatural angle and she was grinning maniacally at me with her fangs flashing and her glossy hair hanging down, ready to pounce on me from above. The humanness of her fashionable designer clothes and cover girl beauty made quite a striking and disconcerting contrast with her extended panther-like incisors and freakishly demonic inverted stance. Her eyes seemed to glow. She hissed like a cobra.

Holy mother of all hell.

Well, that settled the whole vampire question once and for all. As if I wasn't sure before.

Athanasia's leather pants creaked as she shifted, ready to launch at me. 'You ruined everything, and now you're mine!'

I was already up and running for the elevator, and the next thing I knew I was grappling for the loose piece of broken ironwork and spinning round to witness Athanasia in full flight, speeding towards me through the air with her fangs bared and her hands outstretched like claws. I held the broken rod of iron out in front of me, wielding the pointed lilies of the fleurs-de-lis like a weapon, but before I could steady myself she flew straight into me and we both hit the ground with force. We slid across the tiles entwined, and my head hit the iron cage of the lift hard enough to make me yelp.

I felt Athanasia's fangs graze my exposed neck. I let

out a blood-curdling scream and fought against her surprising weight.

And then I stopped.

Her head rolled to one side, lifeless and heavy against my throat. She was as inanimate as a rag doll.

Goodness.

I wasn't dead. I wasn't even undead.

I was, however, positively drenched with blood. There were torrents of the stuff everywhere, pouring over me, streaming across the tiles around us, more blood than one body could possibly contain. The air smelled weirdly salty and metallic in a way that made me want to retch. The still weight on top of me was oppressively heavy – a dead weight, so to speak (or undead weight, really) – and the fleurs-de-lis was clearly visible, sticking out of Athanasia's back, dripping with icky stuff.

'You staked her,' Lieutenant Luke said from the stairs, always helpful.

My goodness. I have.

It seemed I had impaled my bloodsucking nemesis through the heart with a broken piece of ironwork shaped like the former royal arms of France.

'Looks like it,' I replied.

My new vampire friend Samantha slunk out from the shadows by the mezzanine level, and came down the stairs unsteadily, wearing my polyester grey suit from Gretchenville. She held her fingers to her mouth, obscuring her extended fangs.

'Oh, Pandora!' she exclaimed in a more or less human way. 'She came looking for you. I think she figured you had something to do with that article Pepper wrote.'

The article. So vampires read women's magazines. Great.

With a struggle I managed to get myself out from under the supermodel's inanimate body. Lieutenant Luke rushed over and helped me up, now more solid to the eye and finally able to move freely. He checked to see if I was okay (thankfully, I was unpunctured) and we both stared at Athanasia, neither of us saying a word. After all I'd seen over the past couple of weeks I half expected her to burst into flames or float away as ashes like they did in the movies. But she didn't. This vampire just lay there on her face with a rod of iron sticking out of her back.

Darn.

And the day had started with such promise.

CHAPTER
TWENTY-TWO

I rode up in the old elevator with Lieutenant Luke in post-traumatic silence.

He stood in the little carriage with me even though he didn't need the building's machinery to get from A to B. We'd left Samantha in the lobby, curled up on the steps. I wondered darkly whether the Fledgling was licking up the blood or something gross like that. There was nothing cheerfully optimistic about these Sanguine, I reflected. Luke stood watching me with his military cap in his hands, looking handsome and protective, his Union uniform spotlessly clean. He didn't try to hug me or talk to me. I think he could see I wasn't in the mood.

The carriage stopped and the doors slid open on Celia's floor. We both got out.

I knocked and stepped into the penthouse. Luke stayed on the landing outside the lift, looking deeply worried. His angular jaw flexed and his brows were knitted together. 'I'll be here if you need anything, Pandora,' he told me in a tender voice. 'Just call for me any time. Well...any time after dark,' he amended.

Supernatural rules. I didn't understand how it all worked, or just how a blood-sucking homicidal super-model managed to contain a ghost soldier in some trance or spell, (was it like *Rock, Paper, Scissors* with these supernatural beings? Vampire beats ghost. Ghost beats...? Who knew?) I nodded a thankyou and closed the door.

I took a breath.

'Hi Celia, I'm home,' I called out. I stood in the entryway wearing my great-aunt's silk dress and cashmere coat, now coated in fresh blood. I felt a rush of relief to be back in the safety of Celia's penthouse, but I couldn't bear to make a move. I'd already ruined her beautiful clothes and I didn't want to ruin her beautiful penthouse floor, and her beautiful penthouse walls, and her beautiful penthouse furniture.

I stood immobile, feeling shocked and uncertain. Did this bizarre and rather violent turn of events make me a murderer? Or a vigilante? A vampire slayer? Well, it had been in self-defence, I reminded myself. Athanasia had proven herself to be a not-very-nice person, with fangs and what looked to be a 360-degree rotating neck. I'd not really had a choice about impaling her, as things played out, and it had happened so fast I hadn't even known at first that I'd done it. Some survival instinct had kicked in, that was all. Still, I had killed someone and that someone was right now lying in a convincingly human-like state of recent slaughter in the lobby of Celia's building with an iron 'stake' sticking out of her chest. What to do now? I could hardly imagine trying to explain this turn of events to the New York Police Department. Imagine how they would respond to a story of vampire models, fraudulent face creams and friendly ghosts? Ha! They'd have me in a padded cell on mind-numbing medication faster than I could say 'supernatural'. So did this mean I would be one of those people who decided to 'dispose' of a dead body? What do people do in these situations? And what would I tell Celia?

My head hurt, and I was no closer to a solution – or an acceptable state of cleanliness.

'How did it all go, darling?' came my Great-Aunt Celia's voice from the lounge room. Now that I had pulled myself together a bit, I noticed her toes were visible from my vantage point. She was in her usual spot under her reading lamp, reclining in the bookish alcove in her leather chair, feet up on the hassock. The curtains remained open to let in the moonlight through the tall windows of the room. I could see the silhouette of the Empire State Building in the distance, framed black against the faintly bluish urban haze of the Manhattan night sky. New York was carrying on as usual, but my outlook on the world was forever changed.

Celia shifted position and turned to face me. Despite my conspicuous appearance she observed me without a hint of surprise.

'Oh, you got her,' she declared simply, as if she'd already known everything that would happen.

'I killed someone!' I blurted loudly, not able to help myself. *Oh here it comes. The freakout.* I began to shake. Tears welled up.

'Oh, darling, that model was already dead, anyway.'

Yes. Right.

I blinked back my tears. I regained a bit of composure.

Celia placed her feather bookmark in her novel and closed it. She balanced it on the right arm of her chair, uncrossed her ankles and placed her feet on the floor. 'I knew you'd get her, darling,' she assured me.

I nervously ran a hand over my face, and then looked at my palm. It was bloody. *Oh... nasty.* 'I should go wash up,' I managed, my head reeling and my stomach doing unpleasant little somersaults. I didn't know what else to do.

'Oh, I wouldn't bother till you've finished with her,' Celia informed me.

'Pardon?' I said.

'You haven't cut off her head yet, sweetheart.'

I'm afraid I reacted rather badly to this statement.

'*WHAT?*' I shrieked. 'You want me to *WHAT?*'

Celia calmly rose from her chair and slipped her stockinged feet into the pair of fluffy, high-heel slippers she had lined up next to her chair. They had those cute little ostrich feathers sewn on the front. She walked over to me, looking elegant and unruffled, and stopped just a couple of feet away. Celia looked me in the eye and sighed. 'My darling Pandora, you staked that vampire but you didn't kill her. She's only resting.'

'*WHAT?!*'

'Don't shout, darling. It's not necessary, really,' she told me. 'I'm right here.' Her voice was calm and even. I grew quiet. 'Sweetheart, they only stake vampires to keep the body still while they cut off the heads and stuff the mouth with garlic.'

Sometimes I am given too much to grapple with and I just have to deal with it. This was one of those times. 'Oh,' I replied in a dull voice. I stood silent for a while. 'I thought you said it was bad manners to call them "vampires"?' I said next, once my mind was clear.

'Oh yes. But it's rather warranted in her case, don't you think? Nasty.'

She had a point there.

'Athanasia had it coming to her. Anyone will be able to see that,' Celia declared confidently. But her choice of words made me wonder about reprisals. Would hordes of vampires try to kill me now, for murdering one of their own? And what about whoever was behind *BloodofYouth*? Was it just some con artist I'd drawn attention to, or was it Dracula's latest business venture? And who was that woman with the high collar I'd seen silhouetted in the back of the limousine? Just how far did my naivety about the supernatural world extend, exactly? With a shiver, I imagined how many vampires – or Sanguine – might be in New York. Were there hundreds? Thousands?

'Am I in danger, Great-Aunt Celia?'

'For staking her? Oh, I shouldn't think so. That girl didn't make herself too popular. And besides, they can't come up here, anyway.' She made a gesture to indicate the penthouse. 'It's forbidden.'

'You're absolutely sure they can't get in here?'

'Yes, darling. Sanguine can't come in if they're not invited.'

There were those mysterious supernatural rules again.

'Although, I suppose you might want to be careful coming and going after dark for the next little while,' she added as an afterthought. 'I don't think Athanasia's employer will be in good humour about the recent turn of events. But I'll talk to Deus about it, and I'm sure he'll sort it out.'

Oh good. My great-aunt will talk to her immortal friend and sort it all out.

I thought about the body in the lobby. 'Is it because I didn't use a wooden stake? Is that why she isn't um . . . dead?' (Or dead-dead? *Fully* undead dead?)

That's what those vampire hunters in the movies always seemed to use. But like the rest of the mythology surrounding these creatures, I didn't know what to believe. If vampires could reflect in mirrors, and could be photographed (she was a supermodel for goodness sakes!) what other pop-culture folklore about them was wrong?

'Oh, no, sweetheart, you did fine,' Celia reassured me. 'Like I said, the stakes are just to hold them while you do the decapitation. You'll need an axe for that. The garlic part . . . oh, I think it's overrated and unnecessary in most cases. I can't stand the stuff.'

I had noticed.

'The axe will do, I should think,' Celia continued. 'And don't worry; once you've finished her off all that grisly mess will vaporise like magic. There won't be a lot to clean up, I shouldn't think.'

Like magic? Looking down at my clothes, I found that hard to believe.

'Although, the silk dress may need a dry-clean,' she added thoughtfully, bringing a fingertip to her chin.

So I have to cut off Athanasia's head. And not so long ago she'd been cackling about having my head. Fantastic. What has my life become?

I dropped my blood-splattered satchel on the floor with a dejected thud, and tried to mentally prepare myself to *head* (ha, ha, ugh) downstairs to finish off the macabre business of killing a vampire.

'What have you got in your satchel?' Celia asked me cheerfully. I couldn't believe she could change the subject so casually, especially when I was standing next to her drenched in blood.

'Uh, the magazine,' I replied. 'It came out today.'

'Let's have a look then,' she suggested.

In a bit of a daze, I leaned over, unclipped the satchel and pulled out the new issue of *Pandora*. I handed it to my great-aunt with a distinct lack of enthusiasm.

There it was, my big story on the cover:

BLOODOFYOUTH: MIRACLE BEAUTY CREAM OR FRAUD?

The headline was bold across the stunning face of Athanasia – who was now dead in the lobby downstairs because I had staked her.

I sighed.

'Oh dear,' Celia said.

I'd already seen the issue. I already knew.

She was referring to the by-line, of course. *An exposé by Pepper Smith.* To Pepper's, ahem, *credit*, she had told me she would take my notes and write her article, and she had done precisely that. She'd taken all the information

I had gathered and written her own piece, and a watered-down one at that. It was a cover piece, and a real coup for the magazine. But it wasn't my coup. In small letters, on the final page, it said: *Additional research by Pandora English.*

Gee, thanks. Additional research? Additional to what?

'Don't worry, darling. Your day will come,' Celia said and handed the magazine back to me.

She spoke as if she had already known about the article. And she'd spoken as if she had already known that Athanasia would come after me, too, and that I would hold my own and do just fine. She'd known I would get the job at the magazine. If Celia knew all those things, perhaps that statement was one I could take to heart?

Your day will come.

'This is just the beginning,' she told me. 'You know the industry will start questioning this product now, thanks to you. The FDA will doubtless re-evaluate it soon, and darling, when they discover the secret ingredient in *BloodofYouth*, well...' She gave a small, wicked chuckle, clearly amused, and patted me on the arm in a more or less non-blood-soaked spot. 'There will be hell to pay.' Celia turned and made her way down the hallway, pulled open a closet door, leaned in and started searching for something.

'Secret ingredient?' I said.

'Oh yes, darling,' Celia replied casually. 'And I don't think the public will take it too well...'

I stood holding the magazine, marvelling at her calm. Was this why I'd had those strange feelings about the product? Because there really was some secret ingredient?

'No false advertising there,' Celia added cheerfully, and I frowned, confused.

And then my wise and beautiful Great-Aunt Celia walked over to me. She had something big in her hands. 'Sweetheart, here's the axe,' she said, and handed it to me. 'Have fun.'

I noticed that she was not offering to come downstairs with me. I was the one who had gone and upset a very nasty vampiric supermodel and then had to defend myself against her with a makeshift stake. This was my fight. I held the axe in both hands, and blinked. I was about to do something truly horrible.

Come on, Pandora.

'Oh, and why don't you take some rice with you, in case your friend has one of her moments?' she suggested blithely, and handed me a small bag of plain white rice.

'Good idea,' I managed, and took the bag of rice.

With every grain of courage I possessed – and few grains of rice besides – I left the safety of Celia's apartment and got into the tiny gothic elevator, carrying Celia's axe and rice. I pressed the button for the ground floor. Truthfully, it was the last place I wanted to go.

The little lift fired up, and the doors rattled closed. Slowly, I began my descent. I watched the third floor go by. Samantha might be back there by now. Would it be traumatic for a Fledgling to stand around next to a staked vampire? I wasn't sure. Samantha had a few issues (fangs, Fledgling blood thirst) but she was a nice girl. It seemed to me that not all vampires were bad. There was no sign of her as the landing passed and the old lift continued its descent. I bit my lip as I passed the second floor. Here, for the first time, I caught movement from the corner of my eye. By the time I did my double take there was nothing to see, and the elevator was slipping through the floor and into the lobby.

There sure was a sight waiting for me there.

'No!' I said aloud. I covered my face with my hand. 'No...'

I stepped out of the elevator and observed the lobby through the laced fingers of my hand. This was bad. This was very, very bad.

Athanasia was gone.

I stared at the streaks of blood across the tiles, my worst fears realised. She wasn't 'resting' anymore, was she? Someone had pulled the stake out of her back — or maybe she had done it herself? Was such a thing possible? In any event, I'd made a very powerful enemy. There was one seriously annoyed vampire supermodel after my blood. She'd already tried to kill me once. I had little doubt she'd have another go.

'Why didn't you stop her?' I asked Samantha in frustration.

'I couldn't,' Samantha said sheepishly, her arms crossed and her voice low. 'She's my mother now.'

I gaped. 'She's not your mother...' Was Athanasia her mother? 'But, Samantha, she killed you and then abandoned you!'

'I guess she's a bad mother,' Samantha said quietly, and I felt so bad for her I didn't have the heart to protest. 'Anyway she didn't really abandon me,' she said defensively. 'She lives downstairs.'

I gaped again. I hoped I hadn't heard that right.

'Well, downstairs from me,' she corrected herself. 'You know, on the second floor.'

The boarded-up second floor.

Any remaining blood drained from my face. Oh great. Athanasia had taken up residence here in Spektor, in Celia's vampire-free-for-all building? But of course she had. She was a visiting vampire. That was why Samantha was here. Athanasia had taken her home, had her 'meal' and just left her. Perhaps she'd taken her clothes out of greed? Or perhaps they were already gone, for some sinister reason? Perhaps Athanasia hadn't even intended on turning Samantha? Perhaps she was new enough to make a 'child' by accident? Perhaps she was only a Fledgling herself? Everything about this was bad.

I heard the elevator come to life. It moved up through its iron cage and disappeared above the lobby ceiling. Had Athanasia called it? I stood to the side of the lift door, gripping the axe in both hands. Samantha stole her way up the stairwell and crouched down, covering her eyes.

After several long minutes, the elevator reappeared through the iron lacework.

It held my Great-Aunt Celia. I breathed a sigh of relief and closed my eyes for a moment. The doors opened and she stepped out.

'Oh, dear,' she said on seeing the blood streaks across the tiles of the lobby. ''Tis a bit of a mess, hmm?'

I nodded.

'Don't worry, darling, you'll get her another time.'

At seeing my elderly aunt in her ruined lobby, a wave of guilt rushed in on me. 'I'll clean this up, I promise, Great-Aunt Celia. And I'll clean those cobwebs up.' My mother may have denied my 'gift' but she raised me right, darn it.

'You are a dear,' she told me.

It was the least I could do.

Without another word, we stepped into the elevator together and Celia pressed the button for her floor. It was going to be a long, ugly night. I'd need rubber gloves, buckets, scrubbing brushes. Ugh.

'I guess you'll have to meet Deus after all,' my great-aunt mused.

My eyes widened. I turned to her. 'Deus?'

'Yes. This is tricky, you see. Your purpose as the seventh; it looks like it may have already begun.' The corners of her mouth turned down. She didn't seem pleased.

The seventh? My purpose?

'You are the seventh Lucasta, darling,' she explained. 'The seventh has a very special purpose. I'd hoped we'd have more time for you to settle in before all this began.'

'I don't know what you mean,' I protested. 'I've heard of the seventh son of a seventh son and all that, but I can't see how that would—'

'Oh, darling,' she said, and patted my arm. 'That seventh son stuff is child's play. Boys! You are the seventh Lucasta *daughter*. Much more important.'

I was riveted by what I was being told, but then I saw something that stunned me so completely, I couldn't think. We watched the second floor go by, and the second floor *watched us* – or, more specifically, me. Three women stood near the lift cage as we passed, each more beautiful than the next. They were slim, tall and dressed like fashion models, swathed in barely-there designer couture, despite the winter chill in the old building. One was blonde, one brunette and the other ginger-haired.

They all had fangs extending from beneath their lips.

My god!

I recoiled against the back of the lift and clenched my axe with white knuckles. 'Did you see that? Did you see those women?' I cried as the elevator slipped through the second floor ceiling and the nightmarish women disappeared from view. My heart was thumping wildly.

'Oh yes,' my great-aunt replied, unperturbed. 'Athanasia's friends are angry, I suspect. Quite unfair, mind. I mean she was the one who started it, wasn't she? Of course, there was that article you 'helped' Pepper with, but that's fair play...'

Athanasia's friends!

'She'll take a few days to recover from her little staking,' Celia said thoughtfully. 'Those vampire supermodels are all the rage at the moment,' she continued. 'Makes them arrogant, if you ask me. In my day, we preferred a woman with curves. And we preferred them living.' She sighed. 'Don't worry. I'll call a meeting with Deus.'

Don't worry?

I fell silent. The third floor passed. No seething Sanguine supermodels. No Samantha.

My wise great-aunt cast her eyes my way. 'I guess that dress is ruined after all. Never mind...'

CHAPTER
TWENTY-THREE

'*M*iss Pandora?'

I woke, disoriented, at the sound of my name. The room was dark, and I was clearly not alone. I reached across the sheets and my fingers ran over something soft and warm. I was startled until I realised it was Freyja, curled into a ball asleep on my bedclothes. Funny kitty. My eyes flashed over the glowing hands of the bedside clock. It was very early, nearly seven. I rolled onto my back and propped myself up on my elbows. My door was open a crack, I noticed. That was how Freyja had snuck in. But there was a third presence in the room, and he didn't need an open door to enter.

Luke.

As my eyes adjusted to the low light I saw that Lieutenant Luke was indeed standing near the wardrobe, resplendent in his officer's uniform, the brass buttons shining. I was happy to see him, but I did have something to get off my chest.

'Luke, I was wondering if we could, I don't know, schedule our visits or something? So I know when to

304 · TARA MOSS

expect you?' Not that he wasn't pleasant to wake up to, but it was a bit creepy being watched while I slept.

'I'm sorry,' Lieutenant Luke said. 'Because I do not exist in the physical world, I can't read time,' he explained.

Oh.

I rubbed my eyes. Luke, with his unchanging 'physical' appearance – the sandy hair long around the ears, that strong, chiselled jaw and those striking blue eyes – looked as appealing as ever, but his handsome face was tinged with sadness I noticed. A moment of panic pulled me out of my dreaminess. 'Oh, Luke, I didn't mean to insult you. Of course you can't read time. Is everything okay?'

'You didn't call for me but... Miss Pandora, I just had to let you know before the sun comes up that I am sorry.' His voice was full of regret. He bowed his head a little and such was his sorrow that he actually got down on one knee next to the bed. It was a touching, if old-fashioned, gesture. His cap was in his strong hands, and he gripped it with tension.

'You're sorry?' I swung my legs out of bed, felt the cool floor beneath my feet, and cool air around my ankles. Freyja lifted her head, looked at me and then at Luke with her dazzling pink eyes, before snuggling back into the covers contentedly, evidently unfazed by my ghostly guest. *Was that right? Could she see Luke?* Though I was only in my white nightie and not exactly dressed for visitors, I got up and stood next to the bed. It seemed awkward and perhaps rude to remain in bed during a visit – of any kind.

Luke got to his feet. 'Will you accept my apology?'

'Luke, what are you sorry for?' I asked.

'Miss Pandora, I deeply regret what happened this evening. I should have assisted you when you were in danger, but—'

'Oh, Luke. It's okay. I understand.' Well, actually, I didn't understand at all, but I did know that he would have helped me if he could have. That much was clear.

'That lady hexed me in some way. It was a very strange happening,' he continued.

I let out a little snort. Calling Athanasia a 'lady' was probably being more polite than was necessary.

'What? Did I speak oddly?' he replied.

'No, not at all.' I shook my head and moved a step closer. His nearness made my skin come over in goose pimples for a moment, and I felt my cheeks grow warm. 'Luke, I've heard that vampires can hypnotise people,' I managed to say, to make him feel better. I'd heard a lot of things about vampires that weren't true, of course, but that wasn't the point. Nor was it important to think about how Luke might not really be described as a person.

Luke nodded in response, and then frowned. 'I should have protected you. I have disappointed you.'

'No, Luke. It's not your fault,' I said, and brushed my hand across his arm. It felt cool and misty, and now the goose pimples rose up all over my body. It was an oddly pleasant sensation, and I found my gaze wandering over his clothed form – the strange 'realness' of it. He had almost a hyper-real quality when he was like this. I looked up into his blue eyes and saw that we were closer than I'd thought. Our gaze locked. I don't know how long we stood that way, with my body covered in goose pimples, our lips only inches apart.

'I should leave you now, Miss Pandora,' he said. 'I hope you will call for me.'

And then he vanished from my room just as the first rays of sunlight began to filter in.

CHAPTER
TWENTY-FOUR

know it's wrong to wish for the demise of another being just so I won't have to clean up their blood. Still, I found myself wishing Athanasia's blood had vanished 'like magic', as it supposedly would have had I finished the grisly task of offing her.

Maybe I am not as nice a person as I thought?

Cleaning Celia's entryway was most unpleasant. Being daytime, Celia was nowhere to be found. Not even Samantha had been able to help clean it the night before, because of her reaction to the blood. Sure, she had wanted to help, but the blood made her a little crazy and she'd had to keep her distance. On Celia's advice, I'd waited till morning to start cleaning on my own, though that meant I'd have no help, and by then the blood had dried adamantine on the tiles and hardened in every minute crevice.

It took me an hour to clean and scrub the floor to my satisfaction. I'd also cleaned up some of the cobwebs and dust, as I'd promised I would, and in the end I'd felt utterly drained both physically and emotionally. Celia had assured me that I was totally safe from Athanasia and her fanged friends in the daytime, as vamps can only walk by night and are cursed to sleep while the sun is out, or some such thing, but I'd still felt the edge of fear every moment I'd been down there. Besides, from time to time I thought I heard something move beneath the floor.

I was freaked out and exhausted now. The entryway, at least, shone.

Soon it would be time for me to get ready for my date with Jay, though to be honest I felt somewhat less enthusiastic about it than I had when I'd accepted his invitation. I felt bone tired, for one thing, and I hadn't fully recovered from my ordeal the night before. Nor could I tell my date about what had happened right after we'd kissed goodnight. (Imagine how that conversation would go!)

Also, I felt close to Luke after his last visit, even closer than I had before, and it felt somehow like a betrayal to go on a date with someone else. That wasn't fair, of course, considering most people would not regard Luke as even real, but still, it was there pressing at my heart.

He was ever more real to me.

I took a nap and bathed, and when the time came I emerged in the stunning red dress I'd worn to the launch of *BloodofYouth*.

Celia was waiting for me in the lounge room.

'Ta-da,' I said.

My great-aunt frowned and shook her head gently.

'What's wrong? I thought you said this dress looked good?' I protested. 'Jay likes it.'

'Darling, it does look wonderful on you, but you wore it very recently to an event where you spent time with the same man. And there was a red carpet, was there not?'

I nodded, not yet comprehending.

'You simply cannot wear the same dress, so soon, for the same crowd. It is not done. It is considered a faux pas.'

I hadn't had to consider fashion faux pas in Gretchenville. 'Well, what should I wear then?' I asked, disheartened.

Celia smiled. 'I have an outfit in mind for you tonight. Something more modern. It will suit this crowd, I think.'

I raised an eyebrow. *Something modern? From Celia?*

'Slip that dress off, and I'll be in your room in a moment,' she instructed. I did as she said, and stood in my underwear with my arms crossed over my body. The room was cold.

Celia soon emerged in the doorway with clothing slung over her arm. 'Try on these pants,' she instructed, and handed me a pair of black pants. They had four pockets; two deep pockets in the front and two more shallow ones in back. They were made of some kind of wool blend, with a slight stretch, and came just to the ankle. 'They are cigarette pants – the only cigarette that's good for you,' she quipped. 'Wear them with your ballet flats.'

I looked in the mirror on the tall wardrobe. 'I like them,' I said. They sat on the waist just below my belly button, and tapered down the leg to the ankle. They were slimming, and I thought they made me look a little taller than I was.

'And now this top.' She held out a white cotton blouse

for me. It had long sleeves with an exaggerated folded cuff and an elegant, crossover design that sat low on the bust and tied with a crisp sash at the waist.

'Perfect,' she said when I fastened the sash. 'And now for your jacket.'

This was the final layer, and she handed it to me with a look of satisfaction. It was made of the same black material as the pants, with a very slight stretch. It was long and split in the back and short at the front. There were two tiny pockets at the front with little ruffles under them, and stiff silk lapels along the neckline. I slipped it on and secured it with a single round metallic button at the waist. It fit like a glove. The French cuffs on the shirt poked out from the long jacket sleeves. The effect was boyish and playful.

This tuxedo-look sure beat the heck out of my bland grey suit from Gretchenville. 'Great-Aunt Celia, why do all your clothes seem to fit me so well?' I asked.

'You are a Lucasta,' she replied, as if it were a simple matter of genetics. 'Now, darling, you need to wear this with confidence. Use the pockets. Wear it casually, like you aren't trying too hard. Don't be precious about it.' She squinted at me, evaluating what she saw. 'We will leave your hair out this time. No jewellery, and not too much lipstick, but you should wear some kohl around the eyes, I think.'

I nodded, though I didn't know how to do that.

'I'll do it for you,' she said, before I had to explain.

Was there any other young woman in world who could boast a great-aunt for a stylist and makeup artist?

By the time she was done, I was thanking my lucky stars. My makeup was natural, but with striking dark eyeliner rimming the inside of my eyes. It drew attention to the reddish 'cognac' colour of my eyes, and reminded me of the girl with the cat eyes on the cover of *Mia* magazine – not that I was going to think about them anymore. And not that I had to! I had my own job now, and I was about to attend my first fashion show in a funky, boyish tuxedo.

'I got you something special,' my great-aunt said, once I was ready. 'To celebrate.'

'What are we celebrating?'

'Why, your successful move to New York, of course. And here in Spektor.' Celia handed me a small deep red velvet bag, tied with a thin gold silk cord, and she smiled proudly from beneath her veil. The bag fit well in the palm of my hand. Whatever it held was curved and light. From the feel of it I couldn't imagine what it might be. 'It is time to give this to you now. You'll want it tonight, I think. This is a special gift, Pandora.'

Two weeks. It was impossible to register all that had happened in that time.

'Go on, open it,' she urged.

I had hesitated, but now I untied the cord and slid the object out of the bag. It was bronze and round, not quite flat but slightly domed, and had a clasp on one side. I flipped it open, wondering what strange thing it held.

Oh.

I saw my own reflection. It was a makeup compact.

'Darling you must carry this with you everywhere you go,' Celia told me firmly.

I nodded and smiled to myself. She wanted me to look good at all times on this exciting night. It was sweet that she cared about that sort of thing. It was a nice gesture. 'Thanks. It's lovely. I'll be sure to use it.'

'Yes. Why don't you slip it into your pocket, along with your lipstick and key?'

'Um, sure,' I said. I guessed Celia wasn't going to lend me a purse this time. The red one would have been okay with this, wouldn't it? Or perhaps not. It was a bit girly and didn't really match the black and white, I guessed. I'd have to go purse shopping when I could afford to.

'You look like a modern Marlene Dietrich without the top hat,' Celia observed proudly. 'Go on now.'

I gave Celia an enthusiastic hug, patted Freyja as she rubbed against my feet. 'Thank you. Thank you so much, Great-Aunt Celia. I shouldn't be too late tonight,' I said.

Before I left I filled my tuxedo pockets with grains of rice, just to be sure.

After all, I had nowhere to hide an axe.

The address Jay had given me was a slick, dimly-lit bar on Fifth Avenue. It looked expensive and very fashionable, with low-slung leather lounges and a white, avant-garde, spiral chandelier in the centre. At one end of the intimate room was an illuminated cocktail bar lined with liquor bottles. I'd never seen such a place before, and it all struck me as being like something out of a James Bond movie. Any minute a villain with a glass eye and a scar down one cheek would walk in and start speaking in a foreign accent.

My date was already there. I spotted Jay's tall, broad-shouldered silhouette at the bar. I walked up to him.

'Hi.'

He swivelled around. My appearance seemed to surprise him and I experienced an unsettling moment of wondering if the boyish tux was appropriate for the evening. Had I avoided one faux pas only to commit another?

'Oh, Pandora. You look beautiful,' Jay told me in his deep, honeyed voice.

'Thanks.' I melted a little, relieved, and I grinned broadly. 'You look nice too,' I replied. He looked better than nice, but I felt that any more extravagant compliment would be awkward. He wore a black velvet jacket, dark jeans and polished black shoes. He looked rich and stylish. *At least I look stylish*, I thought. I took the stool next to his.

'So . . .' I began, but the bartender was on me in a moment. I looked up to see that he was emaciated and looked as young as I was. He seemed to have dyed his long eyelashes.

'What'll it be?' the bartender asked me, sounding unreasonably bored.

'She'll have a sparkling mineral water with a twist of lime,' Jay cut in, and pushed a few dollars over the glowing bar.

I bit my lip. I wasn't used to people ordering drinks for me. Perhaps he just didn't want me to feel uncomfortable at the bar, but it had seemed a high-handed gesture.

'The show is in the Garment District, not far from here, in a disused warehouse,' Jay informed me while I waited for my mineral water.

'Oh good,' I said. I tried to contain my excitement, but I was sure Jay could see right through my feigned casualness. *My first-ever fashion show, my first-ever fashion show...* I kept thinking. I'd seen so many of them in magazines and on blogs.

My drink arrived in a tall glass. I nervously gulped the entire thing down, which did not sit well with my stomach. I'd forgotten it had bubbles.

'Did you sleep well?'

'Hmm?'

'After I dropped you off – did you sleep well?' Jay asked.

Oh yes, I slept well after a homicidal supermodel vampire attacked me, I stabbed her with an iron stake, and she went missing.

'Yes, thanks,' I replied.

'That was such a strange suburb.' He shook his head and frowned, as if trying to remember something. 'I can't even remember how I got home,' he remarked quietly, almost as if he hadn't meant me to hear.

Spektor. I probably shouldn't have let him drive me home, but Celia didn't warn me that it would be a problem. I made a mental note to ask her about that later. I had a lot to ask her, actually, especially all this stuff about my being 'the seventh'. I didn't really understand it all.

'Um, do you know the designer for tonight's show?' I asked Jay casually.

'Everyone in New York knows him,' he declared, as if I should have known. 'He has taken over from Alexander McQueen as the new *enfant terrible* of the fashion world.'

What an odd thing to say, I thought. 'Unruly child of the fashion world,' I repeated back, translating directly from the French.

Jay gave me a strange look. 'It means he's a genius.'

Jay and I walked the three blocks to the Garment District, and arrived twenty minutes after the show was supposed to start. I had begun to feel on edge about the time, but as it turned out, I needn't have worried one bit.

This time there was no red carpet.

Relieved, I walked a step behind my towering date as we entered a warehouse the size of an aeroplane hangar packed with flocks of fashion types. Bleachers were set up across the space, bringing to mind a school assembly, but these faced inwards to a shining white elevated runway, the first catwalk I had ever seen. Only about one third of the seats were filled so far. People were taking their time getting seated, checking each other out and generally making spectacles of themselves. My eyes were sure busy in this crowd. Every second person was a celebrity, or thought they were one, and photographers moved among them taking pictures of the famous, the fashionable and the outrageous. There were a lot of well-groomed, expensively dressed men and women, each cooler and more hip than the last. Some of the outfits made me

318 · Tara Moss

stare; I saw a woman in a leather corset, fishnets and
what was either a skirt or French knickers, it was hard
to tell. Her hat was larger than the rest of her outfit,
and featured an entire stuffed bird and a length of tulle.
I saw a man in a full-length black fur coat and huge
bug-eyed sunglasses, and strings of gold chains hanging
around his neck. Whoever he was, he had a small circle
of sycophants around him.

Who are these people?

'Here's your ticket,' Jay said, and pushed a stiff
cardboard ticket into my hand. It said B7 and I thought
fleetingly about the number seven, my favourite number,
and what my great-aunt had said about me the night
before. But Jay grabbed my hand and led me through the
throng, and soon I was distracted from my wonderings.

We had second-row seats and a great view. A media
scrum was assembled at the end of the runway with
hundreds of lenses prepared to capture every moment
of the show. There was a bit of a kerfuffle as the last
people took their seats, including an apparent altercation
regarding the owner of a certain front-row spot. Two
petite women argued heatedly until two taller women in
matching black T-shirts sorted it out. The interloper was
led away, the lights dimmed until the entire warehouse
was thrown into darkness.

Lights flashed over the runway, pulsing to the techno-
rock beat, and the first model walked out to a clash of
cymbals and a heavy drumbeat. The letters G R A F T
flashed up against the walls. I watched the first model
move towards us, and I admit I gaped. She was tall and

platinum-haired and built like a giraffe – an alarmingly thin giraffe. She had heavy makeup on, which I supposed was commonplace on the catwalk. It was theatre, after all. But this makeup was as white as snow. She looked suspiciously dark under the eyes. I cocked my head. Was she... *undead?* Surely not. The model progressed down the catwalk, crossing her ankles as she placed her feet. Her face was slack and expressionless. I closed my eyes and let my instincts be the judge. No. She wasn't undead. She just looked like it.

Way to give me nightmares.

'This is all the rage,' Jay explained.

'You mean wan anorexia?'

Jay flashed me a look. 'You crack me up. No, not wan anorexia, neo-goth. The vampire look.'

I swallowed heavily, and hoped Jay didn't see the flash of fear in my eyes.

It was just a look, right? Just because Athanasia was the face of the hottest beauty product in town didn't mean that vampires were running rampant in the fashion industry. Did it? It was just a look, thanks to a slew of vampire books and movies. Sure enough, a male model began his walk down the runway, clothed in Byronic, romantic goth wear, borrowing heavily from Anne Rice's Lestat and Louis. The outfit looked good on him, I had to admit. Next came a similarly dressed woman, again with the pale makeup and dark eyes. Her lips looked faintly bloodstained. To these people it was just a fashion trend, nothing more.

I tore my eyes from the terrifying vampiric models

and spotted a familiar face in the crowd. Two, in fact. Though Jay had snagged us second-row seats, I saw that Skye, my boss, was in the front row on the opposite side of the runway, wearing a yellow and black outfit, her hair pulled back into a neat ponytail. From what I could see she looked well, evidently recovered from her mysterious bout of sickness. The deputy editor and article-thief Pepper was actually in a seat behind her, so I supposed that competition for the front-row seats must be fierce. The two exchanged whispers and Skye went back to watching the show, notepad in hand. I noticed Pepper snapping photos with a small digital camera. It occurred to me that Pepper might get a visit from an angry vampire model. Should I warn her somehow?

When I looked back at the runway I saw that things had gone from bad to worse – or, rather, from deathlike to undead. One out of three models were actually Sanguine. I could feel it. *There, the blonde friend of Athanasia's!* Was I the only one who noticed she was dead? *And there, the redhead from Celia's building. And the brunette, too!* The dark-haired vampire stopped at the end of the runway, the split in her long leather gown falling open to reveal a pale, perfect leg... and she grinned. Her fangs glittered in the spotlight.

No. No!

The crowd applauded. The photographers clicked off a thousand flashes. I thought I would be ill.

When the lights came up, Jay and I left the bleachers. I couldn't wait to get out of there. Despite the clusters of people talking loudly here and there, the place seemed to be emptying fast. The music was still pounding, but it was clearly time to go. The media scrum had packed up and were rushing off somewhere.

'Shall we head to the after party?' Jay asked.

I felt my throat tighten. Would the models be there?

We had walked only a few steps from the bleachers when a familiar voice stopped me. 'Well, fancy seeing you here.'

It was my boss, Skye. She was wearing an intricately designed dress of stretchy neon yellow and black with futuristic stitching. It brought to mind a cocoon, and from the neck down she looked like she might soon turn into a butterfly. From the neck up, she looked like someone who was wearing a bit more makeup than usual to camouflage the fact that she was recovering from a bout of sickness. She was no longer magically glowing, and I suspected she'd stopped using *BloodofYouth*. From her expression, she looked a tiny bit impressed to see me. Not so the thief, Pepper, who stood next to her, glowering. Wasn't I the one who should be doing the glowering? Pepper eyed my handsome date and then looked back to me.

Oh...

'Wasn't it a good show?' I said cheerily. 'I'm glad you're feeling better, Skye. Have you met Jay Rockwell?' I did the polite introductions in my best professional tone.

'Nice to meet you,' Jay said, sliding straight into character as the charming date. He shook Skye's hand. 'Good to see you again, Pepper,' he said with a nod, and my heart did a funny tumble. They knew each other. How exactly did they know each other? He turned back to my boss. 'Is that Gaultier?' he asked. 'You look wonderful.'

Pepper sidled up to me. 'Nice catch,' she whispered into my ear, in a not-so-friendly tone. 'He's such a player, though. You ought to be careful. I'd hate for you to get hurt.'

I felt waves of jealousy coming off Pepper, and I wondered what it was all about. I was shocked by her words and I needed a moment to collect myself. *A player?* I'd sensed he might be. But just how well did Pepper and Jay know each other? Perhaps this wasn't the time to warn her that some employees of *BloodofYouth* had visited me, and might also want to 'chat' with her.

'Excuse me, I'll just be a moment,' I said, and turned to leave the trio to talk while I went to freshen up. I needed a moment to collect myself. Two women walked past at that moment, and I automatically followed them through an entryway, presuming they were going to the powder room.

The two strangers ahead of me talked as they walked.

'What did you think of the gown for me?'

'The leather?'

Halfway down a white, industrial-looking hallway they pushed on a door marked *Private*.

'And those fake fangs!'

I nearly stumbled in after them, but the shorter one stopped and gave me a sharp look, and I quickly realised my error. I kept walking down the empty corridor, as if I knew where I was going.

Darn it. Don't they have signs in these places?

I heard footsteps echoing behind me, and that familiar cold feeling settled in my stomach.

I turned.

Thankfully it was Jay. 'It's this way,' he said with a broad, appealing smile, and held out his hand.

'Thanks,' I replied, embarrassed. I'd been flustered by Pepper, and now I smiled and walked towards him.

But something felt wrong.

I heard other footsteps in the hallway. I was halfway to him when I saw three women walk up behind my date and stop. My heart sank into my stomach. It was the three models – *the three vampire models* – from my building. The redhead, the blonde and the brunette who had been in the show. They still had their white makeup caked on, as if they needed it to look deathly chic. They were dressed head to toe in their own cute designer outfits; a trio of perfectly beautiful horror, like the lethal Spice Girls, except they were all Scary Spice. We were lucky there weren't five of them. Maybe Jay and I could take them on, if that's what it came to?

'Where did you think you were going, virgin?' the blonde hissed.

'That's none of your business,' was my swift retort. I took a few steps closer, and folded my arms. I was still a few metres away from Jay, who looked confused but not nearly as scared as he ought to be.

I wondered what they would do.

I didn't have to wonder for long.

'Hey, ladies,' my date began with a smooth smile. Sensing the thick atmosphere of hostility, he raised his hands, palms up, and spoke in his most charming voice. 'There's no need to—'

Redhead grabbed Jay by the throat and lifted him up against the wall. I could hardly believe what I was seeing. He was a big man, strong and very tall, but she lifted him like he was weightless. Jay was so tall that his feet didn't exactly dangle, but his body hung limp. I thought it strange that he wasn't struggling with his arms or legs. His face was turning more purple by the second and his eyes bulged, locked in a stare with his beautiful attacker. I wondered if she was hypnotising him.

'Put him down!' I demanded, and took a step towards them.

Brunette and Blonde turned to me and assumed poses of readiness. They looked like they planned to fight me. Interesting that they thought it would take two of them.

'Ms Báthory has plans for you and your friends,' Redhead said, still gripping Jay's throat and not breaking the stare. I wondered how much longer Jay could take it before he passed out.

'Let's leave the man out of it,' I said, and looked around me. The models were blocking the way we'd come, and there was a doorway at the end of the hall behind them. There was the door up the corridor behind me which I'd almost followed the two women through, possibly leading backstage or to a room for the fashion show's staging staff. I could make a run for it, but I couldn't leave Jay with those fanged femme fatales, not even for long enough to get help. He could be dead by then. Or undead.

'Look here,' I said, and bolted towards them, emptying

my pockets as I bridged the distance between us. My paper seat ticket fluttered to the ground, catching the eye of the blonde and brunette vamps, and after it, grains of rice hit the floor and bounced. The models reacted with a peculiar 'Ohhh' sound, and crouched to the floor to begin counting. 'One, two, three, four...' Redhead turned from her victim to see what her evil cohorts were doing, and when she spotted the rice she too crouched to the ground and began counting, as if in a supernatural trance. Jay slid to the floor, holding his throat.

Supernatural rules. *So* weird.

'This way, Jay!' I called out and nearly tackled him in my attempt to get him up and moving.

'She had... teeth...' he stuttered, perhaps finally realising the fangs were real.

We scrambled along, Jay clutching his sore throat in one hand while I gripped the other, pulling him as fast as I could towards the far door – a fire door with a big metal hand bar – hoping it led outside where I could flag down help. I hadn't been able to fit a lot of rice in my jacket pockets, and the models would soon finish counting. I pushed the bar down and burst out the doorway, dragging my date behind me. It opened into a disused loading bay. I was not staring at a bustling New York City street, not at traffic and life-saving yellow cabs; I was looking at a disused back alley in the Garment District. It was dark, but not uninhabited, I quickly discovered. Oh no, it wasn't uninhabited at all.

Vampires liked alleys, apparently.

The long black limo was there, along with the familiar

yellow sports car that belonged to my nemesis Athanasia – who stood only metres away in her leather pants and a tight T-shirt that was totally inappropriate for the weather, looking as if she'd never been staked. And she had friends. Big, scary, dead friends. Two males – both pale, ugly, neckless and looking like they'd been Russian body builders in life. One of them – a bald, nasty-looking man with muscles that seemed ready to burst out of his suit – held two bodies, one over each shoulder. I stifled a scream. It was Skye and Pepper.

Then I noticed Athanasia's smile was slick with fresh blood.

Oh no. No, no, no, no...

I could barely take in the grim spectacle as the hulking creature slung my editor and deputy editor into the trunk of the limo like they were sacks of potatoes. And maybe that's all they'd been to Athanasia: food.

Upon my arrival on the scene the rear door of the limousine had opened, and now, slowly, a figure emerged; a figure more beautiful and terrifying than any I had seen before. It was a woman clothed in a long, black dress with a tight, corsetted bustier and draping folds of luxurious fabric that fell to the pavement. She had a high forehead and aristocratic features, and although she was no taller than me, her presence was commanding. Her skin was luminous, pale and flawless, and her dark hair was pulled back behind ivory-skinned shoulders to reveal a long slim neck and a collar of blood-red lace. Her dark eyes were malevolent, somehow mesmerising, and the power of her dark beauty seemed to overwhelm that of

Athanasia, who looked plain next to her master, even after her fresh feed.

This, I knew instinctively, was the woman behind *BloodofYouth*.

'Good. You've come, Pandora English,' the woman announced in a richly accented voice. 'I am Countess Elizabeth Báthory.'

I blinked at her, aware she was trying to hypnotise me. I felt her mind push into mine, and I pushed back. I refused to let her influence penetrate. She kept her eyes locked on mine, and she smiled.

'I was told you are not all you appear,' she stated. 'This was correct.'

Báthory, Báthory, Báthory . . .

I turned the name over in my mind. Athanasia had mentioned her mistress Báthory, as had the red-haired vamp, and here she was. The name Elizabeth Báthory was familiar. It had been in my mother's books. It came up frequently alongside the name of Vlad Tepes, the supposed inspiration for the fictional figure of *Dracula* in the novel Celia despised so much. She was from Eastern Europe. Yes, Romania, or Hungary, but long ago, centuries ago. And unlike Count Dracula, she was very real and she had committed some truly terrible real-life crimes, crimes so heinous it made her a dark legend. There was some talk of a wrongful trial. No, she was of noble blood and thus *could not* be tried, I now recalled.

This is Countess Báthory, the Blood Lady C˘achtice. This is the Blood Countess.

When I was younger I'd read about the legendary Blood Countess, and had asked my mother about her. She was notorious for being the most prolific female serial killer in history, accused of having killed many hundreds of her virgin servant girls at her castle – as many as six hundred. She could not be tried because she was of noble blood, so in a strange version of justice she was walled into her castle for her crimes, and there she supposedly died. There was some dispute among historians and academics about whether she had really killed all those girls. My mother had believed her to be the victim of a conspiracy. But if this was Báthory, clearly she had not died in her castle, as history suggested. She was turned into a vampire, a Sanguine, or perhaps she already was one before they caught her.

A centuries-old celebrity murderess.

With shaking hands I reached into my pockets, found only a few petty grains of rice left. *Darn it. Darn it!* I closed my eyes, said a little prayer, and feeling quite ridiculous, threw the grains at Báthory's feet. All of us present watched the grains hit the pavement, bounce. Báthory looked at me, her crimson lips curling up at the corners into a horrible smile. Her minion, Athanasia, cast her eyes to the ground and I saw her lips move. *One, two, three, four...* The others were, sadly, unaffected.

Athanasia stopped counting at nine.

'If you were hoping to effect me, you are quite mistaken, mortal. I am no Fledgling.' Evidently neither was her muscle. One of them stood protectively next to Báthory, while his bald counterpart moved towards me, intent on taking me down, and perhaps slinging me in the back of the limo as he'd done with my colleagues. I stiffened, and turned to Jay for assistance.

He was staring in Báthory's direction, entranced.

Oh, HELL!

'Jay?'

He didn't respond. He was evidently hypnotised.

Why are the men in my life so useless when these creatures are around?

I turned to run back towards the warehouse, and found that the three models had finished their counting. Blonde, Brunette and Redhead were already at my back and they had me in their clutches in seconds. I flailed violently like a fish but they held me still while the pasty-faced bald man with the formidable muscles moved close at a lumbering pace. He smelled nauseatingly like sulfur and decay. Undead BO. Without a word, he put his hands around my neck in a stranglehold.

'No! No!' I protested, but could say no more with the slow crushing of my windpipe. I thrashed against my assailants, but they had me contained and I would be unconscious in seconds, I knew.

'Don't damage the neck, Augustine,' the Countess instructed calmly. She glided towards me, serene and menacing. 'Open her mouth.'

Muscle tried to open my jaws and I gritted my teeth like a stubborn animal.

No…

'Open up, little *morchilla*,' came a voice from one of the fanged models behind me. She pinched my nose.

'Ha, ha, little blood sausage!' one of the others said, and laughed.

I continued to grit my teeth, holding my breath.

'Stubborn, aren't we?' Báthory remarked, and waited patiently for me to open up. 'I can hold my breath forever. I have no need for breath. But you, mortal girl, you must open...'

Eventually, inevitably, I gasped for air. The Sanguine caught my teeth and prised my mouth open. My tongue fought uselessly with the air. Languidly, and with a sense of great satisfaction, Báthory leaned in, placed her hands over my open jaws and flipped open an ancient ring on her index finger. Something light and powdery landed on my tongue. *Bitter.* Before I could spit, my mouth was forced closed.

I swallowed involuntarily.

'There,' she said. 'Augustine, put her in the car.'

When the trio of supermodels let go of me, my body fell limply into his arms. My head felt foggy. I could not feel my limbs. I was a rag doll, paralysed and terrifyingly helpless.

'As for that one,' I heard the Blood Countess say, 'erase him.'

CHAPTER
TWENTY-FIVE

I'll admit that back in Gretchenville I dreamed I might one day ride in a real limousine. I never imagined, however, that my new boss would be in the trunk, or that I would be sitting in the back with a four-hundred-year-old murderess.

Elizabeth Báthory reclined across the seat of her limousine before me, self-possessed, nefarious and unnaturally alluring. The limo seemed cavernously large inside, and it was new enough to have that new-car smell. It was a welcome change from the sulfurous rot of Báthory's henchmen, one of whom was in the passenger seat up front, and the other – the bald one – was driving. This vehicle even had a bar, and rows of shiny, clean champagne glasses resting on purpose-built holders along the inside. There was no actual champagne, of course. I guessed that champagne was not this woman's beverage of choice. Thanks to whatever poison she'd forced me to swallow, I had no use of my limbs, and I was slumped awkwardly in a seated position opposite her, my head resting against the frosty window. When the vehicle turned a corner, I slid around a little and my cheekbone rubbed uncomfortably against the cool glass. Thankfully they had seen fit to strap me in with the seat belt. For a bunch of murderers, this seemed an oddly solicitous touch.

'Now, tell me who you are,' the Blood Countess commanded.

I opened my mouth to respond, but was dubious about my ability to form coherent words in my unnatural state of paralysis. Sure enough, the first syllables came out slurred. 'Paaaaaaaan...'

Elizabeth Báthory folded her arms. 'Yes, yes,' she replied impatiently. 'I know your name, Pandora English. But who are you? How is it that you managed to stake my mannequin Athanasia? She is still young but she has fed often. She is far more powerful than any human.'

Fed often. Yuck.

Elizabeth Báthory was interested in me, it seemed. This didn't seem to be a positive development. *If only my mother could see me now,* I thought darkly. But then her interest in me might be the reason I wasn't crammed in the trunk. It might even be the reason I was still alive. Were Skye and Pepper unconscious? Paralysed like I was? Dead? *Undead?* I hadn't heard a peep from back there. No thumping, no moaning. I turned my eyes to watch the increasingly barren cityscape pass outside the window. We'd crossed a bridge and were no longer on Manhattan Island, but I wasn't sure what direction we were travelling in. Were we in Queens? Jersey? From my vantage point I could not pinpoint our direction from any landmark, or from the position of the sun or moon. The sky was dark, and the streets filled with identically depressing strip malls, rundown neon signs, thinning traffic. I saw some graffiti on the sides of derelict buildings. This was not good.

I opened my mouth again. 'Where ... are ... we ... going?' I managed slowly, but with somewhat better voice control. I sounded drugged and very, very weak.

Báthory ignored my question as if it had not been asked. 'You don't *look* powerful,' she observed, sounding intrigued. She tilted her head to one side, and dark, perfect waves of hair fell over one shoulder. 'Tell me how you knew about *BloodofYouth*? The blonde one, the coward,' she said, indicating the trunk behind me, 'told me she did not even write the article. She says it was you. Athanasia suspected as much. She said you were poking around. It is true? But how did you know to seek out the actor? And why? Are you so brave? Did you not know there would be consequences? Tell me,' she demanded.

'It's...fraud,' I answered, saving my energy. Despite my terror, I felt petulant about her little game of Twenty Questions, under these less-than-fair circumstances.

'The product I have created is a fraud? Oh, but it is not a fraud at all,' she corrected me. '*BloodofYouth* does precisely what it claims. It *is* precisely what it claims. It restores youthful beauty for as long as the human uses it.'

'Secret...ingredient,' I croaked weakly.

She laughed quietly. 'Did you really think anyone would care what's in it? Humans are not so squeamish about what makes something work, so long as it does.

They choose not to examine their ethics when it comes to what they really want. Surely you already know this about your pathetic, hypocritical race? Do you know the ingredients of everything you eat, use, rub on your skin? Do you know where it comes from? Who suffered for it? I think not.'

Admittedly I was nowhere near knowledgeable about all the products I used or the provenance of every last morsel of food I ate, but that hardly meant that her reasoning was sound.

'There have been a few complaints of allergic reaction, but we'll soon fix that.'

I thought of Skye and her mysterious illness; and Toni Howard's 'allergy'.

'Do you know that we sold out across the country the day *BloodofYouth* hit the stores? When people couldn't get their hands on it, it went on to the black market immediately. We get our best prices there. If your little attempt at *journalism* amounts to anything – which is doubtful – and *BloodofYouth* becomes illegal, it will only boost my profits. I should thank you.'

I blinked.

'Humans will do anything to maintain the illusion of youth. I know this better than most,' she said, and a small, bitter smile crossed her lips.

Legend had it that the motive for Báthory's cruel crimes had been vanity; that she had tortured her victims and bathed in their virgin blood to maintain her youthful beauty.

BloodofYouth. The secret ingredient.

'No false advertising,' Celia had said.

My stomach lurched as the pieces fell into place. Could it be?

'Humans will kill for it if they have to. But they don't have to, because I do the killing for them,' the Countess said, and gave a short, chilling laugh.

CHAPTER
TWENTY-SIX

I don't know how much time passed before the limousine finally slowed. If I had to guess, I would say we had driven for well over an hour. Perhaps even two.

There didn't seem to be anyone following us; no rescuers, not Jay – for whom I was gravely concerned – not even Countess Báthory's minion and muse Athanasia, or her model friends. The landscape had become gradually bleaker and darker as we went, until there were now no other vehicles on the roads, and only a scattering of industrial buildings set against stretches of grazing land and pastures. If this was some kind of agricultural setting, it looked nothing like the farms back home. I hadn't seen a homestead for miles.

Our driver slowed and diverted from the main road just as a ghostly structure loomed on a rise ahead of us – a large white factory surrounded by high, barbed-wire fencing. We followed a winding, single-lane road towards it. From my position, slumped against the window, I could see the foreboding structure was rectangular, with four smokestacks and a few outbuildings. It stood out from the surrounding dark rural landscape like a spectre. I noticed a sign on the side of the road, torn down and left on the grass, the paint faded and peeled away. The setting here had a neglected and malevolent air about it, but this was no abandoned factory, as I could see from a faint greenish smoke that billowed eerily from the mouths of the smokestacks. There was something in there, something being made, even now at this dark hour. And I thought I knew what it was.

Death.

I sensed the presence of death as surely as I'd ever felt anything.

This was a terrible place, a place of nightmares. I could feel it in my body, in my bones, in the sudden coldness in my belly.

Finally the limousine halted on gravel at the gate next to a small security booth. This change of pace, the nearness of doom, made my heart speed up. The increased terror seemed to clear the last of the drugged fog from my mind. I would need every ounce of my wits if I were to survive what was ahead. I took in every detail of my surrounds, everything I could see from my position against the glass. My eyes flicked over the structure ahead, the security lights, the guards in black standing in pairs at the entrance to the factory.

The window nearest Countess Báthory lowered with an electronic hum. She peered out into the quiet night.

After a moment I heard footsteps on gravel. A male guard walked over to the gate and unlocked a padlock with a key attached to a chain on his belt. He was strong-looking – again pale and lumbering, and dressed in black. *Undoubtedly undead*, I thought. He pulled the gate open, as expressionless as a drone, and we drove through. Báthory's window was raised. She had not spoken a word. In my peripheral vision, I saw the gate close behind us, saw the creature refasten the padlock, and my heart sank. Thanks to Báthory's mysterious poison, my body was still rendered incapable of flight, but even if I *could* outrun these brawny guards, I could not scale so high a fence and make it over the barbed wire. I'd need to get that key from his belt, and exit through that tall gate.

The limousine drove slowly to the rear of the factory, out of view of the winding road we'd travelled. As we neared it, I saw that the painted concrete of the structure had faded and peeled away, much like the sign on the road. How long had this place been derelict before Báthory took it over? From our position on the rise, I saw that the closest lights were in the far distance. This location had been chosen for its privacy and isolation.

The car stopped. The engine cut.

The front doors of the limousine opened and the driver and his partner stepped out onto gravel. I saw movement and heard the gravel crunch under their feet. We'd stopped by a rear entrance to the factory. The entrance was large enough for a truck to back in, and it too was guarded by more of Báthory's underlings – large hulking male vampires, no doubt chosen for their might and obedience. These were ugly creatures, nothing like the unnaturally beautiful model vampires she'd left with Jay in the Garment District. How many guards was that now? Four, plus the one at the gate, the limousine driver and his partner. *Seven henchmen. Perhaps more inside.* The bald driver opened the door and Báthory alighted from the vehicle gracefully. For a few seconds I was alone. I took the opportunity to attempt to move my middle finger, just a fraction.

There.

It was only a centimetre, but it was something.

On the drive I'd realised my toes had begun working again. I'd wiggled them inside my ballet shoes and I'd even managed to bend my ankle a little. The mysterious paralysis was wearing off. Báthory was confident enough that she hadn't bothered to otherwise restrain me, and with so many guards, and given the isolation, would it really matter if her powdery potion wore off now? Where could I possibly run to?

The bald driver opened the door, unbuckled my seat belt and slung me over his shoulder.

'Thanks,' I said facetiously into the middle of his back, but he didn't respond. The smell of sulfur and rot filled my nose, and I gagged.

Helpless, I watched gravel pass beneath us until the ground became concrete. I smelled decay and dust, and something else that was impossible to define. I turned my head and saw a concrete wall. *A corridor.* Before I managed to crane my neck for a look the other way I was through a doorway into an unlit room. *Oh.* In sharp contrast to the factory, this room smelled sweet, like perfume or incense. The guard flipped me unceremoniously over his shoulder. I landed somewhat gratefully on the soft, cushioned surface of a bed. The bed was covered with an ornate brocade throw of deep burgundy and gold. There was a Persian carpet on the floor, with luxurious cushions thrown here and there. A vanity. A mirror. *Odd.* That was all I managed to take in before the bald driver, Augustine, stomped out of the room and closed the door behind him, throwing the space into total darkness. I didn't hear him use a latch or a key. The room was windowless and now the sweetness in the air was cloying. There was a trace of mustiness, and more of that indefinable thing that filled me with dread.

The cold feeling in my belly was ever-present, and increasing in intensity.

Báthory's temporary lair.

With effort, I twisted my body on the bed. *Must. Get. Up.* I could circle my ankles, my wrists, but the rest of my body was yet to respond. I rotated a shoulder, managed to get my knee to bend in slow, unsteady movements. I knew I could not walk. Not yet. I certainly couldn't run. Minutes passed in darkness as I felt like a fly caught in a web. I wondered how long I would be left there, willing my body to save me. Now my hands could fully flex. That was something. The feeling was returning to my knees, my elbows. I hated to stay where I had been tossed – like a waiting meal – and I thought of wriggling to the edge of the bed and off, hoping I could catch myself, hoping my reflexes would spring into action, but the likelihood of falling helplessly to the hard floor stopped me. One foolish move on my part could ruin any chance I had of survival.

'She'll drain you.'

I drew in my breath sharply. 'Who's there?' I asked, and noticed my voice was working again.

'She'll keep you here, to have her fun.' The voice was female, and somehow distant. 'She'll drink from you as she pleases. She'll chant and do strange things. It's a ritual for her. Foreplay. And then, when she's tired of you, she'll drain you.'

My eyes searched the pitch dark and found only a faint white shape. 'I can't see. It's too dark. Who are you?'

'Alice. I was like you, before she drained me.' I felt a chill in the air next to me, and then a cool, misty hand. Fingertips stroked mine to comfort me, but her words were anything but comforting. 'She will keep you paralysed and awake. She has the power of Isis. She bathes in blood...'

One of Báthory's victims. This room was where she killed them, and then...

My mother had told me that Báthory's reputation was probably unfounded. Báthory had been an educated woman, and she had ruled her husband's lands effectively in his frequent and extended absences. After he died at war she had continued business as usual with her serfs, and refused to pass on her vast landholdings to her male heirs while she still lived. She'd been a businesswoman back when the very idea of a businesswoman was unacceptable, and what she got for her entrepreneurial spirit was her terrible legend. Or so my mother had suggested. It seemed my mother had been wrong.

'Can you help me?' I pleaded. Perhaps this ghost could try to protect me, as Luke had when Samantha went for my neck.

'She is coming,' the girl said. 'Goodbye.' And the chill air around me returned to normal.

Light footsteps were approaching.

I heard the doorknob begin to turn, and suddenly the room was aglow. Rows of candles lit of their own accord – a most devilish and bizarre show of black magic. There were hundreds of them. I wondered how many women had been sacrificed in this room. That's what this was, wasn't it? The sacrificial chamber of the entrepreneurial Countess Elizabeth Báthory? Now, to my right, I saw an open doorway. It led to a bathtub.

I felt a fresh shiver run through my body.

Báthory.

There was no time to react. My captor was through the door, and it shut behind her, though I was not even sure she had shut it with her hands.

'See my power, Pandora English?' she said, rolling the R. Doubtless she had seen the shock and horror on my features. 'The blood is the life, and I have had so many lives, right here...'

I was careful not to flinch.

'You must know why you are here, yes?'

I had no adequate response. I was not sure why she'd bothered to bring me so far, to what seemed to be the local centre of her devilish operations.

'Count...esss,' I replied, laying on the drugged voice a bit thick. I defied my every impulse to move and remained totally still on the bed as she approached.

Báthory appeared pleased. If she had been Freyja, she would have purred. With an air of majesty and triumph she moved to the end of the bed, leaned in. I resisted an instinct to try and kick up with my legs. The Countess grinned, and sniffed the air delicately. 'Don't think you can hide it from me, girl. I can smell it. You're a virgin.'

Oh...

From beneath her lovely, terrible mouth, two sharp ivory points appeared. Just tips. I recoiled.

She inclined her head. Those dark eyes took me in. 'But first, I have been admiring your jacket,' she said, smiling at it and running her eyes over the fabric. 'It would be a shame to ruin it. Take it off.'

I didn't move.

'Oh, that's right. *You can't.*'

I lay limp and passive while Báthory unbuttoned Celia's tuxedo jacket and pulled it off me, stretching my arms above my head. I watched in silence as she admired it by the light of her strange candles. 'Oh yes. It is a marvellous jacket. I think I'll take it.'

'No...problem,' I muttered.

She threw it on over her dress, pulling one arm through the sleeve. 'What a darling tailor you—'

While her arms were tangled in the jacket sleeves I sprung from the bed as if I'd been tightly coiled. I bolted to the door.

Báthory made a startled sound, her left arm still

tangled in the jacket sleeve. I threw the door open. Unlocked. *'Yes! Go, Pandora! Run!'* I urged myself aloud, and did precisely that. One of my legs was half-asleep now the paralysis had worn off, and I cried out in pain. The next issue would be how to escape the factory, and as I looked around me I doubted that would be an easy task. There were two guards to my right, down the corridor leading to the car. I ran the other way and saw a huge metal catwalk above large steaming vats, and at every exit, a hulking, pale vampire guard.

Darn it. Darn it...

The guards turned in my direction with eerie coordination, and they began to move in at a lumbering pace. The reek of sulfur and rot filled my nostrils as they approached. I couldn't tackle those creatures. I couldn't fight them. *No exit.* I felt a cold metal ladder at my back, and instinctively I began to scramble up it, awkwardly but with the speed of desperation.

As I arrived at the top, Elizabeth Báthory appeared at the end of the metal catwalk, wearing Celia's tuxedo jacket and a look of quiet rage. Flanking her were four guards with guns strapped to their belts. I turned to see four similar guards behind me. I was trapped.

'You are quite the actress,' Báthory said with displeasure, her imperious voice echoing through the factory. 'Come now. Who are you really? My potion wore off far too quickly...'

'I'm Pandora English. A writer,' I called over the din of the vats below.

Báthory's eyes narrowed. 'You are no normal human

girl,' she accused, moving closer. 'Don't even pretend,' she said, walking up to me slowly.

I watched her expressionless henchmen, who stood at each end of the catwalk, and at the base of the ladder up which I'd climbed, and something clicked. *Samantha*. She hadn't been able to help me clean up after my run-in with Athanasia because she couldn't contain herself around so much blood, yet these guards were strangely unmoved. 'These aren't vampires,' I said.

'Of course not,' Báthory replied. 'They're zombies.'

My stomach lurched.

I had only just come to terms with the existence of vampires. I hadn't yet imagined that zombies were real, or I'd have noticed how different they were before.

'At one time it was not so rare, but the labour in this country just isn't what it used to be. Not since the Civil War,' Báthory explained. 'You Americans got it all wrong,' she sneered.

Civil War?

I thought of Luke, the Union soldier who had lost his mortal life in that war. If vampires were in the South back then, doubtless they wanted slavery to remain. They could remain holed up in their huge mansions, their zombie slaves working the fields. Could that be?

I was silent for a time. Contemplating.

'So, now that you've had your little tour, do you like my factory?' Báthory asked me. By now she and I were in the centre of the long catwalk. I had edged back towards the four guards behind me, but I knew I couldn't take them on any more than I could out-muscle Báthory herself. She could see I had no weapons, no stakes. She was more powerful than I. She faced me on the catwalk, alone and magnificent.

'This is where I keep up the stocks of *BloodofYouth*,' she declared proudly, and swept her hand through the air to indicate the dark, metallic-smelling vats of boiling liquid below us. 'You seemed so keen to know what makes *BloodofYouth* unique. Does it please you to witness the secret ingredient for yourself? Before you become part of it?'

I was up against the railing. From the ends of the catwalk, and from the doors below, her zombie guards watched impassively. I counted ten of them. There would be more at the other doors. Their dead eyes followed our movements, their expressionless faces slack, their bodies as lifeless as puppets. This was business as usual, I supposed. I was to become just another few ounces of *BloodofYouth* and there was not a living soul to witness it.

'No more games. Now I will take what's mine,' Báthory said and opened her mouth in a terrible smile, marred by the fangs that slid out to full length from beneath her lips as I watched, frozen in horror.

'Just one last thing before you drain me,' I asked, stalling. 'I need to know, did you really kill those virgin servant girls, all those years ago?'

'What do you think?' Báthory replied. I could tell she was excited now at the prospect of her virgin feed.

That was a yes, then.

'And you really did bathe in their blood? I thought it

might be a conspiracy because those people wanted your landholdings,' I suggested.

'Oh, you are an *innocent*, aren't you?' Báthory whispered, sniffing my neck. 'Why it was both, of course. I would never have been arrested for my little...quirk, if those men hadn't wanted to seize my land. My son was one of those who betrayed me. Did you know that? He wanted it all for himself. He couldn't even wait until I died. I could have killed thousands more and no one would have cared. They were just the daughters of servants. They were nothing. But yes, they wanted what I owned.' Báthory was angry now, as she recalled her betrayal, and it seemed to fill her with even more fervour as she spoke. She looked me in the eye. 'Those bastard interrogators who sentenced me without a trial – when I broke out of the castle, I made them pay.'

I imagined she had.

It took all my courage not to break her gaze. I was nearly out of time but I had an idea. 'It's a shame that *BloodofYouth* works on everyone else...' She bent over me. 'But it didn't work for you,' I finished quietly as she leaned in, her fangs almost at my throat.

Báthory paused. She had one manicured hand resting on my shoulder, the other against my head, pulling it to one side to better expose my jugular. 'Hmmm?' she murmured. She brushed my skin with the tips of her oversized incisors. I tried not to shiver.

'I said, it's a shame. I mean, you don't look a day over four hundred, but still, I would have thought with all that effort you could have made yourself look young again...'

She pulled back violently and gaped at me, inches from my nose. Hers was a strange expression of puzzlement and desire, fangs extended and brow furrowed. 'What? I am beautiful,' she announced, baffled at my suggestion to the contrary. 'For four hundred and fifty years I have been one of the world's most beautiful women,' she explained.

I shrugged. 'If you say so.' I crossed my arms and shrugged, wearing my most incredulous expression. My hair fell over my neck – an inadequate protection if ever there was one.

I'd struck a nerve. I could feel her rage build.

'Look at me!' Báthory bellowed. She snatched my chin in one hand and forced me to look at her. 'I am *beautiful*. You see my magnificent beauty! You see!'

At the sound of their mistress's agitation, or perhaps at some soundless signal, the zombie guards began to animate again. Slowly they advanced towards us on the catwalk, their dead eyes unseeing. Some of them were armed with guns, I now noticed with dread. I'd be shot in the back if I managed to break away and run for it. Dead footfalls rattled on the metal stairwell as they marched towards us, moving in to protect their unhappy mistress. She had them hypnotised– but not me. I tore my gaze from the advancing undead soldiers and looked into Báthory's dark, beautiful eyes. I had infuriated her, and some of her power slipped.

'Let me tell you what I see,' I told her. 'I see every murder, every sin, every drop of blood you have spilled. I see all of it as plain as the lines and wrinkles on your old, ugly face. Each heinous act you have committed over the past four hundred years shows plainly on your drooping, hideous flesh.' Urged by some instinct I pulled the mirrored compact out of my back pocket and flipped it open. 'Look at how *truly hideous* you really are,' I said, and thrust it in front of her face. 'Look at yourself!'

Báthory's eyes flicked to the tiny mirror, and to my shock, she shrieked.

'My face!' she screamed. 'My beautiful face! No! It can't be!'

The countess clawed at her cheeks, stumbling back from her reflection as she did. She was so consumed by the horror of whatever she had seen in the mirror, that she barely noticed when she stumbled right off the edge of the catwalk and fell head first into the boiling vat of blood beneath us.

'My face!' was her last strangled cry before the blood of her victims swallowed her.

I stood breathless on the catwalk. I gripped the railing in one hand, and in the other I held the compact Celia had given me like it was a live grenade.

What did she see in there? Did she really see what I willed her to see? Did I have that power?

Slowly I dared to turn it my way.

I saw only myself.

With a clatter Báthory's zombie soldiers fell to the ground where they stood, the spell that animated them now evidently broken. Guns clattered against the metal of the catwalk, bodies hit the concrete floor of the factory below.

'*Oh boy*,' I mumbled to myself.

Though the paralysis had long since worn off, it took me a while to move. I kept staring into the boiling vat of blood beneath me, wondering if Báthory would come screaming out of it.

She didn't.

CHAPTER
TWENTY-SEVEN

I found Elizabeth Báthory's long black limousine at the back of the factory, where it had been parked.

I approached with caution, but my stealth was thwarted by the sound of the gravel crunching under my flat shoes. Augustine was in there, waiting. I could see his bald head through the lightly tinted driver-side window. This vehicle was my only way home. I hunkered down behind the car, heart thumping in my chest, and grabbed a fistful of gravel. I said a little prayer to myself and threw the handful of small rocks at the side of the fence to make a noise. Augustine's head didn't move.

Is he or isn't he...?

When he didn't stir I dared to get closer.

Augustine was leaning against the steering wheel. I pulled the door open and he fell unceremoniously onto the gravel, his legs still caught inside the foot well. I'd at first assumed that Báthory's minions had all been vampires, but I'd been wrong. Augustine had been a

360 · Tara Moss

zombie slave, like the rest of them. And now that their mistress was finally, truly dead, I wanted to believe that their souls had at last been released.

Alice.

I turned towards the factory doors, and she was there, next to the prone bodies of two lifeless zombie guards. I could see her under the security light, a watery figure, hauntingly pretty, clothed in a blouse and jeans, her blonde hair in a plait. She looked no older than sixteen. I felt my heart break at the sight of her. Somewhere in this country a family missed her. Many tears had been shed for her. Her family could never know, could never imagine how she had met her terrible end.

'She's gone now. You are free,' I told the girl, through a throat that felt restricted with emotion. I felt a tear slip from my eye.

Alice said nothing, but I thought I felt a certain peace emanating from her before she vanished.

'Goodbye,' I said to the empty space.

I had to get out of there.

Augustine blocked my way. 'Sorry,' I murmured to the man who had earlier held me still while his mistress poisoned me. It was rather icky pushing the rest of him out of the car and stepping over his body to find the mechanism to unlock the limousine's trunk.

Ewww.

Augustine was decomposing at a rapid rate. Bits of him were flaking off.

I raced around to the back of the limo and opened the trunk to find two sets of bloodshot, terrified eyes staring up at me. Skye and Pepper were both still very much alive and awake, and waiting for whatever gruesome plans Báthory had for them once she'd had her fun and made black magic beauty cream out of me. I was relieved to see the two of them, and that was possibly a first. From their expressions I could see that they were positively beyond dread, but unable to do anything about their predicament, despite the fact that they were unbound. 'Where...are...we...?' Skye asked in a drugged, uneven voice. The same paralysing poison still had them in its grip. No wonder Báthory had expected I would be more affected than I was. Why had my body responded so differently?

Though I suspected that I was possibly resistant to the full effects of the late undead Elizabeth Báthory's poisons and tricks, I was soon reminded that I was *not* superwoman. Lifting my colleagues out of the trunk one at a time and stretching them out in the back of the limo was quite a task, and I can't say I did it with much elegance. They were dead weights, paralysed as they were. I am woman enough to admit I am not that strong, and though they are both slim, it was a struggle. I even hit Pepper's head on the lip of the trunk, and she cried out. I am sorry to say I kind of enjoyed it.

They both had gaping puncture marks on their throats and I wondered if they would rise as Sanguine before our night journey was through.

Exhausted, I looked at the ghostly white building and closed my eyes. There were no other signs of life. The zombie guards were deteriorating with bizarre speed.

It was time to go.

I stepped over Augustine's flaky corpse with another mumbled apology, and climbed into the driver's seat. I looked into the foot well, stared at the pedals for one flustered moment. I'd never driven anything more exciting than Aunt Georgia's little Subaru. And this was a *limousine*, for goodness' sake. But the key was in the ignition and I started it up easy as pie, popped it into drive, found the headlights and pushed the pedals gingerly until it drifted forward.

I can do this.

I drove up to the gate slowly.

To my relief, all that was left of the zombie security guard were his clothes and a few flakes of dust. It made finding the key chain much easier.

Hours later I knocked on the door of Celia's penthouse. I had driven for some time along long, dark roads, and just when I thought I was lost I found highway signs for New York. After that it was only a matter of heading for the Empire State Building and then up through the park – and holding my breath every time I cornered the long vehicle. (It had a few fresh dents, but I figured the owner wouldn't care.)

'I'm home, Great-Aunt Celia,' I said as I stepped inside. I could see that she was at her usual spot, reading. Her nocturnal habits fascinated me.

Freyja raced towards me, mewing, and Celia turned

to face me. 'Darling, you are back. I'm so pleased you vanquished the Countess. Well done.'

Such a knack for understatement, my great-aunt.

Great-Aunt Celia rose gracefully, slipped on her shoes and made her way towards me, impeccably dressed in a shimmering black dress and hose. She wore a diamanté brooch and drop earrings. Her veil was in place, as was a slick of crimson lipstick. I wondered if she was going out, or if she had come home from somewhere.

'I have my boss and the deputy editor in a stolen limousine downstairs,' I commented, feeling a little insane as I said it, though it was absolutely true. Strangely, on top of everything, I was sorry about Celia's tuxedo jacket. 'And I lost your beautiful jacket in a boiling vat of virgin blood. I'm sorry about that... Oh, and I desperately need a glass of water,' I added as an afterthought.

I slipped off my ballet flats and raced to the kitchen to get myself a glass of water. I gulped down three full glasses before I gasped for air. I realised I was freezing cold. I couldn't wait to get in a bath, but there were so many things to figure out first. 'I'm worried that... that my date Jay was killed. And that my bosses have been made, uh, Sanguine,' I told my great-aunt. 'They have puncture marks on their throats.'

Celia listened to my concerns with her usual air of calm. 'Don't worry about the jacket, darling,' she assured me. 'Though that's a shame about your date.' She paused. 'And with regard to your colleagues, if they were made food, it doesn't mean they are now Sanguine. *Necessarily*.

We'll see,' she said, leaning casually in the doorway. 'Vlad will take care of them, and the car.'

I raised an eyebrow.

'He will take them to the hospital,' she clarified.

With a name like Vlad, I wasn't exactly sure what 'take care of them' might mean. He had nothing to do with Vlad the Impaler, did he?

'If they are to be undead, at least we'll have room for them,' Celia told me. 'The important thing is that you really did so very well, darling, and you are safe. Countess Báthory was quite a foe. I am so pleased the talisman worked.'

I frowned. 'The talisman?'

'The one I gave you. You used it to conquer her,' she explained. She stepped up to the entryway, pulled on her coat and checked her lipstick in the oval mirror by the door.

The compact. The makeup compact she gave me was a talisman?

'Yes, Great-Aunt Celia.' I pulled the compact from my back pocket and marvelled at it. 'It worked a treat,' I said.

'It won't work on the next one, mind you.'

'The next one?' I said, rushing forward to grab Celia's arm. 'What do you mean, the next one?' I repeated, horrified.

My great-aunt gave me a firm hug, opened the door and stepped out onto the landing. 'Oh, darling, yes. You are the seventh, remember. Your time has only just begun. Look, I'm terribly sorry to run off like this, but I am late for Deus and we have important things to discuss,

as you can imagine! I had to be sure you got home safe.
But now I must run ...'

I gaped. Freyja mewed from my feet.

'You've done well,' my wise and beautiful great-aunt
assured me. 'Rest up now. You'll need it.'

ACKNOWLEDGEMENTS

The ongoing journey of my beloved Pandora English would not be possible without the support of her dedicated fans who would not give up on her, the wonderful Echo Publishing and author and editor Angela Meyer who got on board with her resurrection, and my own 'Great Aunt Celia', my dear Australian literary agent Selwa Anthony. Thank you for believing in Pandora, as I do.

Readers, I truly couldn't do this without you. Thank you.

I imagined Pandora and her world as an homage to classic mythology, old school horror tales and popular stories of the paranormal, but with a twist. Hers is a world where the witches aren't always evil, and for that matter, neither are the fanged undead (though to be fair, they aren't all that easy to live with either) and perhaps most importantly, the women aren't relegated to the role of victim, love interest or innocent young girl who need saving. In Pandora's world, women are powerful and complex, if not always good. They are villains and heroes, but never one dimensional.

I owe some thanks to Bela Lugosi, my first dark crush age 6, Bram Stoker, who has 'a lot to answer for', and the real Elizabeth Bathory, whose story and subsequent mythology was the inspiration for The Blood Countess herself. Thank you also to Wiccan goddess Fiona Horne for the obsidian and circle of protection, and the ethereal mists of the Blue Mountains where I wrote many of these books, for the supernatural mists of Spektor. The supernatural seems always to sit at the edges of the natural world.

To my precious family, Dad and Lou, Nik and Dorothy, Jacquelyn and Wayne, Annelies, Linda and Maureen, I love you. To my daughter Sapphira – who I was pregnant with as I wrote The Blood Countess, and I have now seen grow old enough to read these books to at bedtime – you are a loving, creative and precious human being. Thank you for making my life infinitely richer. To my dear husband Berndt, thank you for the patience, the love, the coffee, and so much more.

Mom, I never forget you.

www.taramoss.com

Praise for *The Blood Countess*:

Popular fiction writer Tara Moss has very cleverly jumped genres ... The story is pacy but there's enough background about vampire folklore and the fashion industry to keep it informative as well ... An entertaining and fairly lighthearted take on the whole vampire infestation of contemporary culture, incorporating some lovely stuff about haute couture. – *Sydney Morning Herald, Australia*

A must-read – *Cosmopolitian Magazine, Australia*

The Blood Countess by Tara Moss is a cool new twist to the traditional tales of supernatural beings. Just when you thought you knew every possible vampire related story; you catch yourself indulging in the captivating plot of this book that effortlessly brings together fashion, New York City socialites, and blood thirsty vampires into one extraordinary tale. – *Patent magazine, Canada*

Moss' writing style made this book a pleasure to read and set my imagination aflutter. Her reinterpretation of classic horror characters separates this book from the others in its genre keeping it fresh and exciting... I can't wait for the next in the series. – *W Channel Book Club*

The book's humour is broad...characters are well written. Pandora is infinitely more likeable than Bella... (*The Blood Countess* is an) amusing blend of horror and haute couture. – *Australian Book Review*

Tara Moss has a new book coming out at Halloween and it is different to her previous novels…[The Blood Countess has] flavours of *True Blood, Vampire Diaries, Devil Wears Prada* and *LA Candy*. I would recommend it … Very good read! High enjoyed. – *Angus and Robertson*

'A beautifully written novel that takes you into the world of the paranormal mixed in with some high New York Fashion … cleverly written … keeps you hooked till the very last page. Highly recommended for fans of *Twilight* and the Blue Bloods series and anyone who loves a great paranormal book.' – *Booktopia*

The novel pokes fun at some of the supermodel stereotype s… Are supermodels blood-sucking monsters? – *ABC radio*

'The funny thing, the witty thing you've done is situate Pandora in the business that is 'defying age'. That is one of the things that makes [*The Blood Countess*] interesting…one of the things that provokes quite a bit of thought …' – *Cath Kenneally, Writers' Radio, Radio Adelaide*

Praise for *The Spider Goddess:*

Moss's unusual supernatural series continues. In a strange Manhattan suburb and in a mansion with her aunt and a dead soldier, Pandora English faces up to her inheritance. Meanwhile, a new designer has ominous ambitions. Fashion has rarely been so haunting. In a word: sinister. – *Gold Coast Bulletin Australia*

Some books have got the ability to capture you… It's terrific reading. – *3AW Australia*

Moss' writing style made this book a pleasure to read and set my imagination aflutter. Her reinterpretation of classic horror characters separates this book from the others in its genre keeping it fresh and exciting... I can't wait for the next in the series. − *W Channel Book Club Australia*

Packed with mystery, evil intentions and things that go bump in the night, Pandora's world is breathtakingly addictive...Moss has created a world that is dark, Gothic, uniquely funny and often downright terrifying without an overt morbid feel. Pandora has fast become my favourite heroine and I can't wait to see what danger she leads us into next.' − *Burn Bright Australia*

Praise for *The Skeleton Key*:

'[Moss] has fashioned an entertaining, original vampire tale. Orphan and aspiring writer Pandora English moves to her aunt's gothic mansion in Manhattan and discovers a strange world in which Hollywood, high society and darker forces merge. In a word: macabre.' − *Gold Coast Bulletin*

'Moss has reinterpreted the traditional tale of vampires and other supernatural beings with a fashionable twist and a captivating plot.' − *Unilife magazine*

The Skeleton Key is the third instalment in the 'Pandora English' series—paranormal adventure stories interwoven with elements of mythology and populated with handsome men, ghosts, witches, vampires and a colourful array of undead folk ... The series is fun and makes some humorous swipes at the fashion and beauty industries.' − *Bookseller+Publisher magazine*